PIPER HOUDINI
APPRENTICE OF CONEY ISLAND

GLENN HERDLING

BALBOA
PRESS
A DIVISION OF HAY HOUSE

Balboa Press books may be ordered through booksellers or by contacting:

Balboa Press
A Division of Hay House
1663 Liberty Drive
Bloomington, IN 47403
www.balboapress.com
1 (877) 407-4847

Print information available on the last page.

ISBN: 978-1-5043-4972-7 (sc)
ISBN: 978-1-5043-4974-1 (hc)
ISBN: 978-1-5043-4973-4 (e)

Library of Congress Control Number: 2016901820

Balboa Press rev. date: 2/18/2016

ACKNOWLEDGMENTS

Cover art and design by John Kissee.

I am grateful to my family for allowing me a leave of absence to write this novel, and to my grandfather, Arthur George Herdling, for introducing me to magic…and inadvertently, to magick.

A heartfelt gratitude to Bill Schu for reviewing the first draft and making many wonderful suggestions, which I actually incorporated! And to Kevin Spatz for reading the manuscript to make sure I don't sound like a simpleton.

This story is true except for the facts. While many of the characters, organizations, and events portrayed in this novel are real, they have been used fictitiously. For a comprehensive list of the reference materials I consulted, please visit http://piperhoudini.com, which was meticulously designed by The Dineen Group. If you would like to discover more about any of the real characters, events, or places in this novel, I highly recommend them all.

Dedicated to the memory of my father, Jay Herdling. Thanks, Dad, for always encouraging me to follow my dreams.

CONTENTS

PROLOGUE

Myrtle Corbin hobbled across the wooden planks, trying not to disturb the delicate bundle clasped to her chest. She was no longer a young woman and her lungs burned with each step.

A painted stork guarding a nest of cherubs peered down at her from a tall gable overhead. Myrtle fell against the door of the building. She had to do something to arouse the people inside!

But she wasn't able to knock. One hand was carrying the bundle while the other pinched the blanket together, protecting its precious contents from the corrosive sun. And because Myrtle was born with a clubbed right foot, her left foot supported all her weight, rendering them both useless as well.

The sun was peeking over the Atlantic horizon, growing brighter with each passing second. The blankets would soon provide no protection at all.

Out of habit, Myrtle looked around to make sure that no one would catch a free glimpse. Then she nudged her hips forward. Two tiny legs protruded from the slit of her custom-made skirt and kicked at the front door like a child throwing a temper tantrum.

The ground floor of the structure was made of brick and the upper floor was a lattice of wood-framed panels. It resembled a half-timbered German farmhouse, but Myrtle knew better. This was a hospital.

Under its tiled roof, a staff of nurses cared for frail or underdeveloped infants that had been born too early. To fund its operation, the hospital doubled as a sideshow exhibit, displaying the premature babies in incubators behind a large picture window so people could gawk at them.

The boardwalk attractions wouldn't open for several hours, but that wouldn't keep Myrtle's family from meddling. Already they had begun to gather.

"Whatcha got there, Myrtle?" Elastic Skin Joe called out to her, bouncing down the boardwalk on his fingers and toes. His spindly arms were wrapped behind even spindlier legs so that he resembled a ball with hands and feet. "The Nightgaunt leave us another present?"

On most days she would find it amusing that these so-called "Curiosities" were in fact the most curious creatures of all. But today she had no patience for their nonsense.

"Yes," she replied, once more striking her tiny shoes against the door. "I found it by the drainpipe next to the Foolish House."

"Figures you'd be the one to find it then, huh?" Joe chuckled, untangling himself and vaulting to his full length beside her. The four-legged woman kicked him in the funny bone with one of her extra feet and the elastic man howled in pain.

"Should've booted him somewhere else," said a girl in a pink dress, poking her heads between Joe's spiderlike legs.

"Must you always be so vile?" asked the girl's other head.

"Charlotte! Scarlet! We have no time for your bickering!" Myrtle chided. "If we don't get into the Hatchery soon, we'll lose another one!"

"The doctor's not in?" Baby Bunny's fleshy face scrunched with worry, making it look like the underside of a pumpkin. As always, she brought up the rear of the troupe with her boyfriend, the Living Skeleton, in tow. The shadow of Bunny's massive frame shrouded Myrtle's precious bundle, offering additional protection from the vicious sun. But it wouldn't last long.

"If they don't open the door, can we eat it before it goes *poof?*" asked Lionel the Dog-Faced Boy, licking his chops.

"There will be no feeding on the foundlings!" declared a voice with a heavy German accent as the door to the Child Hatchery flew open. A pale man in his early forties appeared in its frame, yanking the sash of his robe to conceal his nightshirt. He swatted Lionel on the nose with a rolled-up newspaper.

"I hate when they do that," the hairy boy growled, rubbing his furry snout.

"Dr. Couney! Thank God!" Myrtle exclaimed, still catching her breath. "The Nightgaunt—he brought us another one. But I don't understand why he would leave it so exposed this close to daybreak...?"

"Calm yourself, Myrtle," said Dr. Couney, patting the knees of her smaller appendages. "Despite his own aversion to the sun, I do not believe the Nightgaunt would be so reckless, no matter how much of a rush he was in."

The doctor leaned over the bundle and peeled away the blanket as though he were unwrapping a fragile present. He plucked a wriggling figure from the folds and held it out for all to see. The bright green eyes of a baby girl beamed back at them.

Myrtle and the other Curiosities gasped. Instead of turning to dust, the baby giggled as the sun's rays glinted off her tender white skin and fine red hair. An odd pattern of dots on the infant's cheeks sparkled like glitter and then dimmed as the sun grew brighter in the sky.

Myrtle saw a grin spread across Rosita the Painted Lady's face. Like an artist struck with inspiration, the tattooed woman glanced at the insides of her wrists and nodded. Other than her face, they were the only remaining spots of unmarked flesh on her body.

Beneath the brim of his floppy fur hat, Zip the What-Is-It peered at something shiny in the blanket. He sunk his huge hand into the soft fabric and pulled out a silver padlock. Running his fingers over some cursive letters on the lock, Zip reached under his cap and scratched the tuft of hair on his scalp. Myrtle knew that Zip didn't like words.

A young girl beside Zip—whose head, like his, was shaved except for a patch at the tip to emphasize its small size—extended a frail arm from her pink muumuu and reached for the babe.

"No, Elvira," Dr. Couney said, gently swatting her wrist. Elvira withdrew her hand, bit her lip, and lowered her tapered cranium.

In the distance, the El Dorado carousel chimed its first refrain of "Twelfth Street Rag." Couney turned from his fellow attractions, hoisted the infant girl over his head, and let her bathe in the full glow of the morning sun.

"This one is meant for the light."

THE MAGICIAN'S NIECE

The glow from the distant boardwalk bathed the falling snow in a glimmer of neon. Lacey white fronds peppered the trees and gardens but perished where they touched the street, sidewalk, and other lifeless surfaces.

A small figure sloshed across the street, trying to keep pace with the man who clutched her wrist in his gangly fingers. When they reached the other side, the man thrust an ashen hand in front of the girl. She brushed a layer of icy petals from the brim of her hat so she could see him more clearly.

His face was cleanly shaven except for a handlebar mustache that crept across his upper lip, its tips frayed like a rodent's whiskers. A snowflake twinkled in the glow of an electric streetlamp. It grazed the man's protruding brow and disintegrated.

Prying her eyes from the man's burning glare, the girl turned her attention to the building that loomed before them. An odd blend of hope and despair coursed through her frigid body.

Twelve-year-old Piper Weiss had stayed at large houses before, but the time had always come for her to go. Not that she'd been bad or anything. The problem was, strange things always happened around her and she was always sent back to Hollygrove.

Hollygrove was an orphanage—which the children were told was a "bad" word. The people who worked at Hollygrove called it a "foundling home" or a "happiness home." But that didn't fool the kids who had to live there.

The places that always sent her back were foster homes. Piper had been in and out of them for as long as she could remember. She had liked two of them because they had lots of bugs and she liked to catch bugs. Once, when a foster family had taken her in as a baby, they had to fend off a colony of bats that swarmed around her crib every night. There was no sign of how they got in.

Another time she had gotten into all sorts of trouble playing Hide 'n' Seek. The other kids had been unable to find her so the foster parents called the police. The officers searched the home from top to bottom. They finally found her in the attic, hanging by her knees from the rafters—asleep in the middle of the day.

Despite the long wraparound coat that concealed her slight frame and the brimless cloche hat that covered her head, Piper shivered. A cloche hat told everyone that you had short hair. It was only possible to get a close-fitting cloche over your skull if your hair was cropped short and flat.

That's why it looked so awkward on Piper. Her mop of red hair grew all over the place. The hat was pulled well over her big green eyes and Piper had to hold her head at a clumsy angle just to see where she was going. Foreheads were unfashionable for girls in the 1920s.

Not that Piper cared all that much about the latest fashion trends. While wealthy women still continued to wear beautifully embellished silk garments and the masses were reveling in their new-found sophistication of fashionable flapper clothes, Piper's wardrobe consisted mostly of hand-me-downs from the Salvation Army.

The few rags that she owned fit comfortably in the small suitcase that she lugged down the slushy sidewalk. Beneath her wraparound coat, Piper wore a pair of faded blue overalls. She envied the carefree flapper style of the middle class but she didn't think any sort of fashion trend would transform her miraculously into another Coco Chanel.

That's because Piper was small and skinny. She had a thin face and bony knees. The only thing she liked about her appearance was the set of ten evenly-spaced freckles on each cheek that formed two stars if you connected the dots.

Piper gazed at the odd-looking townhouse in front of her. It stuck out like a sore thumb amidst the extravagance of New York's Coney Island.

She stood silently because she didn't know what else to do. The old doubts and fears nagged at her. What sort of place had she been brought to? What kind of people lived here? What sort of grim adventure had she embarked upon this time? Everything was happening so fast that it seemed like a wonderful dream and a horrible nightmare all rolled into one.

The house's dark contours provided a jagged contrast to the bright, snow-feathered lights of the Manhattan skyline in the distance. Piper felt an odd vibe around the building, a mystic vapor, dull, sluggish, and barely discernible.

The house's most prominent feature was the hexagonal skylight that graced its roof. The grille crisscrossed the hexagon in such a way that it looked like a wavy "H." It was by far the brightest window in the house and even the snow would not invade its preternatural glow.

"Welcome to your new home, Piper."

The words spilled like gravel from the throat of the man who had accompanied her all the way from Hollygrove.

It had happened shortly after dinner, when the other kids were either doing their homework or getting ready for bed. Piper had finished her homework early and, as usual, she wasn't interested in going to bed. She had been playing alone on the staircase when there was a knock at the door.

Mrs. Buckley pushed the chair out from under her ample bottom, mumbling something about the front gate being improperly locked. She didn't like visitors at this hour.

The plump caretaker stormed across the reception room floor and threw open the door. The visitor didn't flinch. He wasn't very tall, but his stiff bearing gave the impression that he towered above Mrs.

Buckley. His complexion was pallid and his eyes were like two black caves that seemed tortured by even the faintest light.

"I'm here for the girl Piper Weiss." His voice seemed to echo as though it were coming from a sewer. "I am her father."

Mrs. Buckley glared at the man. She knew, of course, that Piper had been brought to Hollygrove more than twelve years ago by a man named Dr. Couney. She had been abandoned beside a drainpipe near his wondrous hospital for premature babies. Only a tattered blanket and a silver padlock engraved with the name "Weiss" had accompanied the orphaned child. Piper had worn the lock around her neck for as long as she could remember.

"You can't just waltz in here and claim custody of a child without the proper paperwork..." Mrs. Buckley began.

The gaunt man ignored her. A red glow emanated from the dark pits of his eyes as though a fire had been stoked inside them. He held Mrs. Buckley with his fiery gaze and said, "Piper Weiss is my daughter."

"Oh...of course," Mrs. Buckley stammered, dropping her hands to her sides and walking numbly to her desk. She filled out several forms and handed them to the man who claimed to be Piper's father. Then she leveled her empty eyes at Piper, who had been watching the entire exchange through the baluster posts.

"Go get your things, child," she said without inflection. "Your father is here."

So Piper had gathered up the few possessions that she owned and walked silently out into the snowy twilight with...whom? Her father? Surely, Mrs. Buckley wouldn't release her into the custody of a stranger if his claim hadn't been true?

"Keep going."

The man's snarl returned Piper to the moment. They stepped across the slick sidewalk and her father pulled open a wrought-iron gate. The rusty hinges squealed like frightened rats.

"And don't touch anything," the man cautioned as they walked up the stone path.

Piper hardly heard him as her attention wandered from the odd-looking house to the flower garden. Somehow, it was in full bloom…in the middle of winter! Wondering if the ice-blue roses were real or artificial, she reached out to touch one. She slid her fingers along the silky underside of its petals and then jerked her hand back when her index finger snagged a thorn.

"Ouch!" Piper gasped, pressing the injured digit to her lips. "Guess it's real," she giggled.

She pulled the finger from her mouth and a tiny droplet of blood trickled down it. Her father was not amused. In fact, his eyes blazed with demonic fury. And was it her imagination, or did Piper see froth forming at the corners of his mouth?

"I told you not to touch anything!" the man growled.

Something had been nagging Piper about her father's appearance. Something less obvious than the gray pallor of his complexion and the hollowness of his dark eyes. Piper had known kids who'd lived on the streets. They had come to the orphanage with that same look on their faces. It was the look of deep, insatiable hunger.

The hunger consumed the man who claimed to be her father. It transformed him into a monster before her eyes. His front teeth extended into two curved barbs.

Piper could see he was struggling with some sort of inner demon. Every nerve in her body told her to run. But fear, confusion, and downright cold rooted her to the spot.

Perhaps it was self-pity that petrified her. The first rule of being an orphan is that you have to let go of the dream that your parents will show up for you any second. She had allowed herself to fall prey to that fantasy. After all these years, she believed she was about to become part of a real family. And now it was being torn from her in the worst way imaginable.

The twisted figure leaped at Piper like a rabid hyena. She gulped and clenched her eyes. But the agony she anticipated never came.

A tremendous wind whipped around her several times and then lift her in the air. She heard her father roar as she soared past his clawing hands. The gust blew her through the front doors that had somehow swung open from what should have been the hinged side.

Piper landed harshly on a tiled floor. She looked up and found herself staring into the billowing tails of a black tuxedo laced with blood-red trim. The tails of the tux fluttered around the figure of a short, sturdy man. Piper could only make out the back of the man's head, which was peppered with gray curls.

The stranger stood between Piper and her father, his stance bold and challenging.

"What foolishness is this?" he demanded with a baritone voice that pierced the dark chill of night like a knife. He made a peculiar gesture with his right hand and the wind simply dissolved.

The curly-haired man relaxed and softened his tone when next he addressed the intruder.

"Hello, Willie. To what do I owe the honor?"

Piper got to her feet and hid behind the man's tuxedo. She tried to keep an eye on her father while shielding herself from his ravenous stare. The two men obviously knew each other.

Willie? Willie Weiss? That was her father's name?

But if he wasn't dead, where had he been all these years? And why had he brought her to the doorstep of this bizarre individual only to attack her?

Question after question shot through Piper's mind as she continued to watch from behind the expensive cloth of the stranger's garb. Piper's father—Willie—seemed to cower slightly, wiping away a string of saliva and covering his mouth as though he were ashamed.

"Not going to invite me in…Harry?" he asked, a lugubrious chuckle in his unearthly voice.

"Hardly," said the man called Harry, as though acknowledging a sick joke between them. He swept his hand aside to indicate Piper but never looked back to address the child directly. "And this…dinner, I presume?"

Piper felt her insides somersault and let out an audible gasp. Were these two men in league with each other? Was this some sort of conspiracy, some organized cult that plotted to make gourmet meals out of young, abandoned orphans? She slid behind the heavy oak door for protection.

"No, dear brother," Willie replied. "This young lady is going to be your house guest for a while. You will take her in—as a favor to me. After all, I do believe you owe me a favor...or two."

"Maybe so," admitted Harry, running his hand through his hair. He turned to study the girl and Piper thought he looked familiar. "But why would I wish to have a prepubescent street urchin running around stirring up all sorts of trouble in my home?"

"She's not a street urchin, Harry," Willie corrected. "She's a twelve-year-old girl who's lived in an orphanage for most of her life. Twelve years, Harry. Do you remember what happened twelve years ago?"

Piper saw the well-dressed man's body go rigid. Willie seemed to enjoy the discomfort that he was inflicting on his brother.

"Her name is Piper. Piper Weiss." He paused, allowing the name to register.

"She's my daughter." Again, he paused.

"Your niece."

Piper felt Willie's crimson gaze turn on her.

"Piper, I'd like you to meet your uncle, Ehrich Weiss...a.k.a., the legendary Harry Houdini."

Harry peered down at the small, red-haired girl and raised an eyebrow. Piper gasped in sudden recognition. He looked a bit older in person, but it was the same strong face, thick nose, and lofty, domed forehead she had seen in newspapers and handbills. His hair, parted in the middle, had grown white at the temples, but it was dark everywhere else, just like in his pictures.

Harry's thin lips quivered slightly. The man who had appeared so strong and confident only moments ago now stood unnerved by the prospect of this child in his midst.

Piper wasn't thrilled by the idea either. The unwelcome look in Houdini's eyes made her freckles burn like tiny branding irons. For the first time in her life, Piper Weiss wished she were back at Hollygrove.

THE AUTHOR'S DAUGHTER

On the edge of Ashdown Forest in Crowborough, England, stood a redbrick Victorian villa that its original owner had christened Little Windlesham. Its current residents had enlarged the house to include fourteen bedrooms and five reception rooms. It was maintained by a large domestic staff—Rogers the butler, a cook, five maids, two gardeners, and a chauffeur. The Lord of the Manor often referred to the place as "Swindlesham" because of the cost to maintain it.

The enormous billiard room, which ran from the front to the back of the house, doubled as a ballroom but looked more like a museum. A harp and a grand piano were on display at one end and the billiard table at the other.

The Earl of Stafford's portrait decorated the wall above one of the room's huge limestone fireplaces and a stag's head draped with a bandolier parlayed the other. An assortment of animal-skin rugs adorned the polished wood floor, and there were two large casts of dinosaur footprints on display opposite the billiard table.

A door along the back wall led to a room that used to be a nursery. Here, Lady Doyle was holding court, charming her husband's many influential friends as he looked on with pride.

Lady Doyle had originally viewed the new Spiritualism with nervous distrust. She thought that dabbling in the unknown was risky and unnatural. But she had recently developed a talent for automatic writing, a means of communicating with the other world. Spirits would manipulate her pen and she claimed to have no control over what she was writing.

The gardeners were busy showing Lady Doyle's guests where to park their cars. Rogers greeted the guests at the door and guided them across the billiard room into the old nursery.

One of the visitors, an older gentleman dressed in gray dining attire, spotted a small girl sitting on the staircase outside the billiard room. She was stroking a faded downy quilt that was lying across her lap.

"Hello, Billy!" the man said.

The girl on the stairs blushed and gave the visitor a shy smile.

"Good afternoon, Mr. Wallace," she replied.

Her name was Jean Conan Doyle, after her mother. But she liked to be called Billy. She liked it even more when adults indulged her.

Billy was a thirteen-year-old girl who enjoyed spending time with her father. She loved playing on the floor of his study and listening to his pen squeak as he worked.

Seven years earlier, on a trip to Australia, her father had told her that there was no such thing as death. "What people call death really means the passing on to another life," he had said. So from then on, Billy always had this peaceful feeling that death wasn't the end.

It was a wartime tragedy that had converted her father to this belief in Spiritualism. Billy's half-brother Kingsley had died in the Great War. About a year later, her father met a medium who said he could put him in touch with his son.

Billy's father was a rational man and somewhat skeptical. So the medium agreed to be tied to a chair. Yet amazingly, Kingsley somehow came back—and even made physical contact with him!

Unfortunately, the man's obsession with his dead son overwhelmed his concern for the living. Shortly after the Australia trip, an eye doctor was stunned that Billy's father had failed to notice her extremely poor eyesight. He was stunned because Billy's father was not only an ophthalmic specialist himself, he was also the creator of the famous detective Sherlock Holmes and should have noticed that without glasses Billy was as blind as a bat.

Rogers ushered the guests into the old nursery. Billy spotted her father beaming behind his walrus mustache at the far end of the séance table.

Sir Arthur Conan Doyle was over six feet tall and heavily muscled, a giant of a man made even greater by the dignity of his warm personality. But for all that, he was something of an over-grown boy.

Billy heard her mother's voice bellow from inside the room. "Rogers, tell the household that we are not to be disturbed."

The butler drew the blinds and then bowed to Lady Doyle and her guests. Stepping from the room, he closed the door behind him and took the phone off the hook. Rogers then whisked past Billy to warn the servants in the kitchen not to make a sound.

Clenching her blanket securely to her chest, Billy slid across the billiard room floor in her stocking feet and dropped to her knees. She pressed her ear against the door and continued to stroke the soft, worn quilt.

Séances had become a highlight of the Conan Doyles' social life at Windlesham. Lady Doyle's spirit guide was named Pheneas, who claimed to have died thousands of years ago in the Middle East, near Egypt. He was a leader of men.

Each time Lady Doyle filled a page with Pheneas's spirit writing, Billy could hear her rip it from her notebook for Sir Arthur to read.

"God has ordained that a great light shall shine into the souls of men through a great external force which is slowly penetrating through into the Earth's atmosphere."

Sir Arthur's booming voice penetrated the heavy door like the sound of a French horn.

"The world of men will not wake otherwise. All the shams and ceremonies must be swept away forever, and only this sweeping power can do that. It will be the biggest thing that has ever happened in the Earth's history, but great blessings will follow. All the shadows will flee."

"What about Houdini?" asked one of the sitters.

Billy pressed her ear against the door. Harry Houdini and her father had been close friends up until about three years ago. Billy had met Houdini a few times during their travels and the magician always treated her nicely. She loved it when he performed card tricks for her.

Then one summer day in Atlantic City her parents invited Houdini to join them in their suite for a séance. Lady Doyle claimed she had contacted his mother, who had died years earlier.

Lady Doyle filled fifteen sheets with automatic writing in English, each page addressing Houdini as "Harry." Houdini was deeply annoyed. For one thing, his mother didn't speak English, she spoke German. For another, Houdini's birth name was Ehrich. His mother had never called him Harry.

"I was willing to believe, even wanted to believe," Houdini had said.

Billy felt sad for Mr. Houdini. He had been tricked and she knew it. That's when Billy began to suspect that Pheneas might not be all that he claimed to be.

She knew Pheneas had lied because Mr. Wriggly had wandered throughout the Otherworld to seek the real spirit of Houdini's mother. It was nowhere to be found. It was somewhere else.

The séance in Atlantic City was the start of a bitter feud between Houdini and Billy's family. Since many of Houdini's fellow magicians had no idea how to explain his tricks, let alone repeat them, Sir Arthur accused Houdini of working real magic rather than sleight-of-hand.

Many people believed that the self-proclaimed "man from beyond" truly was someone who could pierce the spiritual realm at will. One Spiritualist claimed that he had seen Houdini dematerialize during one of his performances.

The magician had been submerged under water in a locked container. The man said he experienced a great loss of physical energy as Houdini used his powers of dematerialization to pass through the glass and transport himself to the rear of the stage.

Sir Arthur asked the public, "Is it not perfectly evident that if he did not deny using real psychic powers, his occupation would be gone forever? What would his brother-magicians have to say to a man who admitted that half his tricks were done by what they would regard as illicit powers? It would be 'exit Houdini.'"

Houdini, for his part, went on a crusade to expose fake Spiritualist mediums. He despised the way that bogus mediums would take advantage of people's grief by pretending to communicate with dead loved ones.

"Money taken for contacting spirits is the dirtiest money ever earned on this earth," he claimed. "These so-called Spiritualists are getting money under religious disguise."

But Houdini's honorable mission quickly degenerated into an obsessive desire to unmask all mediums. He began to exploit their "tricks" by duplicating them during public displays. He boasted that he could expose any medium as a fraud and soon became known as the greatest scourge of the Spiritualist movement.

So it was no surprise to Billy that Pheneas's proclamation would be cruel.

"Houdini is going rapidly to his Waterloo," her father read from the spirit writings. "He is doomed! Doomed! A terrible future awaits him."

Billy wondered why Houdini's destiny was an issue at all. Pheneas had already told them that 1926 would be the year of reckoning. She continued listening to her father recite the frantic scribbling of Lady Doyle's pen.

"In October, the Earth will be shaken from the sky. There will be great loss of life. It will be terrific. All humanity will be shaken to the core. Shams will then fall away. God will come into his own. After that comes the deluge. No one will suffer that should be spared. God is love. Remember that. It will be like a great sieve passing through all that is worthless, retaining only the fruit."

When Billy heard her father's ominous declaration, she knew that time was running out. It was December. The great crisis of the world was at hand—the Earth had less than a year to live. She was in the end times. And somehow it was tied to Houdini.

Billy was convinced that Pheneas's goal was not as noble as he made it sound. Yes, he wanted to bring peace to the Earth by eliminating humanity's destructive urges—but that would only be accomplished by removing its collective soul entirely.

Pheneas would be powerless, however, unless he could get willing instruments to work through. The Spiritualist movement was strong, but was it strong enough? Would Houdini be the savior that would expose the true nature of the movement, shaking it to its very core? Or would his own demise somehow hasten the end of all things?

Pheneas isn't a spirit, Billy thought. *He's something else. Something rotten.*

She rocked on her knees, clutching and petting the blanket in long, quick strokes. Her eyes rolled up into her head until only the whites showed.

Nuzzling the quilt beside her ear, she whispered in a voice altogether different from her own, "Do not take lightly the words of Pheneas the Pretender. There is confusion in the astral realm—the spirits are fearful. The abyss between the living and the dead grows thinner. This once impenetrable gulf is now infiltrated on both sides by demonic forces that have begun to assault the physical and spiritual planes. For the human race to survive, the girl must survive. But for the girl to survive, the magician must die."

Billy's eyes returned to normal and she stopped petting the quilt. She stared blankly at it. "A girl? Do you mean me, Mr. Wriggly?"

She was suddenly aware of the sound of chiffon rustling beyond the door. Lady Doyle had risen from her chair and was smoothing out her dress. Her trance had been broken and the séance had ended.

Billy's mother invited her guests to enjoy a taste of wine and tea in the billiard room. Billy tried to stand. But because she was still leaning against the door when her mother pulled it open, she fell in.

"Billy!"

Lady Doyle was strikingly good-looking for a woman in her early fifties. She retained most of her dark blonde hair, with only a few strands of gray mixed in. Her green eyes fixated on her daughter.

Despite the initial tinge of anger in her voice, the Lady tousled her daughter's hair and dismissed her with a playful affront.

"You little rapscallion! Were you listening in?"

The woman laughed elegantly and, with a pirouette worthy of Clara Bow, she led the visitors single-file past her daughter and into the billiard room.

Sir Arthur was last in the procession and he grinned down at Billy. But she could sense the nervousness behind his façade. Had he been shaken by Pheneas's prediction too?

"Still dragging the disreputable folds of that absurd rag with you everywhere you go, Billy?" His smile turned slightly sympathetic. "I'm sorry to say, it will not bring him back."

Sir Arthur walked away without picking up his head, and she thought she heard him say, "It won't bring any of us back."

Billy scrambled into the nursery, closed the door behind her, and collapsed against it. She pulled the quilt close to her face and dabbed the tears that were dripping beneath her glasses.

"Oh, Mr. Wriggly. I must warn Mr. Houdini! But I can't just call him up—he lives all the way across the Atlantic. Besides, why would he believe me, the daughter of his sworn enemy?"

She thought for a moment, biting her fingernails and rocking back and forth. Then she had a rather clever idea.

"I know!" She jumped to her feet. "If I can't tell him, I'll *show* him! He's a sensible man. How often has Father said that when you have eliminated the impossible, whatever remains, however improbable, must be the truth?"

She bit her lower lip and stared into the thread-worn quilt. "Of course, we'll be risking detention again, Mr. Wriggly. But I hear the new Imperatrix isn't nearly as dreadful as Mrs. Mathers."

Then she glanced around as if someone might have heard her.

No one could be that dreadful, she thought.

★★★★

OPENING NIGHT

Bess Houdini heard the loud thud of the front doors slamming shut. She had been brushing her curly dark tresses in front of a small mirror that had lately become her harshest critic. It reflected the face of a woman she hardly recognized. Though her features were still youthful and girlish, the lines in her cheeks and the dark circles under her eyes betrayed the passage of time.

"Stop thinking that at forty-nine years you are old," her husband had chided her. "Tush-tush—and a couple of *fiddle-de-dees*. We have our best mature years before us."

Bess stood up from the vanity, lifted the hem of her ruby V-necked dinner gown, and hurried out to the foyer to see what had caused the commotion. She expected to see Houdini standing by the front door tapping his pocket watch with a playful scowl on his face. Instead, what she saw made her stop in her tracks.

A red-haired waif in oversized rags stood shivering beside the front door. Thin sheets of snow melted off her droopy hat and baggy coat onto the polished wood floor of the entrance hall. Bess gazed at her and couldn't help but think of a drowned Chihuahua.

"Harry?" asked Bess.

She hardly ever called him Harry. It was always Houdini.

Or a silly little pet name. But in this case, nothing else seemed appropriate.

Houdini skittered toward Bess, his arms held out high in an exaggerated shrug. He appeared to be as baffled as her.

"Bess...this is my niece...*our* niece. Piper, this is your Aunt Bess."

The soggy redhead tried her best to curtsy.

"Pleased to meet you, ma'am."

Bess faced Houdini in stunned silence, urging him to continue.

"Willie's daughter," he said.

Bess crossed her arms. "That's a load of applesauce, Harry Houdini. Henriette never had a daughter!"

Houdini cocked an eyebrow at her. "Yes, Willie's *wife* never had a daughter."

She peered over at the little girl.

"Oh," Bess said as realization dawned on her.

"She's been in an orphanage her whole life" Houdini continued. "An officer of the state just dropped her off. He said that as the next of kin, we've been designated as her legal guardians—at least until other arrangements can be made."

Bess saw Piper wrinkle her brow as she listened to Houdini's tale.

"But how'd they find out Will was her father?" Bess asked.

Houdini seemed to struggle for words. Piper reached behind the top buttons of her coat and pulled out the silver padlock that hung about her neck.

"I've got *this!*" she announced.

Houdini stepped sideways to Piper, shifting his gaze from her to Bess and back again. He glared at the bauble around the girl's neck and stroked it with his fingertip. He turned it over and displayed the printed side to Bess.

"*Weiss*," he said, almost triumphantly. "An old heirloom. It's been missing from our family collection for at least twelve years."

Bess frowned.

"It all seems a bit farfetched," she said after a moment's hesitation. "Your brother lost his life a few months back, poor soul. And now this girl..."

Houdini rushed to his wife's side and put his arm around her, keeping her from saying any more. Bess, however, didn't fail to notice Piper's ears prick up at the mention of her father's death.

"Yes, yes, my dear. We can talk about this later," Houdini hastened. "Right now, I have a show to perform."

The magician trotted over to the front doors and opened them. He hollered into the frozen wind, "Jim, bring the motorcar around!"

Houdini closed the doors again, blew on his hands, and then fumbled with the loose ends of his bow tie, trying to make them even. Finally, he threw his hands up.

"Bess, would you mind...?"

"I swear, for an escape king, sometimes you are the most helpless man in the world."

Bess grabbed Houdini's tie and knotted a perfectly symmetrical bow without even looking at it. Keeping her focus on Piper, she said, "Thirty-one years we've been married and I still have to wash his ears every day."

Piper giggled.

"Speaking of washing, young lady, you'd better clean up right away if you want to be in time for curtain call," Bess said. "Of course, those clothes won't do at all. I'll bring you some nice evening wear that my own nieces have worn when they've come to visit. And those shoes..."

With a wave of her hand, Bess dismissed the worn leather boots that covered Piper's feet. "I'm sure there's something in my closet that will fit you."

Bess was a tiny person and had tiny feet. She had plenty of shoes that would fit the girl.

Houdini placed a nervous hand on his wife's shoulder.

"Bess, we can't possibly bring her," he whispered as if Piper weren't there and listening.

"And what would you have us do—leave her here by herself? Her first night with us and you would abandon her? Is that how you'd treat your own child, Houdini?"

Again, the magician struggled for words.

"But, the show is sold out! It's standing room only!"

Bess broke away from her husband's hand and took Piper by the wrist.

"Then she'll have the best seat in the house—backstage with me. Come along, dear," she said, leading the girl down the hallway.

★★★★

By the time they reached the city, the snow had deteriorated into an icy rain. Piper stepped from the backseat of a luxurious Lenox that had been chauffeured by Houdini's assistant, a dapper, somewhat cadaverous-looking Irishman named Jim Collins.

Piper stepped onto the slushy sidewalk in the T-strap shoes Bess had given her. She was wearing a one-piece navy coat dress that looked a lot more comfortable than it felt.

As an orphan, Piper had never been to New York City at night. The lights dazzled her. And the brightest lights on Broadway tonight were those on the marquee of the Shubert Brothers' Forty-Fourth Street Theatre. A simple word blazed from the sign above her in tall letters: HOUDINI.

A doorman escorted Piper, Bess, and Houdini to the side entrance where they climbed a small staircase to the rear of the stage. Once there, Houdini was whisked away by stagehands that were eager to start the show.

Piper and Bess settled into a couple of folding chairs offstage, just out of sight of the audience. Soon Collins rejoined them.

"You'd think they'd reserve a parking spot for the guest of honor," he grumbled, removing the brown derby from his head and brushing drops of rain and sleet off it. He grabbed another folding chair and took a seat to Piper's right.

Bess handed Piper a souvenir booklet that was cut into the shape of a lock. A carefully-combed Houdini in jacket-and-tie smiled handsomely from the front of the program. Its contents described the performance as "Three Shows in One: Magic, Escapes, and Fraud Mediums Exposed."

Through a gap in the quilted blue curtain Piper could see the audience file in. It was, as Houdini had said, standing room only. Piper sat in awe. Less than an hour ago, she had been cold and wet standing in threadbare clothes in a big, strange house. Now she was dressed in gorgeous finery sitting backstage at a performance by one of the world's top showmen, who also happened to be her uncle!

The lights dimmed and the orchestra started playing "Pomp and Circumstance." The curtain rose. The crowd started cheering.

When Houdini entered, the applause grew to a dull roar. He immediately pulled the sleeves off his tuxedo jacket to expose his thick arms. The gesture all but bellowed "nothing up there!"

For the first act, Houdini performed fifteen tricks and illusions. The first of these was called "Paligenesia," which Piper's souvenir booklet translated as "rebirth."

"Lay-dees and gentle-men!" the magician began, each word pronounced with a crisp, staccato delivery. "They say the soul cannot escape the confines of its corporeal trappings until its last fatal hour. But tonight you will witness the daring resurrection of a body *before* its soul has been offered a chance to depart."

Houdini summoned a young assistant from the other side of the stage. The assistant was dressed in a shimmering silvery camisole that exposed eyefuls of legs, arms, and cleavage. Piper noticed Bess looking away when Houdini took the young assistant in his arms.

The magician tied his assistant to an upright door that was set against a dark backdrop. He then held up a large carving knife that he subsequently used to cut through a watermelon and a tin can.

Then, with the same casual movement, Houdini sliced off his assistant's arm with the knife.

The young girl screamed—and so did the audience! Piper wanted to run, but Bess took her hand and urged her to continue watching.

The assistant squirmed and shrieked each time the blade sank into an arm or a leg. But Houdini continued to dismember her, tossing each of the girl's limbs onto the chair.

"And now, ladies and gentlemen—the fatal blow!"

The magician walked beside his assistant, raised the knife menacingly, and slashed it across her neck, severing her head from her torso. It rolled onto the floor with a thud.

Piper leaned out of her chair to see the reaction of the audience, but Collins held her back, keeping her out of sight. She was sure that she could hear people running from the theater in terror.

Houdini set the knife down and placed his finger to his lips, which had the desired effect of hushing the audience. He walked over to the chair, picked up an arm, and reattached it to the body. The audience gasped in unison.

Houdini repeated the maneuver with his assistant's leg. Finally, he grabbed the girl's severed head by her lovely long hair and restored it to her slender young neck. The orchestra started playing an upbeat jazz piece and out stepped Houdini's assistant, celebrating her rebirth by dancing the Charleston in her flapper scanties.

Piper squealed in delight and applauded so loudly that she could barely hear the audience doing the same. Bess patted her thigh affectionately.

For the rest of the first act, Houdini made a clock change size, made a lamp teleport from one table to another, and produced yards of colored silk handkerchiefs from an empty fishbowl that he changed into the flags of all nations. Even from her special seat, Piper couldn't tell how the tricks were done.

"And finally," Houdini said to the audience, "just to prove that I *am* a magician..." he pulled a wriggling rabbit out of thin air.

The audience burst into wild applause and the curtain descended on the first act.

With the energy of a man half his age, Houdini leaped over to the spot where Piper, Collins, and Bess were sitting. He knelt before Piper and smiled.

"Enjoying yourself?" he asked.

"It's wonderful!" Piper exclaimed, petting the bunny in his hands.

He mussed her hair and then took Bess's hand.

"Please do this humble magician the most gracious of favors and assist me in our oldest performance?"

Bess's lips dimpled at the corners. Houdini held her hand as she stood.

"I'll get into my tights," she said, reaching into her handbag.

She skittered off and Houdini winked at Piper.

"I wonder how she knew to bring them?" he asked.

Then, like an excited child, he leaped away to prepare for his second act.

Collins leaned over and spoke into Piper's ear; the words were tinged with a faint Irish brogue.

"Now there's a treat. You get to see the illusion they performed together on Coney Island when they first started thirty years ago."

He settled back into his chair like he had just eaten a satisfying meal. "Married all this time and still so much in love. Only one person the boss ever loved more than her."

"Who?" asked Piper.

"His mam," was Collins' reply.

He looked down his nose at her as if considering her for the first time. "You have her eyes."

The curtain rose and Piper's attention returned to the stage. Her program described the second act as "Feats That Have Made Houdini Famous."

"I am so glad that you enjoyed our first act, ladies and gentlemen. But as they say here on Broadway, the best is yet to come!"

Piper marveled at the confidence Houdini displayed when addressing the crowd.

"Despite the tricks that you have just witnessed, I am here to say that I am *not* a magician. I am a mystifier. To show you what I mean, for my next act, I will need some volunteers."

Houdini invited a committee onstage to witness his next trick up close. They watched as he chewed and swallowed twenty-four sewing needles.

"A little iron is good for the blood," he quipped. "But they taste a little sharp."

He followed that by swallowing some white linen thread until only the end was visible in his throat. Opening his mouth, Houdini slowly drew forth the knotted thread. Somehow it had passed through the filament of each needle! The volunteers pulled the end of the string all the way down the line until all two dozen needles were dangling from it.

Piper peeked out from behind the curtain to watch the crowd cheering at each of her uncle's stunning performances, their mouths upturned like awestruck children.

Houdini barely allowed time for the audience to catch its breath before sliding into his next act.

"My dear friends, for over thirty years, I have eluded every chain but one," he began, extending his right hand to the far side of the stage.

"And far from complaining, might I add! Every day I congratulate myself on the solidity and inalterability of the conjugal link. Please join me in giving a warm welcome to my beloved little helpmate, Miss Beatrice Rahner, a.k.a., Mrs. Harry Houdini!"

Bess sauntered onto the stage, taking Houdini's hand and curtsying to the audience. Piper marveled at how youthful she looked in her tights.

Houdini paraded his "little helpmate" around the stage as the audience continued to clap and whistle.

"In all my fights, whether she thinks I am right or wrong, Mrs. Houdini is alongside me, helping to cover me," he said, stepping into an open steamer trunk.

Bess fastened a pair of handcuffs to his wrists and then pulled a white canvass sack up and over his head. She yanked the drawstring tightly, and tied the cord in a double knot.

Houdini's muffled protest could be heard through the sack. "This isn't quite what I meant by 'cover me!'"

Bess glanced off stage and winked at Piper as she guided the bagged Houdini into the trunk. She closed the lid over him, locked it, and sealed it with a net. She then draped a curtain in front of herself and the trunk to conceal them from view.

Bess stuck her head out of a slit in the curtain. "Ladies and gentlemen!" she announced. "Behold, a miracle!"

The curtain snapped closed, then just as quickly Bess's head reappeared.

"One!"

Her head withdrew behind the curtain again, and then re-emerged.

"Two!" Again Bess retreated.

All of a sudden, like a champagne cork Houdini's head popped through the slit in the curtain.

"*Three!*"

Piper jumped at the sound of the baritone voice. The curtain was pushed aside to reveal a liberated Houdini standing triumphantly in front of the sealed box.

Before the hurrahs of the audience could build to a crescendo, Houdini shushed them with a finger pressed to his lips. Then, with the dexterity of a cat burglar, he unlocked the trunk and beckoned the bagged figure within to arise.

The sack dropped to the floor and Bess stepped out of its folds, her wrists shackled in cuffs.

The crowd roared, and so did Piper. She kicked her feet up so high that she almost toppled the folding chair.

With a kiss, Houdini removed the cuffs and soothed his wife's wrist. Bess took a bow, waved to the audience, and then ran offstage.

The orchestra played a drum roll and the theater lights dimmed. The applause died down.

"Lay-dees and gentle-men!" Houdini began, his voice vibrating like that of a radio announcer. "Introducing my or-ig-inal invention… the Wa-ter Tor-ture Cell!"

The stage hands wheeled out an oversized box that looked to Piper like a giant fish tank. Jim Collins, dressed in fishermen's oil-skins and Wellington boots, appeared onstage still wearing his derby hat. Piper had been so enthralled by the previous act that she hadn't noticed his departure.

Collins mounted a brass-bound stepladder, climbed to the top of the tank, and began filling it with a high-pressure hose and buckets of water that other assistants handed up to him.

The sight of the apparatus gave Piper the heebie-jeebies. She had a fear of confined spaces, and this contraption looked a lot like a small glass coffin.

Filling the tank was a slow process. Houdini covered the stage-wait by escaping from a straitjacket. Then he bounded toward his dressing room and returned wearing only a blue bathing suit.

"I am ready!" he announced to his assistants. "Begin!"

The magician lay down on a mat and Collins clamped a thick stock over his bare feet.

"Size seven and a half," Houdini declared proudly. Piper heard nervous titters from the audience.

The stock nested securely in a frame, securing both ankles. Ropes descended from flies above the stage and Collins hooked them to steel rings on the corners of the frame.

From behind her, Piper heard the sound of a winch that hoisted the stock, frame, and Houdini off the mat. The sound continued until Houdini hung upside down by his ankles directly over the cell.

He called out to the spectators, "I invite the heartiest of you to hold your breath while I remain submerged in the Water Torture Cell."

Inhaling deeply several times, Houdini threw his head back and closed his eyes as the winch lowered him into the tank. Once inside, the escape artist folded his arms across his chest. His hair swirled like seaweed and his cheeks bulged like a blowfish.

Piper could tell this was no illusion—her uncle was imprisoned underwater. To complete his confinement, Collins padlocked a steel lid over the top of the cell, leaving only his bare feet exposed, soles up.

The stagehands quickly drew a curtained cabinet around the cell to conceal it from the audience. Piper's view was also obscured, but she noticed Collins standing outside the cabinet holding an ax—just in case.

The orchestra began playing a menacing version of "Asleep in the Deep." Piper heard members of the audience exhaling in defeat as seconds turned to minutes. The tension continued to mount until it became nearly unbearable. She heard shouts and murmurs from the seats:

"Did he drown?"

"He's breathing through a hose."

"It's not real water."

"It's all done with mirrors."

"No! We examined every last inch of it!"

"Aww, there's a trick to it."

"No, he's magical!"

A wave of dizziness came over Piper. But not because she was holding her breath. It felt more like something was sucking the energy from her body. No, it felt like something was moving *through* her body and trying to take a piece of her with it!

The next thing she knew, she was on her back staring into the large soulful eyes of her aunt.

"Wake up, little one! Wake up!" Bess cried, frantically slapping her wrists.

"I'm all right," Piper said sheepishly, rising to a sitting position. She hadn't been this embarrassed since the police had found her asleep in the attic hanging from her knees.

"Oh, you poor dear!" Bess said, helping Piper to her seat. "I was so concerned about what to dress you in that I didn't even think of feeding you! You probably haven't had a decent meal all day!"

Piper could barely hear her over the raucous cheering that suddenly filled the theater.

She lifted her head and saw Houdini standing triumphantly outside the cabinet, which was still sealed and filled with water.

Nerts! she scolded herself, *I missed the whole thing!*

Houdini was drenched. He was smiling for the audience, but Piper could sense that he was somewhat shaken. Through bloodshot eyes, he glanced in Piper's direction and his smile dimmed ever so slightly.

The curtain fell and Houdini rushed to his niece's side.

"What happened, child?"

"Nothing to concern yourself about," Bess reassured him, placing an arm around Piper. "The poor thing is famished. I'll get her something to eat. You go get ready for your final act."

With a slow pivot, Houdini headed toward the dressing room. But he continued to look at Piper over his shoulder. The tension in his forehead was so pronounced that it made his bushy eyebrows look like bat wings.

During the intermission, Bess bought Piper a hot dog and shared a bucket of popcorn with her. Piper was uncomfortable with her aunt making such a fuss. She was convinced that her dizzy spell had nothing to do with hunger—but the hot dog was certainly delicious!

Sharing popcorn reminded Piper of the time she had played hooky to sneak into a Valentino flicker with two other Hollygrove girls. They couldn't afford three tickets, so Piper combined their lunch allowance to pay for one. Then she slipped her two friends in through the back door.

The girls were able to scrimp enough pennies to buy a small popcorn and a Grape Nehi. Piper loved Grape Nehi almost as much as she loved Valentino.

Three weeks later, the two girls were adopted. Piper never heard from them again.

The lights in the theater fluttered, indicating that the third and final act was about to begin. Piper flipped through the program again. The third act was entitled "Do the Dead Come Back? An Exposé of Spiritualist Deceit and Trickery."

The curtain rose as the crowd was still filing back into the theater.

"I have all reason to believe that this is the most important part of the evening's entertainment." Houdini's tone was a bit more somber than it had been during the first two acts. "Long after you have forgotten everything that has gone before, I hope that you will not forget some of the things said and done in the next hour or so.

"This whole psychic thing is taking over," he continued. "I am not denouncing Spiritualism, ladies and gentlemen—I am merely showing up the frauds. I cannot show up an honest medium. But trot her out."

There were many cheers from the audience, but Piper could also hear boos and hisses.

"My feats depend on iron nerve, dexterity, and perfect coordination. But they're all done by natural means. People lack the true ability to see. If they could only educate their eyes, they could readily see through almost every one of my so-called miracles."

Houdini invited two volunteers onto the stage and demonstrated how fraudulent mediums did their slate-writing trick. He took out a pair of blank chalkboard slates and showed it to the audience.

"I want you to watch me very carefully, ladies and gentlemen, because if things are right, this will be a very extraordinary experiment—if things are right."

He bound the slates together so that the chalkboards were facing each other and then asked the first volunteer to hold the slates over his head. The magician picked up a standard dictionary and asked the other volunteer to drop a playing card into any part of the book that he desired.

"Since it is a very thick book, it would be impossible for any human being to give me the correct page numbers that the card has been inserted between. So I had to call upon the spirits to give me a sign of their presence. Spirit, I command you to read the first and last numbers on the two pages."

He looked at the volunteer. "My good sir, please tell the audience what are those page numbers and what are the first and last words?"

The man told Houdini that the pages were 116 and 117, and that the first and last words were "crowfoot" and "ice."

Opening the slates, Houdini said, "I have called upon the spirits to give us a sign." The numbers "116" and "117" were marked on the first, and the words "crowfoot" and "ice" were marked on the second.

Piper had never put much thought into whether Spiritualist claims were true. Throughout her life, she had been at the center of many bizarre incidents, some that had kept her from being adopted by a loving family.

Mrs. Buckley had been convinced that these incidents had supernatural implications. But Piper always insisted that there were logical reasons behind them. Of course, bats don't usually hover over a baby's crib and attack foster parents. But maybe something in the attic had scared them into the room and they couldn't escape?

And earlier tonight, did the man who claimed to be her father really sprout fangs or was that just a trick of the light? And that sudden gust of wind that lifted her across the threshold—surely there was a rational explanation for that?

Houdini invited a volunteer to sit opposite him at a small table. He placed a black velvet hood over the volunteer's head to simulate the conditions of an unlit séance room. While holding the volunteer's hands in his own, Houdini levitated the table with his head, rang a bell with his foot, and tapped the man's shoulder with a rod protruding from his mouth.

The volunteer was amazed, but Piper and the audience got to see how each effect was performed. Throughout the course of the third act, Piper counted forty-three times that the audience interrupted her uncle's performance with deafening laughter and applause.

"You don't know what you're talking about!" protested a lone voice from the audience.

Houdini shielded his eyes from the blinding stage lights to seek the source of the outburst.

"Then come up here and tell the audience," he called out.

A middle-aged man with a pale complexion and thinning hair ambled up to the stage. Piper couldn't help but notice the size of his lips—they seemed three times too big for his head.

"History repeats itself," the man uttered through his sausage-shaped lips. "Christ was persecuted by the Jews, and now we Spiritualists are being persecuted by one. Someday, as in the case of Christ, the people will see the light!"

"But Christ never robbed people of two dollars, did he?" demanded Houdini.

"Your tricks are frauds," shouted the man. "You're duping the public exactly as you claim Spiritualists are. You are a medium but you won't admit it!"

Members of the audience hissed at him. "We know he's deceiving us!" said one.

"He gives us illusions for entertainment!" said another.

"We like trying to figure out how he does it!"

They all joined in to defend Houdini and ridicule the man. It took five minutes for Houdini to restore order.

"These are feats of endurance and knowledge, not mysticism," the magician said. "I've dedicated my life to discrediting fake spiritualists, medicine men, and bunko artists—exposing them for the frauds they are."

"Just as I have dedicated my life to protecting our Spiritualist Church," the man declared as he walked off the stage amidst an onslaught of boos and razzing. "When November comes around, Harry Houdini, you won't be here!"

"And until that day, I will continue to protect the public from scoundrels like you," Houdini concluded.

The crowd's cheers sounded almost ferocious. Houdini touched his hand to his forehead in a salute to the audience.

"And remember, ladies and gentlemen—all this talk of the supernatural is pure rubbish. I get letters every day from ardent believers in Spiritualism who prophesy I am going to meet a violent death soon as a fitting punishment for my nefarious work."

Houdini took a final bow and concluded his show by saying, "Will wonders never cease?"

The curtain fell and the audience jumped to its feet, shaking the walls with their thunderous applause. Bravos and whistles went up to encourage an encore. But Houdini had been more than generous with his time.

He approached Bess, Collins, and Piper, who stood on her chair giving her own standing ovation. Houdini leaned forward in an exaggerated, playful bow. But when he turned his attention to Collins and Bess, his mood became sullen.

"Bess, our guest is exhausted. Please get her to bed. I will be home soon, but there are matters I must attend to." He took his wife's hand and kissed it. Then he grabbed Collins firmly by the arm.

"Take them directly home. Do not stop for anything."

If Houdini had been expecting trouble, it never appeared; the ride home was uneventful. Despite her uncle's assertion, Piper didn't feel at all tired. In fact, it was Bess who dozed in and out. Piper amused herself by watching the city's incandescent skyline get smaller and smaller as the car made its way back across the Brooklyn Bridge.

Collins unloaded his passengers at the front door of the house. Bess unlocked it and Piper smiled to see that it still opened from the hinged side. She hadn't imagined it.

Aunt Bess led her niece up two flights of dark stairs. On the second flight, Piper shivered and clenched the banister. A chill passed through her body as though she had walked through a curtain of icy mist.

Bess steadied her as though she feared she might fall down the stairs.

"I'm all right," Piper said. "Believe me, Aunt Bess—I don't make a habit of passing out."

Bess stifled a smile and escorted Piper into a small bedroom in the back of the third floor. It was a clean, pleasant room with a big, soft bed and a gilded French chair. Lace curtains decorated the lone window, and an Oriental rug covered the polished wood floor.

Piper removed her borrowed dress and put on a flannel nightdress that Bess had laid out for her. Then she slipped between the comfy silk sheets. Bess tucked her in and, almost as an afterthought, knelt beside the bed. She lowered her head, folded her hands, and recited a child's bedtime prayer.

"Now I lay me down to sleep.

I pray the Lord my soul to keep.

If I should die before I wake,

I pray the Lord my soul to take."

Not very reassuring, thought Piper.

Hollygrove wasn't a religious institution, so the children there rarely said prayers. At least not out loud. Some of her foster parents had been devout Christians and prayed before supper and bedtime, usually either "Our Father" or "Hail Mary." A few reasoned that Piper's last name might be Jewish. But most of them chose to ignore that detail and tried to advance their own beliefs on her.

One family had been considerate enough to ask her what an appropriate Jewish prayer was. Piper had no idea! She had never considered herself to be Jewish, Christian, or anything else. She was just Piper.

She heard the sound of a clock on the wall. Its tick-tock echoed in the uncomfortable silence that hung between her and her aunt. Bess brushed the hair back from Piper's forehead.

"You have her eyes," she said.

"His mother's?" asked Piper.

Bess answered with a simple smile. She pulled a quilt up to Piper's chin, stroked her cheek, and then walked out the door, clicking off the light on her way out.

"Good night, little one."

Despite the dark, Piper could see that the hands on the clock were approaching twelve. She lay on her back, nuzzling against the soft warmth of the sheets. At first, sleep didn't come easy. Piper's thoughts were racing through the events of the night. She was afraid to allow herself to believe it had all been real. As an orphan, she had learned early in life not to get too caught up in a new living situation, especially when it seemed too good to be true. Was she truly home now? Was Bess truly as warm and caring as she had been tonight? Did she really belong here?

Folding her hands over her chest, Piper finally closed her eyes. Despite the thoughts racing through her head, the day's events had finally taken their toll. It was the first time that she could remember falling asleep before midnight.

THE WITCH'S SON

As snow gave way to rain in the boroughs of New York, a foul north wind continued to unleash a thick shroud of white on the narrow gaslit streets of Boston's Beacon Hill.

Two boys trudged up the slick road, past the decorative doors and ornamental ironwork that adorned the brick row houses of the Georgian storybook neighborhood. Despite the cold, the boys did not huddle together by choice. A pair of handcuffs shackled them together, biting into their wrists like icy razor blades.

Two women in police uniforms accompanied the boys. The snowstorm had immobilized the city and the male officers were busy handling the major crises. The Department had appointed the policewomen to work with juveniles, so it was their duty to escort the runaways back home. Of course, the patrol wagons had been reserved for the men, so the ladies had been forced to walk the entire stretch from their headquarters on Berkeley Street.

The policewomen led the boys to the front door of an old, four-story home that stood on the flat of Beacon Hill where the street met the bay. Standing on the stoop with her shoulders bent against the snowstorm, the officer with the auburn hair pinched the brass knocker with her gloved fingers. She gently tapped it against the door, as though she knew about the house's macabre history and was afraid to disturb it.

Number Ten Lime Street was an address that had become synonymous with the occult and supernatural among the enthusiasts of Boston's upper class. Guests who attended the frequent parties at the home always marveled at its warm and inviting decor, inside and out. That's because the lady of the house was a meticulous housekeeper.

A slim woman in her late thirties threw open the elegant door. The bob of her sandy-blonde hair reflected the shimmer of the nearest gas light. When she saw the policewoman, her first instinct was to grab the door frame, steeling herself for ghastly news. Then she glanced down at the smaller figures behind the officer and melted with relief.

Brushing past the policewoman, she seized the smaller boy by the shoulders.

"If you ever…!" she began.

Then she clutched the shivering child to her breast and her voice softened. "Oh, Alan! Your father and I were so worried!"

"He's not my father," the boy replied through chattering teeth.

Alan Rand knew that his mother liked to indulge him in every way possible. He was the center of her universe. To her, only his love mattered. He could persuade her into believing practically anything.

But making her understand why he'd run away was going to be tricky. He wasn't even quite sure why he'd done it himself.

"Mrs. Crandon? I'm Officer Irene McAuliffe, and this is my partner, Officer Bohmbach," said the auburn-haired officer.

"Oh, I'm so sorry," Mrs. Crandon replied, extending her hand to shake the officer's. "Where are my manners? Please come in—you must be frozen to the core."

They brushed sheets of snow from their uniforms, stomped their boots several times, and stepped into the hallway. The warmth of the interior had an immediate effect. The police officers removed their gloves and blew on their hands. The taller boy pulled off his knit hat and cupped his ears.

Alan wiggled his nose. It felt like someone was stabbing it with a thousand needles. A good sign—no frostbite. The last thing he needed was another unsightly blemish.

Alan had a strange face. His cheeks were pitted with pockmarks that resembled a pair of coiled serpents. The blemishes looked like acne scars, but they had been there since birth.

"Can I get you some tea?" Alan's mother asked the police officers.

The uniformed women looked at each other. Alan guessed there were regulations that prohibited them from accepting food or drink on the job. But their desire for something warm quickly outmatched their adherence to protocol.

"That would be wonderful, Mrs. Crandon," Officer McAuliffe conceded.

"Please, call me Mina."

Mina Crandon was a glamorous woman, standing nearly six feet tall in her high heels. She dressed well, and the fashion trends of the twenties were good to her. Her sea-blue eyes conveyed a delicate yet mischievous loveliness that was as arrogant as it was penetrating.

Mina led the police officers and two boys into a spacious kitchen and poured them each a cup of tea.

"We tried to reach you by telephone, but the line was busy," Officer McAuliffe said.

"Oh, that would be my husband," Mina replied. "He's been on the phone with your desk sergeant to see if there was any news on the whereabouts of these two scoundrels."

The officers stopped in mid-sip. Officer Bohmbach returned her cup to its saucer.

"Ma'am, we just came from headquarters. If someone had been in contact with your husband, we would have kept the boys there overnight and you could have picked them up after the storm had passed."

Mina scowled. She looked up at the ceiling and bellowed, "Roy!"

When Alan was 5 years old, Mina divorced his true father, a small-time grocer named Earl Rand, charging him with cruelty and abuse. Shortly thereafter, she married Dr. Le Roi Goddard Crandon, a sophisticated Boston surgeon who was twenty years her senior.

In the seven years since, Alan's mother had gone to excessive lengths to ensure that she and her son would never again return to the meager life of a grocer's family. Alan felt a mild victory at the anger she now expressed toward his stepfather.

The sound of footsteps, followed by a low, disdainful voice, echoed from the stairwell in the next room.

"I told you they wouldn't get far in this storm."

A slim, scholarly looking gentleman ambled into the kitchen. Light gleamed off his wire-rimmed spectacles, highlighting the gray in his mustache.

"Welcome home, boys," Dr. Crandon sneered.

Raising his hand in a halfhearted greeting, Alan inadvertently lifted the hand of the other boy to whom he was cuffed.

Mina gasped. "Handcuffs?"

She turned on the officers. "Did you have to treat them like a pair of hooligans? They're not even teenagers!"

"I'm sorry, ma'am," said Officer Bohmbach, approaching the boys with her key.

She sat them down on opposite sides of the kitchen table with the chain dangling between them. "We didn't want them to hurt themselves by trying to make a break for it in the snow. They gave us quite a chase before we caught them."

The officer tried to put her key in the slot of the handcuffs, but she couldn't fit it all the way in.

"Something's jammed in the hole! I can't open it!"

The two boys smiled conspiratorially at each other.

"Too bad Houdini's not here," Alan said.

Crandon's face grew red. He stepped toward Alan and raised his hand in a claw-like gesture.

"I told you to *never* mention that name in this house, you ungrateful whelp!"

"Roy!" Mina shot her husband a reproachful look and nodded toward the uniformed ladies behind him.

Crandon lowered his hand. He turned and grimaced at the two policewomen.

"Officers, I thank you for the safe return of my boys, Alan and Edward—particularly in this ghastly weather."

Alan glared at him. "We're not your boys."

"And my name isn't Edward," the other boy pleaded in a distinctly British accent. "It's Horace. Horace Newton."

"Contemptuous lad," Dr. Crandon said, shaking his head at the officers. "We brought him over in consideration for adoption. We offered him the sanctuary of our home. But as you can see, he doesn't quite appreciate the auspices and warmth of our hospitality. I am afraid that once his visa expires, we will have no choice but to ship him back."

Horace wasn't the first "Edward" in the Crandon household. Alan knew of at least fifteen other children whom his stepfather had called by that name.

"It will be much pleasanter for them living in our house to have a name we have provided them," Dr. Crandon had insisted.

All the Edwards had come from orphanages, mostly in foreign countries. They had all been about the same age as Alan. And they had all been "shipped back," at least according to Roy Crandon.

When Horace arrived at the Crandon household last summer, Alan kept his distance. Too often he had grown attached to an Edward only to have the Edward sent back. This usually happened after Dr. Crandon had diagnosed the Edward with some sort of illness and had performed a surgical procedure on the child.

But Horace had lasted longer in the house than any other Edward, and Alan began to accept him as a member of the family.

On this particular day, the falling snow had been so thick that when the boys got out of bed and looked out the window, they couldn't see the bay at the bottom of the hill.

"Of course it would be snowing," Horace said.

There was no sign that the blizzard would subside, so the boys decided to stay inside and play hide-and-seek. Alan was "It" and Horace scampered downstairs to hide.

The house was a virtual Shangri-La for hide-and-seekers. It teemed with closets, cubbyholes, shafts, and crannies. Horace had at first contemplated hiding in the cellar, but Dr. Crandon had declared that part of the house off limits.

Instead, he decided to hide in a hallway closet. But his shoelace had come untied and it protruded from the crack under the door.

"A-ha!" Alan screamed as he yanked open the door.

The English boy was so startled that he hit his head on the shelf above him, knocking over a rack of photographs. The boys burst into laughter. But when they started to gather the fallen pictures, Alan fell silent.

"What's wrong?" Horace asked, wiping the corner of his eye with a knuckle.

Alan held up a photograph. "I knew this boy."

He rifled through the other photos. There were over a hundred pictures of little children.

"And this one!" He tossed a photo of another face he recognized into a separate pile. "And this one!" he repeated with each toss.

When he was done, he had a collection of more than a dozen photographs.

Horace looked at him. "Who are they?"

"The other Edwards."

Horace cocked his head. Alan explained that the Crandons had tried to adopt other children, but they were always sent back.

"Why?" Horace looked concerned.

Alan shrugged.

"It always happened after Dr. Crandon examined them and found something wrong—like an illness or a weird skin condition. He'd operate on them and then ship them back before I could even say goodbye."

Alan gazed at the pile of photographs. "I never heard from any of them ever again."

Horace turned white.

"What's the matter?" Alan asked.

"The doctor examined me last night," the taller boy said.

Alan waited.

"I have tonsillitis," Horace ran his fingers along his neck. "My throat doesn't even hurt—but the doctor says he's got to remove my adenoids."

"When?" But Alan could see the answer in Horace's eyes.

"Tonight."

That's when the boys decided to plot Horace's escape. They knew that they wouldn't get far by foot, especially in the snow. So instead, Alan and Horace sailed up the bay in a raft they had built the previous summer. The current would carry them much faster and further than any land transportation.

But navigating the waters of Winthrop Bay can be treacherous even on a calm summer day. In the midst of a wintry northeast gale, it's practically impossible, especially for two inexperienced boys.

"Good thing they didn't get very far," Officer McAuliffe said, taking a turn with her key in the jammed handcuff lock. "Their skiff crashed along the shores of Deer Island."

"Where the prison is?" Mina gasped, grabbing her son's shoulder.

Officer McAuliffe nodded, dropping the boys' handcuffed wrists on the table in defeat. "By the time they reached the walls of the prison, they were like two soggy ice cream cones."

Officer Bohmbach smiled. "They're the only two people who have ever tried to break *into* jail."

Roy Crandon let out a phony chortle that did little to hide his annoyance. He rested a hand on the lower back of each officer.

"I assure you, ladies, that if I can salvage your handcuffs, I will return them to you as soon as the storm lets up."

He prodded them toward the vestibule. Officer McAuliffe and Officer Bohmbach barely had time to stretch their wet gloves over their fingers before Crandon ushered them out the front door.

"My wife and I thank you once again for bringing our sons back home safely. I will be sure to mention to your Sergeant how helpful you have been."

Crandon shut the door on the two policewomen but not before Alan caught the confused looks on their faces. The doctor wasted no time opening an adjacent door to a storage closet. He rummaged through the contents of the closet and pulled out a hatchet.

Running his finger along the edge of the blade to test its sharpness, Crandon turned with a grimace. He took several menacing steps toward the boys and raised the tool above his head.

"No, Roy...!" Mina screamed.

Alan cowered and Horace raised his free hand in self-defense. Crandon brought the hatchet down with a crash, cleaving a fissure in the center of the kitchen table. Shards of steel clinked to the floor as the chain between the boys exploded.

Crandon grabbed Alan's face, digging his fingernails into the soft flesh of his serpentine birthmarks. "Next time, it will be your hand."

Mina pulled the boy to her bosom. "Stop it, Roy! Can't you see that he's been through enough?"

"It's for his own good," Crandon retorted. "Someone has to discipline the child."

"Oh, please," Mina scoffed. "If you cared so much for Alan's well-being, why weren't you on the phone with the police department? Whose call did you take that was more important than the welfare of my son?"

Crandon pursed his lips. "If you must know, I received a call from our fish-lipped friend in New York. He attended Houdini's opening on Broadway this evening."

Mina raised her eyebrows. "I'm sure it was well attended?"

"Standing room only," Crandon replied. "Our informant tells me that anyone in the audience who may have been on the cusp of believing in our cause would now be totally convinced otherwise as a result of Houdini's little demonstration."

"Swine!" Mina growled through clenched teeth.

"But that wasn't the reason for the call," Crandon continued. "It seems that there was an incident on stage—or rather, I should say, off stage. There was a child, about Alan's age, sitting in the wings with Houdini's wife. She fell off her chair during the water torture routine."

"So?" Mina countered. "The man loves performing for children. And his wife has nephews and nieces who have attended his performances in the past."

"If that were the case, why wouldn't he reserve a seat for the child in the front row? Why did he take extra precaution to keep the child from view? Why all the secrecy?"

Mina rubbed her chin. "Maybe it does bear a closer watch. But not by your stool pigeon—his appearance draws too much attention."

She stopped and thought for a moment. Then she narrowed her eyes. "Let Flapper do it."

"My dear Psyche," Crandon grinned, "you just read my mind."

Psyche was Crandon's pet name for Alan's mother. It was the all-encompassing Greek word for soul/mind/breath/life. Alan's skin crawled every time his stepfather said it.

But the name he despised even more for his mother was the one by which the residents of Boston, the United States, and even the world had come to know her: Margery, the Witch of Beacon Hill.

Like her disciple Lady Doyle, "Margery" claimed to receive guidance from otherworldly adepts. But unlike her British counterpart, Margery drew her knowledge not from remote prophets who lived 3000 years ago in ancient Egypt, but from loved ones who had just passed over. Number one among them was her own brother, Walter.

"I'll send a wire to Master Therion to see if Flapper is available," Crandon said. "But first, I have other pressing matters to which I must attend."

He turned to Horace.

Horace glanced from Crandon to Mina, who avoided his gaze.

"I want to go back home," he pleaded.

"Of course, dear boy. And so you shall!" Crandon reassured him. "But there's still the matter of your adenoids that I must remedy."

He grabbed Horace by the wrist and opened the door to the cellar. Horace looked at Alan with desperation in his eyes as the doctor led him down the wooden stairs.

The English boy disappeared into darkness and Mina pulled her son even closer, as though fearing that he might try to follow.

Alan stifled a sob.

"Until today, I've never done *one thing* against Dr. Crandon's wishes!" his voice croaked. "Why won't he allow me to have a friend?"

"Hush, child. One day, you'll understand," Mina said in a reassuring tone. She kissed the top of his head. "Until then, you must understand, you owe everything you have to Roy Crandon."

Alan understood more than his mother knew. He recognized that his very existence was the result of a failed experiment by Dr. Crandon.

Over the years, he had learned that early in their relationship—before they were married—Crandon and his mother had made a sinister pact. In return for allowing him to perform some sort of surgical alteration on her, Crandon would create a new life form...a soulless vessel that would house the spirit of Alan's dead uncle, Walter.

But when Alan was born, his body was not the empty abode that Walter had expected to occupy. It had a soul of its own, and a strong one too. Even as a babe, Alan wouldn't allow it to be evicted without a fight.

Alan was certain that his blemishes were the result of some sort of demonic brand when he was still in his mother's womb—a constant reminder of Crandon's first failure.

Not that there was anything special about him. Sure, he had "talents" that the other kids at school lacked, but most of these were derived from the macabre books that his parents had accumulated over the years.

Alan had shown a special aptitude for performing the enchantments in these ancient tomes at an early age. He had once invoked a minor fire elemental that had set fire to the school bathroom. He had never revealed any of this to his mother or Dr. Crandon. But someone had found out and he was punished several times for his unauthorized practice of the dark arts.

Alan also knew that somewhere in the world was another person his age whose power rivaled his own. One whose power was innate, not the result of some incantations in a book.

Releasing her hold on her son, Mina stepped softly across the kitchen and closed the door to the cellar—but not before a scream escaped from its inky depths.

No more, thought Alan.

He knew that his mother was inextricably linked to the doctor by a pair of psychic handcuffs. And it would take more than a hatchet to release her.

If he could learn the whereabouts of the "other," or if he could somehow find the means to merge the disembodied spirit of his uncle onto a new life form, then she would be free. And no more Edwards would be experimented on.

Alan was not aware of any magic that would reanimate a body with a new soul. But he knew someone that might be able to help.

The chubby voodoo kid, he thought.

Alan would probably wind up in detention again just trying to get to him. But unlike Mrs. Mathers, the new proctor was a push-over. He could wrap her around his finger as easily as he had done with his mother.

Dr. Crandon always says that sacrifices have to be made for the greater good, Alan Rand thought.

His pulse quickened and the tiny serpents on his cheeks grew hot.

I am the greater good.

HOLIDAY HOCUS-POCUS

The following morning, Piper was up by five o'clock. So she was surprised to hear the sounds of activity in the house. She grabbed a fluffy white robe that Bess must have hung on the bedroom door while she slept. She snuggled it close to her body in case the chill that she had felt the night before was still lingering in the stairwell.

Piper passed an elaborate bathroom adorned with the initials HH on the floor tiles. It was the only bathroom she'd ever seen with a sofa in it. She walked down the hall and peered into the master bedroom. The bed was already made and there was no sign that anybody had slept there the night before.

Then she heard a voice calling from the bedroom. It was a horrible mournful voice that sounded like someone sobbing.

"Poor, poor Stoker, he lost all his magic, oh my, oh my." Piper looked around for the source of the whining voice. Hanging from the ceiling was an elaborate cage. She stepped inside the room and stood on the bed to take a peek.

Piper expected to find a parrot or a parakeet perched in the cage. Instead, a strange-looking creature poked its nose between the bars, and Piper almost lost her footing.

The animal looked like a fox, but it had the wings of a bat and it was covered in downy white fur. It hung upside-down from the bars at the top of the cage.

Piper thought it must have been a majestic looking creature at one time. But now its body was riddled with scars, its left eye was missing, and the tender skin of its right wing was shredded beyond repair.

"Poor, poor Stoker, he lost all his magic, oh my, oh my," the creature whined again.

The sight and sound of a talking bat made Piper lose her balance and she almost fell into the glass door of a gold-leaf curio cabinet. Inside it were treasures she had never seen before—a gold Faberge ladle, a monstrous set of handcuffs with six sets of locks on each cuff, silver engraved rice bowls with Chinese markings, and a tiny ivory baby carriage with a satin pillow and coverlet.

Everything looked so old yet so beautiful. It reminded Piper of a museum she had once visited with her fellow Hollygrove orphans. She had felt as out of place there as she did here. She was so afraid of breaking something that she tiptoed out of the room, making sure to touch nothing.

Piper walked toward the staircase with every intention of descending to the main floor. But there was a third flight of stairs that she had not noticed the night before, so she decided to explore. Pulling the sash of her robe a bit tighter, she climbed the creaky steps as quietly as possible.

When she got to the top, she peered into the nearest room. It was a cubbyhole that opened into a larger, bare-floored workroom. In the center of the room stood a large wooden table strewn with papers, a microscope, a banker's lamp, a typewriter, and a pair of balances.

Playbills, engravings, and photographs featuring Houdini's name and likeness covered the walls, mantels, and even door frames. And each wall was lined with books from floor to ceiling.

The early morning rays of the sun peered through the hexagonal skylight that Piper had seen from the road the night before, casting a shadow of the window pane's stylized "H" on the opposing wall.

Piper scuttled through the cubbyhole and stepped into the workroom. She was familiar with some of the titles lining the walls, such as *The Count of Monte Cristo.* But there was something strange and otherworldly about the others. Their dusty, threadbare leather covers, with broken spines, obscure lettering, and foreign words, were hoary with age. Even their scent was alien. Without even understanding the names of the books, Piper knew this must be Houdini's magical library.

She wandered around the room, browsing the shelves. Some of the works were massive tomes bound in brass. Others were locked with iron clasps.

She noticed the word "grimoire" in several titles, such as *Grimoire Heptameron, Grimoirium Verum,* and even a grimoire named for a pope. There were also several "libers," including *Liber Mysteriorum, Liber Iuratus Honorii,* and *Liber AL vel Legis.*

This last one held Piper's attention because it was newer than the rest and the only book she could find that was written in English. She pulled it off the shelf and flipped through it.

The author of *Liber AL vel Legis* was a man named Aleister Crowley. In its introduction, Crowley claimed to have written the book in Cairo in 1904—rather recent compared to the other tomes. And he signed the introduction with the name *Ankh-af-na-khonsu.*

"You can see that I live in a virtual library," said a voice behind Piper.

She jumped and slammed the book shut. When she realized the voice was Houdini's, she relaxed only a little.

"I don't house my books," her uncle smiled, running his finger along their spines as he surveyed the mess in his office. He was wearing striped flannel pajamas monogrammed with a gray "HH" on the breast pocket. "My books actually house me."

Piper tried to compose herself.

"Good morning, um, Uncle…Harry?" she said uneasily.

The magician rubbed his chin and looked at the skylight as he contemplated her greeting.

"No. That won't do at all. I would like to be known as Houdini. Don't call me Uncle Harry or Uncle Houdini. Just say 'Houdini.' It sounds better, looks better, and is better. I am only called Harry on legal documents…and by my enemies."

"Well, I wouldn't want to be your enemy," Piper said, biting her lower lip. "Houdini."

Houdini chuckled.

"Did you sleep well, child?"

"Oh, yes!" Piper brightened. "This is really a late start for me! I'm usually out of bed long before sunrise."

Her uncle's eyes twinkled a ghostly blue-gray, and Piper thought she detected a note of approval in his voice. "I'm a light sleeper too. I wear a blindfold at night because the least ray of light will awaken me.

"When I was just a tyke, my blessed mother used to worry because I slept so little. Whenever she bent over my crib, day or night, my eyes would be open. Now, if I sleep too long, I'm haunted by... *the dream.*"

"The dream?" Piper asked, perhaps a bit too anxiously.

Piper didn't want to tell her uncle that for as long as she could remember, she had never had a dream, or even a nightmare. The idea of a nickelodeon playing inside a person's head while they slept fascinated Piper, and she loved to hear other people talk about their dreams.

Houdini indulged her curiosity.

"In the dream, I'm just a little boy. Younger than you. My mother takes me to the railroad station. The train rushes in and mother gets on board. Before my startled eyes, the train goes away, leaving me at the station, alone and afraid, not knowing when the next one will come along so that I can join her.

"Now do you see why I don't trust sleep?" he concluded. "I'll get enough of it when I'm dead."

"Well, at least you had a mother that you can dream about," Piper said, her green eyes looking up at him then quickly looking away.

At least you can dream, she added in her head.

Houdini stared at her as if he had just been slapped in the face. He shook his head and changed the subject.

"Did you enjoy my performance last night?"

"Posalutely!" Piper exclaimed, cringing as soon as she said it. She didn't like using modern jargon to express herself.

Hoping her uncle hadn't noticed, she asked, "Can you show me how you did some of your tricks? Please, please, please!"

"Well, young lady. A good magician never tells his secrets."

Houdini inhaled sharply and his eyes narrowed.

"But seeing as you are a little girl and nicely built for illusions, perhaps one day I'll call upon you to be my assistant. So I can reveal a few to you."

Piper brightened. Houdini tried to keep his expression stern but he couldn't conceal a slight smirk.

"Before I share any of my secrets with you, will you agree to swear a solemn oath to me?"

The girl nodded intently and raised her right hand.

Houdini began, "I, Piper Weiss, do hereby solemnly and sincerely swear on my sacred word of honor and before the great God almighty that I will ever hold sacred the secrets of Harry Houdini."

Piper repeated the oath.

"So help me God, and may He keep me steadfast," Houdini added.

"So help me God, and may He keep me steadfast," Piper echoed.

Houdini clasped his hands behind his back and paced the room. He stopped before a large box that looked like a pirate's treasure chest.

"The first thing you should know is that the word 'magic' comes from the ancient Persian word 'magi.' These were the priests in biblical times that had knowledge of nature's power.

"The wise men of yesterday became the sleight-of-hand artists of today." He gestured with his hand and Piper jumped as sparks flew from his fingertips. "Which is why I don't like to be called a magician. I'm simply an illusionist.

"Today's magicians are but actors playing the part of the wise magi. The hand isn't really quicker than the eye—people just *want* to be fooled. The modern magician helps them along by misdirecting their attention.

"As you saw last night, I distract my audience with amusing patter—and my devilish good looks," he winked at Piper.

"The point is, people don't notice what you're really doing because they don't want to."

Houdini opened the chest and its hinges squeaked like rest-less mice. Piper saw that it was filled with card tricks, thimbles, sponge-rubber balls, and other amateur gimmicks. Houdini ran his hands through them like he was sifting through sand for gold. He then pulled an old wand from the chest.

"One, two, three!" he shouted, and the wand transformed into a bouquet of plastic flowers.

Placing his hands on Piper's shoulders, Houdini turned her around to face a full-length mirror. He handed her the wand, and it no longer showed any trace of the bewitching blossoms.

"The secret is to practice in front of a mirror every day," he said.

Piper looked away.

"What's the matter, child?" Houdini asked.

"I—I don't like looking at myself."

"What nonsense! You're a beautiful girl!" He touched Piper's chin and nudged her to peer at herself. But when he saw that she still would not make eye contact with her reflection, he surrendered.

"No matter. It's not your face that you should be concerned about anyway. It's your hands!"

Houdini made a flicking gesture with his wrist and beckoned Piper to do the same with the wand. "One, two, three!"

"One, two, three!" she repeated, gesturing with the white-tipped stick. But nothing happened.

"One, two, three!" she said again, and still the wand refused to produce its festoon of posies. Piper grew more frustrated with each failed attempt and Houdini finally eased the wand from her grip.

"Patience, my dear Piper. Patience. No one can perform magic their very first time out. Practice, as they say, makes perfect."

He laid the wand back among the contents of the box. Piper folded her arms over her chest.

"Those aren't the kinds of tricks I want to know about anyway," she said.

Houdini beamed. "So you want to know how I do the great es-capes? A girl after my own heart!"

He sat down in a large armchair and took a deep breath. He motioned with his arms and legs, pretending to be bound to it. "When I am about to be tied, I always sit a little forward from the back of the chair. If my feet and legs are to be tied to the chair, then I sit so that my knees are at least one one-quarter of an inch from the chair leg.

"It's the same principle with a straitjacket," he continued, his eyes sparkling with pride. "I inflate my chest to make myself bigger when being tied up. Then I compress myself so the bonds are loose. That gives me enough wiggle room to dislocate my shoulders."

"How about your box trick?" Piper asked, wincing at the memory of passing out during his Water Torture act. "A dislocated shoulder won't get out of that thing!"

Houdini's expression changed dramatically. The twinkle left his eyes and his face grew haggard.

"I can't tell you," he said in a voice that was almost a whisper. "I don't know myself, and what's more, I always have a dread that if I should fail, I would not live. I have promised your Aunt Bess that I'd give up the box trick at the end of the season, for she makes herself ill with worry, and for myself I shall be relieved too."

He stood and brushed the front of his pants with his hands. Then his whole body shuddered like someone who had just escaped a nest of spiders.

"Locks!" he exclaimed, stabbing a finger into the air. He rummaged through the contents of the chest once more. "Locks are a different story. I've never met a lock I didn't like."

He plucked a padlock from the chest and tossed it to Piper.

"The most difficult task is to identify the type of lock you are trying to pick. Is the lock a wafer or pin-tumbler? Open as many as you can and study the principles, looking all the time for weak points that are built into the design. Believe me, all locks have weak points."

His hand disappeared once more into the box and emerged with a pair of manacles.

"Handcuffs are just another type of lock. Believe it or not, dear girl, there are only 20 brands of handcuffs on the whole planet. Most of them are in this chest."

He spit on his wrist then snapped the cuffs over them. "Saliva. Makes it easier to slide them off."

"Gross." Piper crinkled her nose.

Houdini laughed.

"Many locks and handcuffs can be opened with properly applied force, others with shoestrings."

He pulled something out of his shoe and started using it to fidget with the lock.

"Always carry keys and picks in your shoes. Or your hair. You've got the hair for it." He brushed his fingertips along his receding hairline. "Not a good place for me anymore."

Even as Houdini smiled, Piper noticed that he never stopped working the lock.

"Sometimes I'll carry picks in my mouth, or in my throat or my gut to regurgitate later...or even in other unmentionable areas."

Piper blushed.

"All seems kinda dangerous," she said.

Houdini scoffed. "Take my advice, my dear Piper—laugh at Death before she laughs at you. People will pay a dollar to see a person in love with Death. But Death just closes doors. I want to see them...open!"

The cuffs snapped open and Houdini exclaimed, "Ta-Da!"

Piper clapped her hands and Houdini took an exaggerated bow. He reached into his pocket and withdrew a gadget about the size of a pocket knife. Piper saw the name "Houdini" prominently engraved across it.

"I always carry this with me. It's got a set of steel lock picks that can open most doors. With it, I have opened thousands of ward locks. Such an implement, if in the possession of an evil person, would be a very dangerous thing. This is a gift that I give to you."

He held the device out to Piper. She carefully plucked it from his open palm and began to inspect all of its various picks.

Houdini continued. "Use it responsibly. It usually lands its beneficiary in jail. But I have domesticated it and refined it until it has landed me before applauding monarchs and paying audiences. You see, it all depends on the lock you pick."

He removed another item from the chest. "And if that doesn't get you out of trouble, this little gizmo will give you the upper hand in any unforeseen circumstance."

At first Piper thought it was a necklace, but then she noticed that the flexible silver wire had a serrated edge.

"This is called a Gigli saw," Houdini explained. "Secret agents have been known to conceal them in their clothing. I prefer to hide them in my shoelaces. You, however, being of the fairer sex, can wear it out in the open as a piece of jewelry."

The magician coiled it several times and looped it around Piper's neck, laying it over her robe and on top of the silver padlock that still hung from her neck. He flinched when he caught his finger on the Gigli's edge.

"I suggest you wear it on the outside of your clothes, because its teeth are sharp!" Houdini said, sucking his finger.

He glanced in the box, furrowed his brow, and reached for something else.

"Hmmm. I have no idea what this is. But I'm sure it will look better on you than it ever will on me."

He tossed her a diamond pin that was shaped like a question mark. It had a rare pearl drop at the base of the punctuation.

Piper's jaw fell. "Are these real diamonds? Is that a real pearl?"

"Of course, dear girl," her uncle smiled. "When you're dealing with Houdini, everything is real. Except, of course, when it's not."

Piper closed her mouth. Her eyes, however, remained as wide as two saucers.

"But why have you given me all these things? Are you afraid something's going to happen to me?"

She recalled Houdini's ardent instructions to his assistant the night before: *Take them directly home. Do not stop for anything.*

"Nonsense, child," Houdini retorted. "But one can never be too careful. In a house this big, with all of the toys I've amassed over the years, there's a whole lot of mischief you can get into! So it's best that you be prepared for any eventuality."

He looked around the library, searching for something. His eyes landed on an ornate gold case displayed in a glass cabinet. It was no bigger than a cigar box. He rubbed his chin and studied Piper up and down. She felt exposed, like he could see right through her.

Houdini unlocked the cabinet, removed the box, and opened it. Piper thought she saw her uncle's face glow for a second, as though the box had beamed an ethereal ray of light on him. He gently lifted a shining object from its housing and presented it to Piper.

It was a key. A golden skeleton key.

Piper took it between her thumb and forefinger. She thought she could feel it throbbing with some sort of power. The key gleamed suddenly and she almost dropped it.

"Wh-what is it?"

"I call it the Key of Solomon. According to legend, it can open any door, anywhere."

Houdini paused and took a deep breath. "But use it wisely, because it will work only once for its wielder. After that, it must be given to a worthy individual—someone who will use its power for good, not ill. That is why I am bequeathing it to you, Piper."

Piper couldn't tell if this was just another one of Houdini's fanciful stories or if he was being sincere.

"So then, you've used it once already?" she asked.

The magician turned from her. "My dear girl. I am the Great Houdini! What need have I for a magical key?"

This time Piper could tell he wasn't being completely honest. But she didn't pursue her question.

"Thank you, Uncle...I mean Houdini. These gifts are really nifty and all...and I hope I'll make you proud of me if I ever have to use them."

She hesitated, trying not to seem ungrateful.

"And thanks for sharing the secrets about how you do your escapes." She held her breath. "But I'm afraid those aren't the tricks I was curious about either."

"Oh?" Houdini raised an eyebrow. "Then what tricks did you mean, my dear girl?"

She paused, as if weighing her word.

"How did you make the wind?" Piper finally blurted.

"The wind?"

"Yes. The wind that carried me away from my fa…that man's claws and fangs?"

Houdini averted her gaze.

"You're mistaken, child. It was windy, to be sure. What else would you expect from a mid-December storm? But that man picked you up and tossed you inside to be done with you. He had long fingernails and horrible teeth to be sure. But no claws, no fangs. I'm sure there was no intent to harm you."

Houdini's chuckle seemed less than genuine.

"And he wasn't my father?" Piper pressed him.

Just then, a high-pitched voice emanated from the bottom of the stairwell. "Young lady…and young man—your breakfast is ready."

Houdini placed a hand on Piper's back and led her out of the library. "Let's adjourn to the dining room. You're going to love your Aunt Bess's cooking. We can continue our discussion later."

Piper followed Houdini through the door of the study and down the stairs. She could tell that he had no intention of ever following up on the conversation.

When the pair reached the ground floor, Houdini greeted his wife, took her in his thick arms, and swung her around the vast kitchen.

When he set her down again, Bess kissed his cheek. Then she greeted Piper with a kiss on the forehead.

"Good morning, my dear. I hope you enjoy tarts?"

She handed Piper a small basketful of bread puffs that oozed with strawberry jam filling. "Eat them quickly—before your uncle steals them."

Houdini smiled. "I've never lost my fondness for pastry."

Bess slapped him playfully on the hand.

"When I'm not looking, he likes to help himself to the cakes in my cupboards. More than once I've found the cupboard empty but locked, with Houdini's visiting card on one of the plates."

Houdini bit into his tart, looking like a little boy who's just been caught with his hand in the cookie jar. Bess had surrounded his dish with the day's newspapers and placed his coffee where he could easily reach it without spilling. Jam dribbled from the corner of his mouth.

Piper looked up and noticed that some of the cabinet doors did indeed have locks. And above the cabinets was an aviary about six square feet with all kinds of birds. There was also another smaller cage with a black-and-gray parrot.

"You sure like birds."

"And dogs, and rabbits. All animals actually," Bess admitted, pouring Piper a glass of orange juice.

"No cats, I hope," Piper said.

"Not presently," Bess replied. "You don't like cats?"

"I'm allergic," Piper admitted, remembering one of the foster homes that she had been forced to leave. It had been a nice place, and the foster parents were pleasant enough. But they owned a number of cats who had the run of the house. Piper had never been sick a day in her life, but when she tried to stay there, she kept sneezing and sneezing.

"What's that bird-thing in your bedroom?" Piper asked, taking a bite of her tart. It tasted so good, she almost forgot her question.

"Oh, so you met old Stoker!" Houdini declared, peering over his newspaper. "You know, Piper, in the East they believe that the bat has a particular affinity for arcane uses. In the Austrian region of Tyrol, it is believed that the man who wears the left eye of a bat may become invisible, and in the German state of Hesse, whoever wears the heart of a bat bound to the arm with red thread will always be lucky at cards."

He paused to wipe jelly from the corners of his mouth with a cloth napkin. The effect looked almost like blood.

"The Arctic snow bat is the rarest breed of all and therefore the most sought after," he said.

"Your uncle saved Stoker from a cruel fate, poor soul," Bess said, taking the napkin from her husband and replacing it with another.

"H-he can talk!" Piper said.

"And why not?" Houdini answered. "His brain is far bigger than a parrot's!"

"So is his mouth!" Bess replied, which made Piper laugh.

In the days that followed, Piper visited Stoker every day. Houdini even let her feed him.

Exploring her new home, Piper couldn't help but think that her uncle's and aunt's marriage was more like a game of two children playing house. Houdini composed a daily love letter to Bess, even when he was at home. He hid them around the house like he was setting up a treasure hunt for a children's party. Then he would playfully invite his wife to find them.

Bess was no different. She was a willing partner in her husband's odd little games of make-believe. And it was true that she washed his ears every day like he was a schoolboy.

"I have to steal his soiled underwear at night to get him to change it," Bess confessed to Piper. "Ironically, the World-Famous Self-Liberator is the most helpless man in the world."

Bess sewed a number of small dolls, dressed them in different outfits, and gave them to Piper. Aunt Bess was fond of her big dollhouse with its variety of carpets and furniture. But Piper had always been more of a tomboy. She was more likely to wind up pitching baseballs in the backyard instead of playing with dolls.

The backyard was perfect for pitching balls because it had a huge fenced-in courtyard. The snow had all melted and Piper would wander the barren gardens and play on a swing that hung from a tall oak.

She also enjoyed exploring the inside of the house. It had a dozen rooms with several fireplaces, baths, and kitchens—plus a cellar *and* a basement. There was a large trap door in the front of the house so that Houdini could get his baggage from the street to the cellar.

But Piper's favorite room was Houdini's vast library, not just because of its secret panels and hidden passageways. It was a veritable fairy-tale sort of a room. Each time she visited, she found something new to capture her attention and her imagination.

Houdini beamed with pride the first time he discovered Piper sitting behind his portable writing desk. "That is the same desk at which Edgar Allan Poe composed his acclaimed works of verse and fiction," he bragged.

But his tone was altogether different when Piper stumbled across two ancient ceramic jars that were in the same glass cabinet where he had kept the Key of Solomon. Each of the jars had a wooden lid that was carved and painted with the image of an animal's head. One had the head of a jackal and the other a falcon.

The mysterious relics were obviously antiques and Piper had no intention of disturbing them. But when Houdini discovered her examining them through the glass, he pulled her back. His words were cold and abrupt. "Not every vessel should be viewed as a trap from which to escape."

Piper quickly learned what Houdini had meant when he had told her, "With all of the toys I've amassed over the years, there's a whole lot of mischief you can get into!" Her favorite piece of furniture was an old electric chair that her uncle claimed had executed the first criminal in America sentenced to die by electrocution. Despite his wife's objections, Houdini had insisted on installing the deactivated machine in their living room.

"I did it purely for sentimental reasons," he explained to Piper.

The house also had an antique iron maiden torture chest. The inner walls were fitted with 600 deadly-sharp spikes to ensure a quick and bloody death. The outside of the tomb-sized container looked like an upside-down ice cream cone with the cast likeness of a woman's face on top. Piper thought that the woman looked like Bess.

Aunt Bess was a funny duck and a free spirit rolled into one package. At night, she would cater to her husband's every wish. "You're getting a special dinner tonight, Houdini—all your favorites. Hungarian chicken, spatzels, and custard bread pudding with bing cherries."

But every morning, while Houdini stayed home to work on his next big thing, Bess would treat herself and Piper to lavish shopping sprees where salespeople actually let her try things on! One time Bess bought them matching coats. Then they ate lunch and laughed at everything and everyone around them.

Bess took turns with Houdini in spoiling their new niece. One day, Houdini took Piper to a general store near the subway station that had a long, winding candy counter. He gave her a one-pound basket and told her that she could fill it with anything she wanted. He also let her get a Grape Nehi to wash it all down with.

When Christmas came, Houdini put up a big tree that Bess and Piper helped decorate with strings of popcorn and cranberries. Houdini added some delicate ornaments that he'd gotten in Germany. They clipped little candle holders to the tree, put candles in them, and Bess helped Piper light them. Bess and Piper sang "Up on the Housetop" and "Jolly Old St. Nicholas." Houdini pretended to join in, but it was obvious that he didn't know the words.

"I've never been ashamed to acknowledge that I'm a Jew, and never will be," he declared, "but other than the Fourth of July, Christmas is the most meaningful holiday to me. I may be the son of a Rabbi, but I married a gentile and I enjoy sending out Christmas cards every year."

He smiled at Piper. "Quite honestly though, since Mother passed away, Christmas has been somewhat empty. Until today."

They gathered around the Christmas tree and opened their presents. Bess gave Piper a sweater, some socks, and mittens that she had knitted for the winter ahead. Houdini gave his niece a few coins, including a quarter that he pulled from her ear. Then he handed her an oval-shaped present that was wrapped artlessly in newspaper and masking tape.

"Did it myself," Houdini smirked.

"Impressive," Bess rolled her eyes.

Piper ripped open the newspaper wrapping to unveil a glass pitcher.

"It's a milk jug," Piper said, almost as a question.

"But not an ordinary milk jug," Houdini replied, putting a finger aside his nose. "It's a magic jug. Here, I'll show you."

He brought the pitcher to the kitchen and filled it with milk.

When he returned, he set it on the table. Then he took a sheet of the newspaper wrapping, rolled it into a cone, and gave the point of the cone a slight twist.

Houdini poured the milk from the pitcher into the cone and returned the pitcher to the table.

"One, two, three…!" He shook the cone so its contents would splash Piper and Bess. They both flinched, but nothing came out. To prove that the pitcher really contained milk, Houdini poured the rest of its contents into a glass and drank it.

"Refreshing," he exhaled loudly, wiping his lips with the back of his hand.

Piper and Bess looked at each other and shrugged their shoulders. "Hurray!" they shouted in unison.

"How does it work?" Piper asked.

Houdini took his niece aside so that Bess couldn't hear. He let her examine the milk jug.

"The pitcher contains a transparent liner," he said, showing Piper the inside of the jug.

Then he tilted the jug. "When you tip the pitcher, a shield on the lip of the pitcher creates a barrier and the milk flows through a cutout into the lining instead of pouring into the cone. When the pitcher is tipped a second time, milk spills over the barrier and pours into the glass."

Piper turned the pitcher around in her hands and then looked at her uncle with misty eyes.

"What's the matter, child? Christmas is supposed to be a happy day!" Houdini said.

She glanced around as though searching for the right words.

"It is! You and Aunt Bess have made this the happiest day of my life! Less than two weeks ago, I was a nobody—I had nobody. Now I'm the niece of the world's most famous magician and his beautiful wife. I'm living in their marvelous house and sharing their wonderful life."

"So, is there a problem?" Houdini asked.

"I just…" Piper hesitated. "I just keep thinking that it's all a big mistake—that somebody's going to come and take it all away." She was trying hard to fight back her tears.

Houdini got down on one knee so he could look his niece squarely in the eyes. Bess placed a comforting hand on her shoulder.

"It's true that God has seen fit not to bless Bess and myself with children of our own, even though Ma prayed for it. But now that her prayers have been answered, we won't let anyone take it away."

He took his wife's hand and squeezed it. "Perhaps it's time for us to rest long enough to raise a child ourselves."

"But I still feel kind of guilty," Piper said. "You and Aunt Bess gave me food, clothing, a place to sleep, and all these amazing Christmas gifts, and I didn't get you anything."

Houdini laughed. "You just learn how to do that trick, and that will be the best present of all," he said, rustling her hair.

That evening, Piper enjoyed the best Christmas dinner of her life. Bess served a fat roast turkey, a mountain of roasted and mashed potatoes, stuffing with sausage, a bowl of almond green beans, cranberry sauce, and a silver boat of thick gravy to smother it all. Everything was hunky-dory.

Over the next week, Piper practiced her magic every day. She discovered that she performed best after one of Bess's spectacular dinners. She even amazed herself a few times with some of her results after a delicious dinner.

By the time New Year's rolled around, Piper was an accomplished amateur. It was 1926, and the country was celebrating its Sesquicentennial over a long holiday weekend. Piper commemorated the occasion by performing for the first time in front of a live audience—her aunt and uncle.

As the last rays of the sun gave way to the modest glow of a half moon, Piper set up her magician's table in the middle of the living room. Houdini sat beside his wife on their gilt-edged sofa.

"I'm glad for once to be in the audience," he said.

To open her performance, Piper took out her wand. She shouted, "One, two, three!" and flicked her wrist. A bouquet of colorful flowers emerged from the wand's tip. Houdini winked at her and Bess clapped in delight.

Piper wanted to impress her uncle in the worst way. But she knew it would be difficult since most of her tricks were pretty basic. Instead, she hoped that Houdini would be proud of the lightness and agility of her hands and the witty banter she had been practicing all week.

Piper performed a few card tricks and some sleight-of-hand illusions with sponges and thimbles. She even managed to escape from a pair of handcuffs, which thrilled Houdini to no end.

For her closing act, she performed the milk pitcher trick.

"I have here a sheet of ordinary newspaper, filled with ads, more ads, and maybe some partial truths. Now I'm going to fill it with something substantial."

Bess and Houdini giggled.

Piper rolled the newspaper into a cone. In her other hand she picked up the milk pitcher and slowly poured its contents into the cone. A few drops trickled out of the bottom of the paper. Setting the half-empty pitcher down, Piper twisted the bottom of the cone and folded the end up tight.

Houdini gave an encouraging nod as Piper emptied the rest of the milk into the newspaper and returned the pitcher to the table. With a sudden motion, she flicked the paper cone at her aunt.

Bess shrieked as white flew everywhere and she lunged to protect the sofa. Piper and Houdini laughed when Bess realized that the white stuff was only paper confetti.

Crushing the newspaper cone, Piper smiled and took a bow. Bess stood and brushed the bits of paper from her dress.

"Enough of that for one night, young lady," she said. "It's time for you to get to bed."

"Aww, Aunt Bess! Why so early?" Piper whined.

"Because you've got a big day ahead of you."

"Why?" Piper knitted her brow.

"Because I've enrolled you in school, dear."

Piper looked at Houdini. Houdini looked at Bess. And Bess stood her ground.

"You didn't think I was going to allow our young ward to remain under our roof only to be fed an intellectual diet of deception and illusion! She's a young lady, Houdini. She needs a proper education."

Houdini sat on the edge of the sofa in silence. He looked like he wanted to argue but couldn't find the right words.

Bess turned to Piper. "Now get upstairs and I'll run a bath for you."

"But my magic tricks..." Piper protested.

"I'll clean up your act. Now scoot!"

Bess picked up the empty pitcher and used the cuff of her sleeve to wipe the ring it had left on the wooden table.

"I have a feeling you may have provided her with a talent to get into more trouble than you know," she said, dropping the pitcher onto Houdini's stomach.

"Ugh!" Houdini grunted. "What did I do to deserve that? She performed the trick admirably and even added a few nuances of her own! It's called innovation, dear Bess!"

"I have nothing against innovation, Houdini," Bess replied. "But the next time she performs that trick, do not let her use one of my good crystal pitchers."

Houdini stared blankly at his wife. Then he examined the exquisite design of the heavy decanter in his lap. It had a Waterford signature etched into its base.

Piper walked up the stairs and paused to glance at her bewildered uncle.

"Good night, Houdini," she said with a twiddle of her fingers.

She lingered a moment longer as Houdini picked up the wand and sniffed the bouquet. She thought that his eyes would pop out of his head.

The flowers were real.

THE ZOMBIE'S BROTHER

A skeletal frame of beams, girders, and columns ascended from the torn landscape along Flatbush Avenue. Construction was well underway and the cornerstone had already been laid. But the colder temperatures had forced all work on the building to come to a halt.

There was about three inches of new snow on the ground and clumps of it blemished a sign that children had used as target practice for their snowball fights. On warmer days, the words "Future site of the Loew's Kings Theatre" could be read on the face of the sign.

Another sign below it read, "Danger: Keep out!"

A boy in baggy tweed pants climbed to the top of the scaffolding where the theater's marquee had already been erected. Salvador Gamache came here when he wanted to read in peace. He dreamed of being an usher when the Loew's King finally opened.

That's because Sal was a "reel boy." He enjoyed the movies. He had been to some of the other "Loew's Wonder Theatres" and could imagine the high curved ceilings, ornate walls and windows, and sweeping staircase that would soon define this one.

The Wonder Theaters had been funded by Marcus Loew to establish his preeminence in New York film exhibition. Loew used extravagant ornamentation to create a fantasy environment that would stimulate the imaginations of average citizens by making them feel like royalty.

Every morning before school, Sal would perch atop the marquee and spend a half hour or so reading something by one of his favorite dime-store novelists. It was a cure for his loneliness and an escape from the sound of his parents arguing.

He would imagine the scenes in his books being played out on the big screen of the movie palace. This morning he was enjoying the latest issue of *Weird Tales,* in which bug-eyed aliens were plotting to take over the world.

Sal wasn't allowed to read the pulps at home. His old *granmé* called it *terib*—horrible stuff—and warned him that it would stunt his growth and turn him into a socialist.

Sal's family had moved in with his *granmé* before the start of the school year. It was always hard being the "new kid" in school. But it was even harder for Sal because he was the new *black* kid.

Not that he was the only black kid in school. African Americans had been migrating from the South to the big cities since before the Great War. Newspapers claimed that the reason for this "Great Migration" was racial tension and the widespread violence of lynchings in the South. But Sal didn't know anybody who'd been lynched.

Yes, racial tension was alive and well in Louisiana, just as it was everywhere else. But in the North, black people could find better jobs and attend better schools. It was also a place where his papa could vote!

Unlike most of his fellow black classmates, Sal's family hadn't migrated to the North looking for work. His papa earned a steady income from the sugar cane farm he owned outside New Orleans.

The Gamaches had come to New York for medical care. Sal's older brother Henri had been stricken with a rare brain disorder that had baffled Louisiana's medical community. The family moved to Brooklyn so that Henri could be treated at Bellevue Hospital, which was well-known for its psychiatric facilities.

Overall, the move had been a good one for Sal. Sure, there were things he missed about Louisiana. But the school he was attending in Brooklyn was definitely a step up. Public schools for black kids in New Orleans weren't as good as the ones for white kids. In New York, however, there were no "black schools" or "white schools." Segregation had ended here over 25 years ago.

The same was true about movie theaters. In the South, black people were required to sit in a separate area—usually the balcony, where the view was terrible. But in New York, the theaters were large enough to support black and white audiences without dividing them. That's another reason why Sal enjoyed reading at the Loew's King. Even though it wasn't finished yet, nobody could tell him he wasn't allowed to be here.

"Hey, you're not allowed to be here!"

The voice startled Sal so much that he almost tossed his *Weird Tales* over the side of the marquee.

He looked up. A lanky figure stood between him and the early morning sun. Sal's eyes took a moment to adjust to the contrast of the dark figure against the bright rays streaming behind it. But his ears had already placed the speaker by the way he pronounced the "here" as "heah."

"Rand! What are *you* doing in New York?" Sal exclaimed, his own speech marked by a slight French Creole accent.

Alan Rand crossed his arms over his chest. He had unkempt sandy-colored hair and an ugly serpentine rash on both sides of his face.

"Whatcha reading?" the boy asked, though Sal could tell he didn't care.

"A magazine."

Rand tilted the periodical back so that he could read the title.

"Any stories in here about the undead?" Rand probed.

He wasn't a big kid, but he was bigger than Sal. Well, taller anyway. Sal's waistline was bigger. He didn't think of himself as heavyset, but he was heavier than most kids his age. He liked to say that he was "stocky" and blamed it on his mom's gumbo. But the simple truth was that Sal was not a big fan of exercise.

"What's it to you?" Sal asked the taller boy.

"My stepdad's a doctor. Heard all about your family's little secret. Strangest case he ever heard. No pulse. No breath. Even some rotting flesh."

"You're all wet, Rand," Sal protested weakly.

Rand ignored him.

"But every time the docs wanna pull the plug, your brother gets up, walks around a bit, and performs a few tricks like a dog. Then he goes right back to bed, without saying a word."

Rand stepped closer to Sal.

"Stranger still, it only seems to happen when you're in the room, Gamache. What's that all about?"

Sal reflexively stroked a sterling silver amulet that hung from his neck beneath his shirt. The pendant had an image of a cross mounted on a tomb flanked by two coffins.

"That where you keep it?" Rand asked, nodding toward the spot where Sal was groping.

"What the hell are you talking about?" Sal demanded, dropping his hand.

"Don't play stupid with me, jigaboo."

Rand reached for the amulet, but Sal knocked his hand away and leaped to his feet.

"Jigaboo? Is that the best you got?"

Sal almost smiled at the irony. The kids in his old school had made fun of him because his skin was too light. Here it was too dark. Sal was actually Creole—a mix of African, French, Spanish, and Native American heritage. Or, as his brother used to say, "We're a bunch of mutts."

"Go visit the south, Rand," Sal said, trying to sound self-confident. "They give lessons in bigotry to ignorant bozos like you!"

Rand grabbed Sal by the shirt and slammed him against a wall.

"You should've stayed in the south! You and all your kind!"

Rand dropped Sal to the plywood floor with a fist to his gut. Then he kicked over the brown leather satchel that Sal always carried with him, spilling books everywhere.

Sal had been in plenty of scraps down in Louisiana. But he never took joy in them like some of the boys in the neighborhood gangs. It's not that he was a coward—he just wasn't good at fighting. He could take a punch but couldn't throw one to save his life. Just the thought of his fist connecting with someone's face—the look, the sound, the feel—was enough to make him puke.

But when Rand started rummaging through his books, Sal felt violated. Something snapped inside him. Rand held up a book entitled *The Book of the Dead: The Papyrus of Ani* by E.A. Wallis Budge.

"Is this it?" Rand demanded. "Does this tell you how to do it?"

Tightening his fist, Sal leaped at his adversary and socked him in the nose. He heard a *crack* but wasn't sure if it was the boy's nose or his own hand.

"Oww!" they both cried at the same time.

Alan Rand held a finger to his nose and Sal saw blood dribble onto it. Rand looked at it and then tasted it as if to confirm what his eyes had already told him.

"You dirty dinge!"

Rand raised his fist to return the blow, but Sal twisted his head so it barely grazed him. The failure to connect just made Rand angrier, and his next jab smashed Sal's lower lip into his teeth. The stocky boy hunched over in pain and he accidentally struck Rand in the chin with his elbow.

Pressing the advantage, Sal lunged at Rand, ramming his head into the boy's stomach. As Rand fell backward, Sal continued to advance, his lungs heaving with each step.

Rand struck his opponent in the nose with the back of his hand. Sal lost his balance but didn't fall. He grabbed Rand's wrist and bit his forearm. The taller boy screamed and pulled his arm away.

"You fight like a girl!" he exclaimed.

"At least I don't look like one!"

Rand fumed. His eyes darted around at the bits of construction debris that littered the area.

"You're not the only one who can fight dirty," he said, snatching up a loose two-by-four and approaching Sal like a demonic samurai.

Sal scampered backward, desperately seeking some kind of protection. His hand fell upon another beam of wood. He raised it just in time to block a swipe from Rand's wooden scimitar.

Sal took a swing at Rand, but it didn't connect. The momentum made Sal lose his balance and he collapsed onto the floor.

The next thing he knew, Rand was pouncing on him like a drunken panther. He knelt on Sal's chest, driving his bony knees into Sal's ribcage. Rand turned red in the face and the snakes on his cheeks turned purple. But Sal didn't think it made his adversary look threatening. On the contrary, Rand looked nervous—like he was scared he might actually hurt him.

"Get your lousy knees off my chest," Sal screamed. He fumbled around him for something, anything, to turn the tide to his advantage. His hand landed in a pile of something soft and gritty.

Sawdust.

He grabbed a handful and threw it into Rand's face.

"Aggh, my eyes!" Rand exclaimed.

Coughing, spitting, and sputtering, he blindly groped for Sal's throat.

Sal turned his head to the side and he felt a tug at the frayed leather band around his neck. It snapped. Before either of them could react, the cord slithered down Sal's neck, slipped between two wooden planks, and fell to the slushy sidewalk below.

Rand scrambled to his feet and ran toward the construction ladder that both boys had used to reach the top of the awning. Sal reached out with his foot and tripped the fleeing youth. He clambered over Rand to reach the ladder first. But Rand blocked him with a knee to the groin and Sal doubled over in pain.

Rand's victory, however, was short lived. Sal teetered for a moment and then collapsed seat-first onto his face.

"Get off me, lardbutt!" Rand's muffled voice demanded. He kicked and swatted at the heavier boy, but Sal didn't budge.

Just then, the adversaries heard the sound of two delicate hands clapping in mock applause.

"Congratulations, boys," said a girl's voice. "That had to be the most pathetic fight I've ever seen."

The first thing that Sal noticed was the girl's hair. It looked like it belonged on a Raggedy Ann doll. She wore a brand-new houndstooth jacket and a black panne velvet skirt that gathered at her knees. Sal could tell by the way the girl fidgeted that she was as comfortable in her clothes as a baby in burlap. But at least her clothes were more flattering than the flapper duds most of the girls in school were trying to get away with.

The redhead was holding a Grape Nehi in one hand and twirling a familiar charm by its leather cord in the other.

"The amulet!" they exclaimed.

"Is this what you boys were fighting over?" she asked.

Sal rolled off Rand's face and both boys jumped to their feet.

"It's mine!" Rand proclaimed. "The spade stole it from me!"

"That's exactly what I figured," the girl said, giving Sal a dirty look. She palmed the amulet and handed it to Rand. The boy stuck his tongue out at Sal.

"No, wait! It's mine!" Sal protested.

The girl ignored him and pressed the object into Rand's palm, closing his fingers around it. She held the blond boy's eyes with her own.

"The cord is ripped. So put it in your pocket and keep it there until you get to wherever it is you're going."

Rand nodded and stuck his fist into his pocket. He turned and scampered down the ladder, giving Sal a wink on his way down.

"So long, sucker!" he taunted before disappearing beneath the edge of the marquee's roof.

Sal groaned.

"Are you all right?" the girl asked.

"Of course I'm not all right!" he replied.

His chest hurt like hell and his nose was bleeding. He touched the tip of his tongue to a cut on his lip and winced. Speaking only aggravated it.

The girl scooped up a bit of snow and pressed it to Sal's swollen lip.

"Ow!" he yelled, knocking her hand away. "Whadja do that for?"

"I thought it might help the swelling. And stop the bleeding."

Sal didn't reply. He was too busy trying to catch his breath. Rand had been right about one thing—he was definitely out of shape.

"Well, at least wash your face with it," the girl said.

She snatched his wrist, turned his hand up, and plopped the snow into his open palm.

"Stop pretending you care," Sal said with a scowl. "You gave that cake-eater my pendant! Us colored boys are always the bad guy, right?"

The girl smiled and opened her hand.

"Not always. Sometimes pale-skinned redheads make better thieves."

Sal's pendant dangled from her finger on its leather thong like a yo-yo string on a string.

"My amulet!" Sal cried out. "How did you…?"

"A little sleight-of-hand my uncle taught me," she boasted.

"If that's the amulet then what's in Rand's pocket?"

The girl took a swig of her Nehi. She drained the last drop of the bubbly refreshment, wiped her mouth with her sleeve, and turned the empty bottle upside down.

"They should really come up with a way to make these things re-sealable," she said, circling the bottle tip with her finger. "Otherwise you gotta finish the whole darn thing."

"The cap!" Sal beamed. "But then, how'd you know the pendant was mine and not his?"

"I've seen lots of fights in the places I grew up," the redhead replied. "I can tell when someone's fighting to take something and when someone's fighting to keep it."

She handed the amulet to Sal.

"Thank you," he smiled gratefully.

"What's so valuable about it anyway?" the girl asked. "Looks like a cheap trinket to me."

"It belongs to my brother," Sal replied, tying a knot in the severed cord. "He's in the hospital—coma. I like to…I like to carry a piece of him with me."

"I'm sorry to hear that," the girl said with doleful eyes. "But why did that other jerk want it so badly?"

"I'm not really sure," Sal said, half-truthfully. "I don't know him very well. He doesn't go to my school."

"Oh? What school is that?"

"The Flatbush School," Sal replied, and then added, "P.S. 90 down the road."

"Ducky!" said the girl. It looked to Sal as though she intentionally bit her tongue as soon as she said it. "That's where I go! I mean, that's where I'm supposed to go. It's my first day. Walk with me?"

"That would be…ducky," Sal smirked.

The girl blushed.

"I'm Piper," she said, extending her hand. "Piper Weiss."

Sal took her hand and shook it. "Salvador. Friends call me Sal. And people too lazy to pronounce Salvador."

Piper grinned at his remark. Sal then crouched to gather his fallen books. Piper knelt beside him and helped put them back in his satchel.

"Wow! How much do you carry in this thing?" she asked.

"How do you think I maintain this Charles Atlas physique?" Sal teased, striking a pose like the famous bodybuilder.

Piper giggled. But she was right, of course. Sal kept his books with him at all times like they were his best friends. In addition to his school texts, he carried works of science fiction like *The Island of Doctor Moreau,* some dime novels by authors like Zane Grey and Bram Stoker, among others.

Piper thumbed through one book called *The Mystery of Space* by Robert T. Browne.

"Science fiction?" she asked.

"Some people think so," Sal winked.

The redhead returned it to his satchel. Then she leaned over to pick up the book that had piqued Rand's curiosity. It had fallen open during the melee and one of its pages caught her attention.

"What's this?" she asked.

"Oh, that's the *Book of the Dead,*" he replied, avoiding her gaze. "Just some mumbo jumbo the ancient Egyptians used to protect dead guys from the creatures they might meet in the afterlife."

"No, I mean *this.*" Piper pointed to a crude illustration of four jars with lids that looked like the heads of different animals.

Sal scrunched his nose and took a deep breath.

"All these people ever thought about was death. Death, dying, and more death. They actually believed that the body would come back to life! So they mummified it and preserved all the vital organs in these four jars."

He pointed to the illustration.

"They're called *canopic* jars and were used to preserve internal organs so their owners could use them in the afterlife. The jars had wooden lids that were carved and painted to look like the heads of the four sons of Horus."

Sal moved his index finger across the page pointing to each of the jars in succession.

"Duamutef the jackal protected the stomach. Qebehsenuef, the falcon, protected the intestines. Hapi, the baboon protected the lungs."

His finger tarried on the final jar.

"And this one, Imseti, has a human head. He protected the liver. It was his job to reanimate the corpse."

"My uncle owns the falcon one and the jackal one," Piper said with a smug expression.

Sal narrowed his eyes.

"Well, I'm sure they're just replicas."

"Oh, you don't know my uncle," she chuckled. "He doesn't tolerate fakes."

Then she closed the book and placed it neatly in Sal's knapsack.

"We should get going," Sal said, securing the bag's rusty buckles and slinging it over his shoulder. "First bell's gonna ring soon, and you don't want to be late for your first day."

Sal went down first because he thought Piper looked a bit unsteady in her new shoes. He figured he'd catch her if she slipped on the ladder—or at least cushion her fall. But when he looked up to see how she was doing, Piper clocked him on the forehead with her heel.

"Stop looking up my dress, you cad!" she barked at him.

At the bottom of the ladder, Sal was pressing his hand to the growing lump on his forehead when Piper jumped from the fourth rung and landed beside him.

"You look a mess," she said.

"No thanks to you," he grumbled. "So much for chivalry."

"Oh, quit your bellyaching," Piper said.

She tossed a snowball at him and ran off.

Sal followed in hot pursuit, but his own snowball missed its mark. Then they took turns skidding down the slushy sidewalk all the way to the Flatbush School.

DETENTION

Public School 90 was a two-story brick building on the southwest corner of Church and Bedford. The main entrance was set behind a porch with a wooden roof supported by two stone columns and a round brick arch. The front wall of the main floor was punched with circular openings and the second floor had a large central window flanked by thinner, round-headed windows.

Piper and Sal sloshed up the wet walkway and stomped their feet on the ground before entering the building. Unlike the schools that Piper had previously attended, the classrooms inside the Flatbush School were large, well-lighted, and ventilated. Its halls and stairways were wide and airy.

Piper was also happy to discover that the toilets had doors. Her old schools didn't believe that children deserved privacy. But here it seemed that the students were allowed to be just as comfortable as the teachers.

The Flatbush School had more than four hundred students. Aunt Bess had arranged for her to be placed in the seventh grade, in a class where there were eighteen other children about the same age as her. Sal was in her class too. He sat in the front row, and Piper noticed that he had a hard time sitting still.

The smells of chalk dust, wood furniture polish, and musty books were familiar and welcome. Piper was happy to sit in a desk all her own—with her own inkwell! Her old schools had double desks and the students had to share an inkwell.

Piper's teacher was a woman in her mid-twenties named Miss Hine. She had light brown hair, a long face, and pale blue eyes. After the usual business of introducing Piper to her new classmates, Miss Hine addressed the class.

"Raise your hands if you can name all the Presidents," Miss Hine said.

Sal's hand went up, but Miss Hine ignored it.

"Anyone besides Salvador?"

The teacher looked hopefully at the newcomer, and Piper guessed that she was tired of Sal being the only person in class who knew anything.

After a few uncomfortable seconds, Miss Hine looked away from her with a disappointed frown.

"All right, Salvador. Please stand up and recite as many as you can," Miss Hine said.

Of course, Sal knew them all, just like Piper knew he would.

"By the end of the week, I expect all of you to know the names of the thirty Presidents," Miss Hine challenged.

The truth was that Piper already knew the names of the Presidents…and the Vice Presidents. But unlike her uncle, she never enjoyed being the center of attention. The kids at the orphanage had called her "smarty pants." So she learned at an early age to be very quiet and not raise her hand.

At lunch, Sal saved a seat for Piper next to him. It was a table that had mostly black boys sitting at it, but Sal was eating all by himself. Piper sat down at the empty seat.

During recess she played jump rope, hopscotch, and still-light with some of the younger girls. They were all dolled up in pretty dresses with bows in their hair, and Piper could hardly stand it. She'd rather have been shooting baskets or marbles with the boys and wearing overalls like them too.

"You boys sure are lucky, getting to wear pants," she told Sal when recess was over. "I wish I could wear something to cover my legs."

"Then how would *cads* like me be able to peek up at your bloomers?" Sal grinned. The grin turned to a grimace when Piper flicked the bruise on his forehead.

Just then, a hand fell on her shoulder and a voice behind her growled, "You must be the new girl, Piper Houdini."

Earlier that morning, Houdini had told Piper, "You'll have to go to school. But leave the name of Houdini behind you. It will not be safe to associate yourself with the fame and notoriety of that name outside this house."

Piper turned her head and glanced up into the unblinking eyes of a well-dressed man with graying temples.

"I'm Piper Weiss," she corrected.

The man cleared his throat.

"My apologies. I'm Principal Kaiser. I spoke with your Aunt Bess when she enrolled you in our school. She asked that I make a lady of you."

He took hold of her hand. "Flicking boys on the head is not proper behavior for a lady," he said, emphasizing each word with a tap on her finger.

Then he dropped her hand and marched back into the school. Just like that. Piper stared after him, wondering what else her aunt had told him.

Sal cocked his head. "Why'd he call you *Houdini?*"

"Probably because I have a knack for getting into and out of trouble," Piper said, hoping that a sarcastic answer would put the matter to rest.

The rest of the school day consisted of a combination of study periods for reading textbooks, writing, and solving math problems. There were also recitation periods where the students *recited* to Miss Hine what the textbook had said or how the math problem should be worked out. Piper thought the whole thing was a bit silly and unnecessary. She did, however, enjoy the film strip lessons because her old schools couldn't afford them.

At the end of the school day, a bell rang to dismiss the students. Piper bent over to pack up her books and when she sat up again, there was an envelope on her desk that hadn't been there before. The words "NOTICE OF DETENTION" were written in calligraphy across the envelope, beautifully delineated in gold ink.

Piper opened the envelope and removed a standard form that had been filled out in the same elegant handwriting and gilded ink that adorned the envelope.

NOTICE OF DETENTION

Name: _Piper Weiss_ will be required to serve a detention...
  _ at regular break time
  X after school hours
in Room _117B_
on _Tuesday, January 4_ for _45_ minutes.

Reason for detention?
____ Disturbance
____ Disrespectful
____ Cheating
____ Off limits
____ Tardy
____ Trouble on playground
_X_ Other: _Reckless and unregistered practice of thaumaturgy_

_____   _____

Date   Signature of parent or guardian

Piper had always gotten good grades in vocabulary, but she had no idea what "thaumaturgy" meant. She continued to study the notice as she blindly followed the other students into the hallway.

The detention was scheduled for the next day. But she wanted to speak with the person who had issued the notice so she could explain to her aunt and uncle exactly what it was that she had done wrong.

The numbers on the classroom doors ascended as Piper made her way down the hall. She stopped when she reached Room 117. It was the principal's office, which was no surprise to Piper. Principal Kaiser probably wanted to discipline her for flicking Sal on the noggin.

The notice, however, said that detention would be held in Room 117B. Piper looked around, but the only thing between the principal's office and Room 118 was a door marked "Cloakroom."

Being sent to stand in the cloakroom was the customary punishment for misbehaving in some of her other schools. So Piper walked toward it and reached for the doorknob. A booming voice stopped her coldly.

"Whatcha doin' there, lass?" asked a man in denim overalls who was sweeping the floor with a wide push broom. His hair and beard were almost as red as his face. A patch on his left shirt pocket identified him as the school's custodian, Mr. McFadden.

"I'm new here," Piper said, dropping her hand. "I'm just trying to find the best place to hang my things." She didn't mention the detention notice because she didn't want the custodian's first impression of her to be that of a delinquent.

Mr. McFadden stopped sweeping and leaned on his broom handle. "You won't be finding any coats in that room, missy. Hasn't been used in over thirty years. Don't even have a key for it no more."

"Why not?" Piper asked.

"Student got locked in there one Christmas break. Wasn't a pretty thing when everyone got back." His eyes bulged as though he had witnessed the tragedy himself. "That's why each classroom now has its own cloakroom—ones with no locks on the doors."

Mr. McFadden grasped his broom handle again. "So let that be your first lesson in your new school, lassie—don't be playin' in locked rooms," he growled, pushing a growing pile of dust across Piper's path that almost soiled her new shoes.

Piper turned to walk into Principal Kaiser's office when she bumped into Sal.

"Hey, Piper! How was your first day?" the boy asked eagerly. But his expression changed suddenly when he eyed the envelope in her hand. "What have you got there?" he asked, narrowing his eyes.

Piper got the feeling that he already knew the answer. Well, of course! If she had gotten into trouble for a little thing like flicking a boy on the head, then a rascal like Sal must have gotten plenty of these notices.

"Detention," she answered, waving the form at him. "I don't know what *thaumaturgy* is, but I'm gonna ask Principal Kaiser if it's some sort of code word for defending my honor against boys who tease me about my bloomers."

"*Thaumaturgy?*" Sal's eyes widened, ignoring her sarcasm. "Dammit, Rand snitched!"

"Rand?" Piper cocked her head. "You mean that boy from this morning? What's he got to do with this?"

Sal stood silent for a moment. Then he snatched the detention notice from Piper's fingers.

"I'll handle it," he said.

Piper started to object, but Sal persisted.

"Look, he's trying to make you out to be some sort of conniving witch. But you were just pulling a fast one to correct an injustice, that's all. I'll go in and explain it was just a simple misunderstanding."

"I can fight my own battles," Piper said, trying to seize the notice from his fingers.

"I know you can, Piper. You've already proven that. But you fought my battle this morning, so let me return the favor. Besides, what will your aunt and uncle say if they find out you got detention on your first day of school?"

Piper hadn't considered that. All she wanted was Houdini and Aunt Bess to be proud of her. After everything they had done for her, how could she look them in the eye if she came home with a detention notice on her very first day? Would they think they had made the wrong decision in keeping her? Would they send her back to Hollygrove?

"All right," Piper conceded. "But at least let me go in with you."

Sal smiled and put his hand on her shoulder. "Believe me, I know how the system works by now. If we both go, Kaiser will think we're trying to gang up on him and we'll get into even more trouble. Go back to your aunt and let me handle this."

Piper slouched. Glancing at Sal through a strand of red hair that had fallen across her left eye, she said, "You'd do that for me?"

"Uh-huh," he nodded.

"Then I've already gotten something on my first day that I've never had in any other school."

"What's that?" Sal asked.

"A friend," Piper said, pushing the hair out of her eye with two fingers.

Sal grinned and Piper turned to walk down the freshly-swept hallway.

"By the way," Sal called after her, "I think your freckles are the cat's meow."

Piper turned the corner and giggled. She didn't even flinch at his use of the corny expression. Perhaps it was a sign that her life had reached a turning point.

Piper had learned to avoid friendship early on because her friends always ended up leaving her. She hardened herself by refusing to get involved with anyone and never asking for help. Because she never bowed down to the bullies who teased her for being a loner, she often came back to the foster home or orphanage with a bloody lip or black eye.

That's why she had helped Sal this morning. When the amulet landed at her feet and she saw the two boys fighting on the marquee, it was a chance for Piper to set things right without making herself vulnerable.

It was a good thing that Sal turned out to be her classmate instead of Rand...

Piper stopped a few feet from the exit. She remembered Sal's words:

I don't know him very well. He doesn't go to my school.

Then how did Rand "snitch" to Principal Kaiser?

Piper did an about-face and marched back to the end of the hall. When she reached the corner, she peered into Room 117. Principal Kaiser sat at his desk but there was no sign of Sal.

Out of the corner of her eye, she noticed a tweed trouser leg disappearing into the cloakroom. Then the door snapped shut.

Room 117B?

Piper rushed to the door and tried the knob. Locked. Just like Mr. McFadden said it would be. But she knew what she had just seen!

Piper glanced at the keyhole. She thought about using the golden key that Houdini had given her, but then rejected the idea. She didn't buy her uncle's story that she could use it only once, but a closet door wouldn't prove too challenging even for her novice lock-picking abilities.

Piper reached into her pocket and pulled out the engraved gadget that Houdini had given her. She withdrew several of the attachments until she found a steel lock pick that looked to be about the right size and shape.

Students and teachers were still roaming the halls and Piper's task was made all the more difficult by having to stop and start over again every time someone passed. Some of the faculty members eyed her suspiciously and she was nervous that Mr. McFadden might return at any moment.

Finally, Piper felt the upper pins of the lock separate from the lower pins. Turning the cylinder with the tool, she finally heard a satisfying "click."

"Ta-da!" she said softly, wishing her uncle could see her.

When Piper was satisfied that no one was watching, she slipped into the cloakroom, making sure to keep the door from closing completely behind her.

At first Piper could make out nothing but a few mops, buckets, and brooms. But her eyes always adjusted quickly to the dark, even when there was no light at all.

Soon she could make out a magnificent mirror propped against the back wall of the tiny room. It was as high as the ceiling with an ornate gilded frame inlaid with gold leaf. The mirror stood on two feet that were shaped like eagle claws.

Piper stepped up to the mirror and touched it. Suddenly, the door to the cloakroom slammed shut behind her, locking her in. Piper's heart skipped a beat. Despite her ability to see in the dark, she wasn't sure if she would be able to pick the lock from the inside. But before panic could set in, the glass of the mirror began to glow with an eerie red light.

Piper looked at the ornate framed glass and expected to see the hazy reflection that always greeted her when she looked in a mirror. But she couldn't see herself at all.

What she observed instead was Sal standing before three people whose backs were to her. From this angle it was obvious that two of them, a boy and a girl, were about her age. But Sal was pleading earnestly to the third person—a woman in her mid-thirties who stood between the boy and the girl.

"It can't be a mirror," Piper muttered. "It's some sort of window!"

But upon closer examination, she realized that the window wasn't attached to any wall. Piper could walk behind it like it was a movie screen. Except there was no projector. The scene playing out beyond the glass was live, in color, and three-dimensional!

Then how did Sal get through it? Piper pressed her fingertips all around the glass for some way to open it. But she could find no latch, no hinge.

She felt around the frame for some sort of lock or keyhole but only succeeded in scraping her finger against a jagged nail where it was connected at the corner.

"Oww! Dumbdora!" she cried out. "I should just cut this finger off—it only gets me in trouble," she said. It was the same finger she had pricked the night she'd met Houdini.

Piper wouldn't let a little cut deter her. Pressing her shoulder to the glass, she gave it a slight shove. The mirror tipped back off its feet, but it didn't allow her to pass.

Steadying the object with one hand, she pressed her other hand against its center. The glass softened like butter where her injured finger had touched it.

At first Piper thought it was just the icky feeling of her blood against the smooth surface. But then she realized that her finger had actually penetrated the window!

She quickly withdrew her hand and gawked at her bloody digit. Then she gradually inserted it through the glass once more. The window melted around her finger but would not allow any other part of her to pass into it.

Piper twirled a knot in her hair. After a few moments, she got an idea. A very weird idea.

Tracing her finger around the glass, Piper smeared her blood to create the outline of an oval that was bigger than her. When she finished, she pressed upon the center of the oval. The glass now felt like gauze and the mirror seemed to turn into a bright silvery mist.

In a moment, Piper was through the glass. A cry of panic caught in her throat as she faded from one world into another where time and space seemed to cancel each other. Her journey carried her no more than a single step, but it was an instant in time that seemed to last forever.

And then, with the same feeling of split-second infinity, she plunged back into reality and landed viciously on her back.

For a moment Piper thought that she was outside because the floor was made of stone and she saw stars above her. But when her vision cleared, she noticed there were lines between some of the stars depicting the constellations.

It was a domed ceiling that had been painted to look like the night sky. Piper sensed that the dome was moving ever so slightly, as though it were keeping up with the position of the stars as they might appear in the afternoon sky.

She sat up and looked around to see if she was still in the cloak-room or someplace else. There was a full-length mirror by her feet. But this one had a polished wood frame and tinted glass that gave it a smoky appearance at its edges.

The place was colder than where she had just been. The only sources of light were lamps and candles that gave everything an orange tint. On the stone wall opposite the mirror hung a magnificent tapestry decorated with emblems of medieval heraldry, floral arrangements, and musical instruments.

Shelves filled with old books lined the other three walls. They reminded Piper of Houdini's library, except these shelves also displayed the bones and pickled remains of animals that she couldn't recognize. There were several empty rectangular tables and a square one that looked like a card table, except instead of cards there were tiles marked with Chinese symbols spread across it.

Just then, Piper heard a familiar New England accent.

"How the hell did she get here?"

Alan Rand took several menacing steps toward her and stabbed a long, bony finger in her direction.

"That's her! She's the one who turned my magical charm into *this!*" Rand held up the Nehi bottle cap between his thumb and forefinger.

"That's bunk!" Sal exclaimed, jumping between him and Piper. "She turned nothing into nothing. The amulet's right here!"

From under his shirt collar he produced the silver charm hanging from its frayed and knotted thong.

Sal reached down to help Piper up but was looking at the woman whom Piper had seen through the window.

"My friend here performed a little sleight-of-hand trick. She substituted the bottle cap for the amulet that Rand was trying to steal… from *me*."

"Is this true, Alan?" the woman demanded, stepping in front of the room's only other occupant, a girl Piper didn't recognize. Rand's eyes shifted from Sal to Piper to the woman.

"I just wanted to borrow it," he said finally.

"My dear boy, I'm not asking you about the charm," the woman scoffed, placing a hand on his shoulder. "It's obvious by its markings that the trinket does not belong to you. Not the type of magick with which you generally consort, now is it?"

She had a vigorous voice with a British accent that possessed a certain degree of hypnotic power.

"I merely want to know if it's true that this young lady bamboozled you…with elementary legerdemain?"

"Leger-wha…?" Rand replied, twisting his face.

The woman sighed and shook her head.

"Stage magic. Did this young lady deceive you with an ordinary parlor trick?"

The girl that Piper didn't know began to snicker.

"The Wizard of Lime Street! Undone by a simple illusion!" Her accent was also distinctly British and her thick Coke-bottle glasses wobbled on her nose as she laughed.

Rand's face grew red. The plump woman held up her hand, admonishing the girl with a single word.

"Silence."

Though it was barely more than a whisper, the girl with the glasses stopped laughing.

"I am sorry, Imperatrix," she apologized, feverishly stroking a worn old quilt that she cradled in her arms.

The woman tensed at the unfamiliar word.

"Please don't call me that."

Then she turned her attention to Piper.

"So, you are Salvador's new friend. I am the headmistress of the Academy of the Inner Light. I am known by several names, but my students call me Miss Fortune."

She was a broad woman, simply and conventionally dressed. She had faded blond hair that was cut into a short bob. At first glance, Piper thought Miss Fortune could pass for the matron of an orphanage, like Mrs. Buckley. But her glittering deep blue eyes suggested something less easily accepted. The headmistress seemed to shine with light and yet Piper could sense bits of darkness within her as well.

"I am curious, young lady. How is it that you were able to activate the *Kefitzat Haderech?*"

"Excuse me, ma'am?" Piper asked, tilting her head.

"The mirror," Sal whispered, pointing his thumb at the mahogany-framed glass. "She wants to know how you jaunted through it."

"Oh, I cut my finger!" Piper held up her finger and then quickly lowered it when she noticed that the digit had stopped bleeding.

"Umm, I made a big bloody O on the magic mirror back in the cloakroom. Then I just stepped into it."

"You can say that again," Rand snorted.

Miss Fortune ignored him. "Sanguine magic. Interesting."

She nodded but Piper wasn't sure if it was a gesture of approval or disapproval.

"Blood is the symbol for life. Yours must be powerful indeed. Tell me, little one, what is your name?"

"Piper W..." she hesitated for a moment. Piper was still confused about everything that was going on. But she knew that extraordinary circumstances rarely tolerated ordinary people. She drew a deep breath.

"Piper Houdini!" she said finally, jutting her chin and folding her arms across her chest.

There was a collective gasp. Piper looked at Sal. His eyes were huge.

"You mean, you *are* related to Harry Houdini?" he asked.

Piper nodded. "I'm his niece."

She wanted to hide from the stunned eyes in the room. Even Miss Fortune seemed unsettled. "So, now that I told you the truth, can you please tell me where I am?"

Sal chimed in before Miss Fortune could answer. Pointing to the dome above their heads, he said, "If the star chart is an accurate representation of where we are, I'd say that this detention hall is located somewhere in England."

"London, to be precise," Miss Fortune acknowledged.

Piper gasped. Somehow, she had traveled over three thousand miles in the blink of an eye!

"B-but, how do I get back to the other magic mirror? I'll be late for Aunt Bess's dinner. It's goulash...and rhubarb pie!"

"Don't worry, child," Miss Fortune said in a soothing tone. "Just as the laws of space do not apply here, neither do the laws of time. You won't miss your dinner."

Piper relaxed, but only just a little.

"But you must understand that there is no 'other' magic mirror," Miss Fortune continued. "The *Kefitzat Haderech* is the only one of its kind...at least as far as I know."

"Then how did I get here?" Piper asked.

Miss Fortune smiled. "You've heard the saying that 'all roads lead to Rome'? In thaumaturgy, all mirrors—in fact all solid reflective surfaces—lead to the *Kefitzat Haderech*."

"Thaumaturgy." Piper repeated. "That's why I got detention. What is it?"

The headmistress looked at her with a serious expression, but her eyes never lost their luster.

"Your uncle practices the craft of magic...with a *c*. Thaumaturges practice the higher art of magick...with a *c k*. We differentiate it because magick...or *thaumaturgy*...is the art of changing consciousness at will."

Piper's nose crinkled like she smelled rotten eggs.

"Does thaumaturgy sell out the Shubert Theatre?" she asked somewhat sheepishly.

"My dear girl, when you change your consciousness, you can change your whole perception," Miss Fortune replied. "When you change your perception, you can change reality. And when reality bends to your will, you can effect a positive change in the whole world. Can your uncle's illusions do that?"

Piper gave a meek shrug.

"Let me give you an example," the headmistress continued. "Before today, did you ever expect that you could travel vast distances through a mirror?"

Piper shook her head. "Of course not."

"But when you saw your friend Salvador on the other side, you understood on an instinctive level that it must be possible. You changed your consciousness. And once your consciousness was raised, events transpired that made it possible for you to join him.

"Of course, it takes months, sometimes years, for most thaumaturges to master the *Kefitzat Haderech*. Jaunting can be extremely dangerous, even in the hands of the most practiced magician. Those who misuse it and live usually wind up in detention for several weeks." She gave Rand a harsh glare.

"Weeks?!" Rand protested. "Get outta here! My mom's gonna kill me!"

"Should've thought of that before you ambushed me," Sal said, scowling at the boy from Boston.

"So that's why you're all here?" Piper asked, looking around. "Driving a mirror without permission?"

Miss Fortune didn't take offense at the jest, but she didn't smile either.

"There are many ways to misuse thaumaturgy, my dear Piper. This used to be a detention hall for wayward youths who toyed with the black arts. My predecessor tried to assert control by punishing them whenever they practiced their fledgling abilities. I, on the other hand, am seeking to train them, to teach them the way of the inner light."

As if on cue, the dark-haired girl spoke up.

"I came to detention today because I have a message for you," she said to Piper, repeatedly combing her fingers along the worn blanket. Behind her thick lenses, under long black lashes, the girl's gray-blue eyes gleamed like diamonds.

"Mr. Wriggly said I would find you here."

Piper looked at Sal to see whether the girl was joking. "Mr. Wriggly?"

"Her cat," Sal replied.

"He sheds a lot," the girl said with a hearty little chuckle. Piper cocked an eyebrow.

"You're not the only one here with celebrity blood flowing through her veins, Piper," Miss Fortune said. "I'd like you to meet Jean Conan Doyle."

"Billy!" the girl corrected her, stroking the bundle with greater intensity.

"Yes, dear. Of course," Miss Fortune said with an apologetic tone. "*Billy* Conan Doyle."

Piper looked at Sal, who nodded once as if to say, "Yes, *that* Conan Doyle."

Piper knew about the feud between her uncle and the world-famous author. She had once heard Houdini joke, "Sir Arthur states that I am a medium. That is not so—I am well done."

During a more serious discussion about the matter, he had said, "Conan Doyle is a menace to mankind because laymen believe him to be as intellectual in all fields as he is in his own particular one."

With everything that had happened to her today, how could Piper not believe that her uncle's crusade was completely misguided? Certainly there was more to the world than mere logic and science could explain.

Or maybe this was an elaborate ploy by Sir Arthur to discredit Houdini. Was everything she had witnessed today just some sort of illusion? If so, why? And how? Until this moment, she had been very careful not to let anyone know about her affiliation with Houdini.

"Um, I don't see any cat," Piper said, peering into the blanket.

"That's because it's invisible," Sal called from behind Billy, trying to suppress a snicker.

"Can I pet it then?" Piper asked, reaching out her hand.

"It's also intangible," Sal said, clearly enjoying himself at her expense.

Piper scowled skeptically.

"Mr. Wriggly said you wouldn't believe me. So he told me to do this..."

The girl shoved the withered old rag under Piper's nose. Before she could react, Piper began to sneeze violently.

"Okay, okay! I believe you!" she said between spasmodic bouts of sneezing. "What's Mr. Wiggly's message?"

"Wriggly, not Wiggly!"

The strange girl did not withdraw the quilt and Piper could barely hear Mr. Wriggly's message over her fits of sneezing. *"For the human race to survive, the girl must survive. But for the girl to survive, the magician must die."*

"All right!" Piper yelled. "I promise!" She sneezed. "I won't save the magician!" She snelled.

Rand was beside himself with laughter.

"That's enough, dear," Miss Fortune said placing a hand on Billy's shoulder and gently pulling her away from the newcomer. "I'm sorry, Piper. I didn't realize she would do that."

Piper hunched over trying to catch her breath. "Who'd have thought," she gasped, wiping her nose with her sleeve, "that I'd be more allergic to ghost cats than real cats?"

Sal stepped forward and patted Piper softly on the back. She appreciated his effort to comfort her, but she wished he'd have given her a little space instead.

"So, she got detention for speaking to cats that can't be seen or touched?" Piper asked, somewhat bemused.

"No," Sal replied. "She got detention for how it got that way."

He made the sign of a hangman's noose and lolled his head to one side.

Piper's eyebrows almost jumped off her forehead.

"And what about you? Why are you here?" she asked, straightening her back and looking Sal in the eye.

"I came to defend you!" the boy said objectionably.

"You know what I mean," she said. "What law of thaumaturgy did you break to get here in the first place?"

Sal remained silent. He turned away from her gaze.

"Let's just say that your boy here also has a fondness for dead things," Rand said.

"That's enough, Alan!" Miss Fortune chided, this time in more than a whisper. "I will not have my students airing each other's dirty laundry."

"We're not students and this isn't no school," Rand jeered. "This is detention! And no amount of ballyhoo from you is gonna change that!"

Miss Fortune rolled her eyes, but Piper could see that Rand had struck a nerve.

"He's right, Imperatrix...I mean headmistress," Sal said as though it pained him to agree with Rand. "And that's why Piper shouldn't be here. She did nothing wrong."

Miss Fortune nodded. "Nor can I admit an underage candidate without first obtaining permission in writing from a parent or guardian. And it wouldn't be wise to invite a well-known skeptic like Harry Houdini into our affairs. He would seek to make us part of his public crusade, and we cannot afford that right now."

She studied Piper.

"Besides, I can see no reason to penalize your new friend, Salvador. She penetrated the *Kefitzat Haderech* in order to aid you. Most of you have used it for far less altruistic motives."

She glowered at Rand.

"You mean you're just letting her go back? She'll tell Houdini everything!" Rand sounded positively dumbstruck.

"Calm yourself, Alan," Miss Fortune said. She looked at Piper compassionately. "Of course, it would be best for everyone involved if you were to simply forget that you had been here."

"I won't tell anyone. I promise!" Piper exclaimed. "If I told my uncle, he'd just think I was on dope or something."

Miss Fortune gave her a wry smile.

"Don't be so sure, my dear. The jury is still out on whether Houdini truly believes in the supernatural or not. I simply cannot allow you to return to him with a clear recollection of all you have witnessed today."

Piper gulped.

"What are you going to do, Imperatrix?" Billy asked. Her voice trembled, as though she had seen cruel things performed under similar circumstances before.

"Calm yourself, Billy. I am not going to harm her," Miss Fortune said. "A simple memory charm will have the desired effect. By the time she goes to sleep tonight, she will have no recollection of us."

Before Piper could grasp what Miss Fortune intended to do, the headmistress placed a finger on her forehead and began to chant.

"On this day and in this hour,
I call upon the ancient power.
Let Piper forget what has been done,
Before the setting of the sun.
By spirit, water, fire, and air,
Such memories she shall never bear."

She removed her finger from Piper's head.

"How do you feel, my dear?"

"L-lightheaded," Piper said groggily.

"That's to be expected."

She turned Piper around to face the *Kefitzat Haderech.*

"Now it's time to get you back home."

Piper stared at herself blankly in the mirror.

"Can I go with her?" Sal asked.

"That would not be wise, Salvador," Miss Fortune replied. "Besides, you and I still haven't had a heart-to-heart about your particular...dilemma."

Sal lowered his head. "Will she forget me too?"

"Of course not! She will only forget the things related to her, ahh...detention."

Miss Fortune said the last word with self-reproach. Then she traced a symbol at the center of the mirror and made the following invocation:

"I conjure thee, Qaphsiel, and thy host,
In the name of the three-times holy,
Carry this one from this place to that
Without harm or folly."

Piper felt a gentle nudge and then there was a sickening sensation in her gut. Then she landed softly on her feet and realized that she was in the same dark room where her journey had begun.

The doorknob was locked, just as she knew it would be. So Piper brought out her set of tiny tools and in less than a minute it was open.

Without giving the mirror a second glance, she opened the door and stepped out of the cloakroom. She didn't care who might see her. But enough time had lapsed since the end of the school day and the hallway was deserted.

Piper paid little attention to the cold as she left the school and walked across Flatbush Avenue. When she passed the construction site of the new movie theater, she smiled at the memory of helping her new friend Sal get the best of that bully.

(What was the bully's name?)

And it was nice of Sal to return the favor by defending her against...

(Against what?)

The rest of the trip was a blur. She boarded the Brighton Line trolley and got off at Stillwell Avenue where she and her aunt had exchanged goodbyes that morning. Bess had wanted Collins to drive her, but Houdini insisted it would draw undue attention.

(Undue attention to what?)

Piper walked the remaining six blocks in a daze. By the time she reached the brownstone with the bizarre hexagonal skylight, she was exhausted. Piper was no longer amused by the odd way the door opened when she turned the knob. She just wanted to sleep.

She entered the foyer, closed the door, and hung her coat on the rack. Then she made her way numbly toward the stairs, passing the kitchen where she knew her aunt and uncle would be waiting.

"Oh, hi Piper! You're just in time for dinner..." Bess said, her voice trailing off.

"Much too close to nightfall, missy. I want you home earlier," Houdini said with mild reproach. Then he peered at her over his afternoon edition of *The Brooklyn Daily Eagle* and his tone changed. "How was your first day of school?"

"Um, I don't feel so well," Piper replied, tottering across the floor. "I'm going to bed."

She wasn't looking in their direction—it was all she could do focus on walking. But Piper knew that Bess and Houdini were looking at each other.

"You sure you won't have a bite?" Bess asked.

"No thank you, Aunt Bess," Piper said flatly, plodding up the stairs with her eyes half closed.

"Did something happen at school?" Houdini asked.

"I have to hit the sack. Everything's hunky-dory."

"But it's goulash," Bess called up as Piper reached the second floor.

"And rhubarb pie!" Houdini added.

"Your favorite!" they chimed together.

Piper said nothing. She didn't want to be rude, but something was urging her to just put the day behind her and start fresh in the morning. She turned the corner and began to climb the second flight of stairs.

She gripped the banister tightly when she encountered the icy veil. Piper had no idea why this part of the stairwell was always difficult for her, especially at night when it felt as though she were slogging through oatmeal. But the sun hadn't fully set and yet it was harder than ever to plod through. She had the same sensation in her stomach as when she had gone through...

(Gone through what?)

Piper didn't remember. And she didn't care.

With a final lunge, she hit the landing on the third floor. Staggering into her room like a drunk, Piper collapsed on the bed. The last thing she saw before falling asleep was the corona of the sun outside her window as it disappeared behind the buildings.

Images of doors and locks and keys swam through her head. One door was protected by a flock of flying coats and Piper heard the cries of "Help me!" coming from the other side.

She recalled the story of a boy trapped inside a closet over Christmas vacation and she raced to the door. The coats immediately began to attack her.

Piper snatched one of the garments out of the air and swirled it above her head like she was fending off a swarm of hornets. She then threw the coat at the others, distracting them long enough for her to slip through the door.

Piper slammed it behind her and heard the *thud thud thud* of coats pummeling against it. Some of them got cinched between the door and its frame and continued their manic attempt to seize her.

She backed away from the writhing sleeves and bumped into something cold. She turned around and screamed.

The pallid, rat-like man who claimed to be her father stood before her, holding a long-stem rose in one hand. His lengthy fingernail pointed to a giant keyhole surrounded by a gilded frame. Then he handed the flower to Piper.

Accepting it without hesitation or suspicion, Piper took a step toward the frame and tossed the flower into it. Its inky depths were suddenly illuminated by a shower of sparkling lights.

Piper walked into the lights and emerged into what appeared to be her uncle's library. She was greeted by a man puffing on a curved cherry-wood pipe. He was wearing a checkered cloak and deerstalker cap.

The man raised a magnifying glass to his eye and said, "When you have eliminated the impossible, whatever remains, however improbable, must be the truth."

Sal was there too. He was engaged in a serious discussion with Mrs. Buckley from the Hollygrove Orphanage. Only it wasn't Mrs. Buckley.

Sal turned his head. When he saw Piper, a horror came over his face. His eyes pleaded for her to run.

Mrs. Buckley spun around to see what he was looking at. But where her eyes should have been there were only two keyholes.

She drew closer to Piper. No—Piper was being drawn closer to her. Drawn into the emptiness of those cold, obsidian eyes. Her mind was filled with a single, all-consuming thought—*Get free! Get ...*

"*Free!*"

Piper bolted upright in bed. Her forehead almost collided with Bess, who had been sitting on the bed next to her, trying to calm her down.

Bess caressed Piper's head and cradled it to her bosom, gently rocking her.

"There, there, sweet girl. Aunt Bess is here. It was nothing more than a dream. That's all. Just a dream."

Piper pulled her knees to her chest and nuzzled against the soft wool of her aunt's sweater. She could feel her lower lip quivering but she couldn't control it no matter how hard she tried.

"Just a dream," Piper repeated.

But she knew that was a lie.

Piper didn't dream.

★★★★

BIMBO AND THE BEAST

Seven miles to the north, another young woman was opening her eyes for the first time since daybreak. She leaned over and kissed the cheek of the rigid figure whose cozy quarters she had shared.

"G'nite, Chawlie!" she said in a high-pitched voice edged with a thick Brooklyn accent.

The girl folded her hands over her chest and her body convulsed violently. Her right arm jerked upward and her left leg kicked forward. *Chawlie* didn't stir.

She repeated the same crazed movement with her left arm and right leg. The wooden canopy in front of her nose began to wobble and open ever so slowly. A dusting of soil trickled into the chamber, but the girl slipped out and slammed the lid before any significant accumulation.

It was this technique—this hermetic performance of the Charleston—that had earned her the name "Flapper." Although there were hundreds of girls within two city blocks who considered themselves "flappers," among her kind she was *the* Flapper.

At least in her own head.

The shadow of the Kamies Monument fell upon her, but Flapper neither noticed nor cared that she was standing atop the highest point in Brooklyn. She gazed at the distant New York Harbor and then examined the ground at her feet.

"Hot diggity! Mother Nature gave the snow a bum's rush," she smiled.

In addition to the way she could sneak into buried caskets, Flapper had also learned how to mentally manipulate a piece of turf so that it folded back like a throw rug. Once she had wiggled into her daytime abode, the turf rolled back into place.

It was an essential skill for dewdroppers who preferred to spend their daylight hours under manicured lawns of five-star accommodations, like the one here at Green-Wood Cemetery. But it was always so much more difficult when a layer of snow blanketed the ground.

With a nod of her head, Flapper beckoned the sod to unfurl. She smoothed its surface as though it were a delicate duvet. When she was satisfied that the grave looked as placid as when she had found it, Flapper stood and patted the headstone of its now lonesome occupant.

It was a simple stone. No dates, no first name, no epitaph. Just the name "Ebbets" carved in capital letters on a rectangular stone slab. Flapper knew very little about the man she had slept with except that he once owned a baseball team that still played three miles to the east in a stadium bearing his name.

When Flapper first came to New York, she had dreamed of becoming a movie star. But her friends told her that the only way she'd become famous would be to sleep with famous people.

The previous day Flapper had cuddled up for the day with Henry Chadwick, another baseball legend she had never heard of. But she could tell that "Hank" had been quite a pip in his day.

Unlike Charlie, Hank had ritzy digs! There were stones shaped like bases in the ground surrounding the grave and a granite baseball that adorned the top of his monument-like headstone.

But Henry had died eighteen years ago, so he wasn't a very cozy snuggle pup. She preferred the recently deceased and their jerky-like texture. Not *too* recent—she hated the smell of embalming fluid. Charlie had passed away less than a year ago, and that was just dandy.

Flapper glided across the cemetery lawn wearing nothing but a petticoat and a low-cut black bodice that flattened her bust beneath a spider-web pattern of lace. She wished that her clothing was as durable as her skin, which repelled soot and soil like polished marble. To protect tonight's ensemble from the elements, Flapper had hidden it beneath the massive brownstone overlay of the Pierrepont family tomb.

It was a sleeveless purple number with sequins that clicked as she snatched it from its hiding place. When Flapper finished putting on the cloche hat, peacock feather, gold lamé, and flapping galoshes, she looked like a walking Vanity Fair ad.

Her nails were long and cut to a point, a style that would endure on her forever. So would her raven hair, which was cut into a perpetual boyish bob.

The makeup on her face always looked immaculate, but that was because she wore no makeup at all. No kohl, no fake lashes—her eyes were naturally dark and alluring. She wore no lipstick to accentuate her mouth because her lips would permanently retain their crimson-colored Cupid's bow shape. And she needed no lily-white foundation because she already had the flawless complexion of a porcelain doll.

Flapper slipped through the towering churchlike arch that graced the main entrance to Green-Wood and the landscape quickly degenerated into a maze of hybrid squalor. She walked up several blocks until the sound of oily waves against the fetid docks of the Gowanus beckoned her down a row of shabby brick houses along 20th Street.

Hordes of scoundrels and lowlifes shouted and sang along the thoroughfare while furtive hands extinguished lights or drew blinds behind barred windows as she passed. A swarthy, sin-pitted face sprung up in front of her, blocking her passage.

In her former life, Flapper would have backed off and screamed. But now she held her ground and even managed a slight smile, though the man's breath was fouler than the stench of the neighboring bay.

"You shouldn't be walkin' these streets alone, doll," the miscreant warned.

Flapper knew the man had no concern for her welfare. His warning was a mere ruse to bait pretty young women so he could bask in the glimmer of their unforeseen dread.

"Never again," Flapper whispered.

The pock-faced man cocked his head. This was not the response he had expected. He pulled his black knit hat halfway over his ears, emphasizing the odd shape of his head. It had the same angular contours as the head of the man who had spawned Flapper's "rebirth" seven years before.

The daughter of a minister in a middle-class Pennsylvania neighborhood, the girl who would become Flapper had strict parents who stressed rigorous studies, good grades and, of course, faith in Jesus Christ. While her father buried his face deep in his Bible, her mother would deem the slightest transgression as an excuse to wield her husband's belt.

Her clothes had been plain-Jane, old-fashioned hand-me-downs, mostly tweed ankle-length dresses that had earned her the nickname "Second-Hand Rose." The girl's mother taught her how to act and sit like a proper lady while her father forced her to take up the violin (even though she secretly wanted to play the saxophone).

When her grandmother in New York City sent word that she had fallen ill, the girl jumped at the chance to take care of the old woman for the summer. She could no longer bear living in a place where people got excited over news of the next church mixer.

Grandmother was an eccentric artist who had distanced herself from the family long ago. No one had visited her in years. But the girl saw this as a ripe opportunity to escape the confines of her repressive heritage and take New York by storm. Broadway. Movie palaces. Shopping! And her parents couldn't argue. After all, helping family members was the Christian thing to do.

The girl arrived at her grandmother's Manhattan brownstone on a mild summer night. She was so surprised at the spirited and youthful appearance of the woman who opened the door that she thought she had been given the wrong address. The woman looked no older than her own mother!

Grandmother welcomed her with a powerful hug.

"Believe me, child, I look far worse by day when my condition bothers me most," she explained.

The older woman took her inside and continued to speak.

"That is why you must never enter my bedroom during the day. My eyes are sensitive to even the faintest light."

The girl had heard that bright light could bother people with consumption, so she never questioned her grandmother's instructions.

Once inside the house, the girl sidestepped a half-finished limestone carving that was propped up on sandbags in the middle of the living room. Upon closer inspection, she could see that it was a life-size statue of a reclining lion with a human head. But the face had no features.

"Do you like it? I modeled it after the one in Giza," Grandmother said with a smile, patting the sculpture on its expressionless forehead. "The face of the original Sphinx is thought to be a portrait of the pharaoh Khafra, so I'm trying to get it just right."

The girl felt a sudden rush of dizziness. She dropped her suitcase and stumbled backward into a chair next to the fireplace.

"Oh, you poor dear! You must be famished and exhausted from your long trip," the older woman exclaimed. She disappeared into the kitchen and returned with a steaming cup of tea.

As the girl sipped the soothing liquid from the antique china teacup, the woman lifted a bronze bust off the mantelpiece and caressed it.

"This is my father, the famous French playwright, Honoré de Balzac."

She peered hopefully at the girl for a sign of recognition. Then she looked away, disappointment etched in the fine lines of her face.

"You see," Grandmother continued, "I am the lovechild of Balzac and an Arabian princess who gave birth to me in the shadow of the giant Sphinx. That is why it fascinates me so."

The girl hid a skeptical smirk behind her teacup. But when Grandmother continued her tale, telling her that she had been weaned in the desert on cobra blood, she spurted hot tea from her mouth and nose.

In the weeks that followed, while her grandmother slept, the girl conducted menial tasks around the house. The chores were not overwhelming, but she would be too tired by the end of the day to join the other neighborhood teenagers when they invited her out to enjoy the big city nightlife.

Her grandmother would emerge from the locked bedroom at sunset each evening and the girl would have just enough strength to help the older woman work on her sculpture. She never saw the woman eat but assumed she waited until after the girl went to bed.

By midsummer, the other teenagers on the block started to poke fun at her.

"I guess rubes aren't allowed to have fun," they would call through the open window.

She had learned enough of the modern jargon to know that a "rube" was a country bumpkin. So when she overheard the neighborhood girls talking about going to a swank party at an opulent apartment overlooking Central Park West, she pinched a few dollars from her grandmother's purse and, ignoring her fatigue, slipped out of the house before the woman awoke.

The girl made her way to an open-air market on First Avenue where obnoxious merchants behind wooden pushcarts peddled everything that a fashionable New York girl would need for a night on the town. Bell-shaped cloche hats, makeup, compacts, cigarette cases, and even those new "nude" rayon stockings that showed off the legs.

She also bought a yellow knee-length dress, a thin leather belt, and a lovely pair of Delman shoes with hourglass heels and a strap across the instep. Finally, the girl picked up a string of white beads to complete the ensemble.

Following her shopping spree, the girl walked down to the Bowery, bags swinging merrily in hand, and stepped inside a beauty parlor. The big decision—to bob or not to bob? To crop or not to crop? Or should she just play it safe and go with a fingerwave style?

In the end, she decided on a simple bob.

When she walked into the rust-colored building on Central Park where the party was being held, none of the kids from her grandmother's neighborhood recognized her. She took delight in teasing them, adopting a squeaky Brooklyn twang to disguise her voice. Even the most ardent flapper found it annoying, but she thought it was oddly liberating.

The girl's loud, coquettish behavior captured the attention of several distinguished gentlemen. But one face in particular caught her eye. It stood out by its lack of emotion.

She thought the face looked like a caricature that one might draw upon the surface of an egg. It was beardless and hairless except for a coiled cylindrical forelock. It had small ears and a delicate nose. Its mouth was large, with thick, moist lips, and big teeth that were white and even.

The face belonged to a big fellow, two or three inches taller than six feet, flamboyantly dressed in a checked tweed suit. The girl guessed that he was in his early forties, but the way he carried himself gave him an air of greater maturity. His neck was like that of a bull and the baldness of his head gave him the appearance of a monk. A very wicked, very sensual monk.

The quiet young rube from Pennsylvania would have turned away to avoid the attention of this dangerous looking individual. But a real New York livewire, one who liked to shake things up, would never turn down a chance to *woof* with such an unusual, captivating stranger.

She strolled over to the beefy man with one hand on her hip and the other dangling an empty cigarette holder between her delicate white-gloved fingers. She stumbled once in her Delman heels, but the man either failed to notice or didn't care.

"Butt me," she said when she was within earshot.

The man pressed a cigarette into her holder and torched the tip with an etched silver lighter. The girl puffed a few times at the other end of the holder and then coughed uncontrollably.

The man suppressed a smile.

"A bit young to be here, aren't you, child?"

His voice, which the girl had imagined would be booming for someone of his bulk, was rather light and high with a distinctly British accent.

"Old enough to know the best shindigs to crash," she replied, batting her eyelashes and looking askance, like the pretty girls did in the flickers. "Young enough not to be a wet blanket."

"Enchanting," was the big man's response.

He touched the side of her face and traced a finger lightly down her neck. His hands were unusually small and well-kept, like the claws of a delicate bird.

"My, what a lovely throat," he said, inspecting it as a physician might. "Tell me, how long have you had these two welts?"

The girl lowered her head and rubbed the side of her neck to hide the marks. She had first noticed the red bumps the day after her arrival in the city but had hoped that pancake makeup would conceal them.

"I-I've been staying with my grandmother," she said, momentarily forgetting her party-girl demeanor.

She quickly composed herself by thrusting a hip forward and smiling devilishly.

"I mean, you know these old New York joints. Probably a couple a' cockroaches needed a soft spot to do the hotsy-totsy."

The man's eyes, which had previously held the sleepy reserve of a sloth, lit up at the mention of her grandmother. He then looked away and deliberately focused his attention on someone else.

"Excuse me, my dear. There is something I must attend to. Please enjoy yourself, but don't get too...what is it you American girls say these days...loaded to the muzzle?"

He smirked, took a slight bow, and backed away to disappear into the throng of party goers.

So that was it then. The gig was up. The rube had blown it for her. Again.

She was just about to reveal herself to the neighborhood girls when a figure stepped in front of her. He was a fashionable gentleman in baggy flannel trousers and a patterned Fair Isle sweater. His face was rather thin and the girl thought it looked like an angelfish—or an axe blade with eyes.

"Do you know who that fella was you were flirting with?" he asked.

"Was it that obvious?" the girl blushed. "I'm guessing this is where he hangs his hat? It's his party, right?"

The man nodded. "But did you know that he's a renowned occultist?"

The girl looked at him sideways.

"I'll remember that if I ever need a pair of cheaters," she said, circling her eyes with the thumb and forefinger of each hand.

The man pursed his lips as he contemplated her statement. Then he raised his eyebrows like a scientist who has just discovered the solution to a particularly troubling equation.

"Oh, my! No, no, my dear. Not an oculist." He took a loud breath through his nose. "Our host is a black magician! People in occult circles call him 'the Great Beast.' Others call him 'The World's Most Wickedest Man.'"

The girl gave him a puzzled look, so he continued. "He throws these parties in order to find lonesome girls that he can use as human sacrifices in his ghastly satanic rituals. And God as my witness, dear girl, he has marked you!"

The man grabbed her thin wrist and began urging her toward the front door. "I've seen this happen before. You're in grave danger! Leave this place at once and come with me. I will protect you!"

The girl was caught somewhere between fear and confusion. What had she gotten herself into? She needed to get out—now! But why?

Before she could sort through the details, she was outside the apartment building and her defender was ushering her into the shadowy depths of the park.

And just like that he was all over her.

He pressed his mouth against hers so she couldn't scream, and she could hear the fabric of her new dress being torn. It was pointless to struggle. She closed her mind to the reality of what was happening and focused instead on blaming the rube for being so stupid to fall for such a ploy.

And the dress. She had looked so good in it, right? She had fooled everyone. Did he have to tear it like that?

She was on the ground. He was on top of her. His hatchet-face inches from hers, his nostrils flaring and assaulting her gossamer skin with staccato gusts.

Then he was off her as quickly as it had begun. Had he finished? She wasn't even sure that he had done anything.

Suddenly she realized that her assailant was curled up next to her, howling in agony. Something had struck him.

No, not something. Some*one.*

"It is poor form indeed to attend a party uninvited," a familiar high-pitched male voice called out. Against the shadows of the trees she could make out an even darker shape. A big shape. A shape she recognized.

The silhouette wielded a slender walking stick that had some sort of metal ornament at its tip. He brought it down fiercely on her attacker's narrow head.

"But when the gatecrasher takes liberties with my other guests— invited or otherwise—there must be a reckoning!"

The man screamed again. He rolled out of harm's way and staggered to his feet to confront his adversary. But as soon as he realized whom he was up against, the assailant turned and bolted through the trees, fumbling with his flannel pants as he ran.

The Beast made no effort to pursue him. Instead, he raised his walking stick and shouted, "A pox on you and your progeny!"

Even though there was no light this deep in the park, the girl could see two ruby eyes glint within the head of a silver cobra.

The Beast extended his hand and helped her to her feet. "Please accept my humble apologies. As your host, I should have been more heedful. The press has often labeled me a hedonist, but I do not encourage wanton carnal activities among my guests if both parties are not consenting."

He had been wearing a Spanish cloak over his checked suit. He flung its red and green velvet lining over her shoulders to conceal her torn dress.

"When I saw you leaving with that cad, I assumed it was under your own volition."

The girl said nothing about how the man had tricked her. She pulled the cloak tight against her chest and asked, "Then why did you follow us?"

The Beast smiled. "I was hoping to catch up with you so that you might arrange a meeting for me with your grandmother. And since you are in no state to walk home alone, I can think of no better time than now."

The girl didn't think it would be polite to question the motives of her rescuer. So with little conversation, the Beast accompanied her to her grandmother's quaint little brownstone.

When the girl walked inside, the woman was waiting for her in one of the two chairs beside the fire.

"I love what you've done with your hair, my girl. Very…Egyptian." She narrowed her eyes at her granddaughter. "How much did it cost me?"

The girl ignored the question. She was annoyed that her grandmother had showed no concern for her well-being. After all, it was pretty clear from her tattered clothes that she had met with foul play. Pushing the door open a bit wider, she invited the Beast inside.

"Grandmother, there's someone here who'd like to meet you. This is…"

That's when she realized that her savior had never given his name. She couldn't very well introduce him as "the Beast."

The big man extended his hand to the woman. "Master Therion. And you are…?"

The woman ignored the man's hand and his question.

"Master, is it? I haven't called anyone 'Master' in years." Nodding to her granddaughter, the woman said, "Dear, why don't you put some tea on for us while I get better acquainted with your friend."

The girl looked at her grandmother like she was soaked with a bar rag. She went into the kitchen to make the tea, but she kept peering around the corner to see what was going on.

Master Therion walked over to the mantelpiece and picked up the bust.

"Balzac," he said, taking a seat across from the woman and examining it.

A look of delight crossed the older woman's face. The girl noticed the Beast was starting to sway in his chair, succumbing to the same sensation that had overtaken her the night she arrived.

The Beast looked up and saw that the woman was now leaning over him. Her hair was scattered in a mass of curls over her shoulders and her fingertips were caressing the back of his hand.

The girl couldn't believe what she was seeing. No longer was her grandmother a woman who looked middle aged. In her place stood a young woman of bewitching beauty.

The Beast quietly stood and acted as though nothing unusual had occurred. He returned the bust to the mantelpiece and faced the woman.

The girl heard them both mumble some words, but she couldn't make out what they were. The conversation had the outward appearance of the politest small talk, but she could see how each of the Beast's words burned the woman like drops of corrosive acid.

Grandmother squirmed away from the man and then approached him again, even more beautiful than before. The woman seemed to be battling for her life. And if she lost, hell would cry out to her—the hell that every once-beautiful woman who is approaching middle age sees before her. The hell of lost beauty, of decrepitude, of wrinkles and fat.

Her dread seemed to imbue her form with a feline grace and agility. She took one step closer to the man and then sprang, seeking to press her crimson lips to his.

"Kiss me, my fool," she pleaded softly.

The Beast caught her in mid-leap and, holding her at arm's length, somehow turned her own current of evil back upon her. That's when the girl realized that the man who attacked her hadn't been lying. Master Therion was indeed a black magician.

And so, it would appear, was her grandmother.

A turquoise glow seemed to dance around her grandmother's head. Her flaxen hair turned the color of muddy snow. Her fair skin wrinkled. And her eyes, which had turned so many happy lives to stone, became as dull as tarnished silver. The twenty-year-old beauty had gone, replaced by a hag of sixty, bent, decrepit, and degraded. She hobbled away from Master Therion, cowering and cursing his name.

The teakettle screamed, startling the girl from her paralysis. The Beast took several strides toward her, grabbed her wrist, and pulled her toward the front door. He raised his walking stick on the way out and struck the sculpture with its cobra tip, shattering the sphinx into fragments of limestone.

Outside, the Beast continued to haul the girl up the sidewalk, his cobra-tipped stick urgently tapping the cobblestones with every third step. When her confusion threatened to overwhelm her, she slipped from his grasp and refused to take another step. "What the hell is going on?" she demanded, unleashing the full fury of her newly barbed Brooklyn tongue.

Master Therion eyed her with a look that was half pity and half amusement. "A fair question. One that deserves an honest answer." His barrel chest expanded as he took a long breath. "It would appear that your grandmother is a vampire. And a sorceress."

He waited for the words to sink in. Then he added, "She was trying to endow that sculpture with life so that it might one day carry out her evil wishes. Your life, my dear. By day, the figure would sap you of your *spiritual* essence. By night, the woman herself would take your *physical* essence." He stroked the side of her neck where the two lumps protruded.

The girl wanted to crumble to the sidewalk. It all sounded so insane! Grandmother was a vampire? She had heard the legends in her churchgoing community. It would explain why she had been feeling so sluggish. Once again, she had been a victim. And once again, she needed to be rescued. She was tired of being other people's playthings. Tired of looking to others to validate her, to define who she was.

"So, what now?" she asked in a voice devoid of hope.

Master Therion raised an eyebrow. "The way I see it, you have two choices." He held up one finger. "You can do nothing and your body will naturally purge all the toxins in your blood. Your *mana* will eventually return to normal and you can resume your old life."

The girl's shoulders sagged.

"Or," Master Therion lifted a second finger and narrowed his eyes, "I can infuse you with the blood of the Lam. It will mingle with your grandmother's venom while it is still fresh in your veins. The resulting synthesis will transform you into something new. Something beautiful. Something *powerful.*"

The girl looked up at him with big brown eyes that told him she had already made up her mind. "Blood of the lamb?" she asked, remembering her Christian teachings.

"Something like that. Come with me, child," he smiled and offered his arm. She took it after only a moment's hesitation.

The Beast led her to Grand Central Terminal where a porter in a blue uniform waved them onto a northbound train. Two hours later they arrived at a station that seemed to be a miniature version of the one they had just left.

The girl accompanied Master Therion to a small clearing on the Hudson where he righted an overturned canoe and slipped it into the river. Therion paddled the two of them across the water to a small, uninhabited stretch of land in the middle of the river.

When they landed upon the shores of the island, the Beast immediately lit a fire outside the mouth of a cave. When the campfire grew bright enough, the girl stifled a gasp. The exterior of the cave resembled a serpent's skull, with two huge stalactites forming its fangs.

"Come, girl. Sit beside the warmth of the fire," the Beast invited. He refrained from speaking until she complied. "I spent forty days and nights alone on this island attempting to invoke certain intelligences into our plain of existence. But power of such nature only manifests through a consenting sacrifice."

He glared at the girl for an uncomfortable moment. Then he disappeared into the cave.

When he re-emerged, he was wearing a robe with a red hood. The girl thought she saw something moving beneath its folds. Moths danced around the campfire as the Beast began to sway back and forth, chanting some sort of ancient incantation.

"There is no moon tonight. There is no air. Look at the trees. Not a leaf is moving."

From beneath his robe, Master Therion pulled a fluttering, white-winged creature that was unlike anything the girl had ever seen. In his other hand he brandished an ivory-handled dagger with a wavy blade.

He held the agitated creature aloft by its feet. Its wings flitted faster as it struggled to fly free. Muttering something in an alien tongue, the Beast slashed the beautiful creature across its throat.

The girl jumped to her feet.

"What are you, crazy or something?"

The Beast flashed his eyes at her. The thrill of magnetism that emanated from their turquoise depths compelled her to return to her seat.

She watched in mute horror as the bat-like creature's alabaster coat turned a deep shade of crimson. The desperate thrashing of its wings slowed to a dull flap.

Flap-flap. Flap.

Poor little flapper, the girl thought. *You won't have died in vain.*

At that moment, the Beast slashed his own wrist with the ornamental blade. He grabbed the creature's blood-soaked carcass in his bloody hand and held it above the girl's head so that the two distinct streams flowed into a single cascade of sanguine liquid.

"Drink," he urged.

"Says you!" she protested, falling backwards off her perch onto the ground.

The Beast thrust the dead animal scant inches from her lips.

"The old woman infused your blood with venom. In time, the repeated abuse would have killed you. Do nothing now, and your body will eventually exorcise it. But consume the combined vitality of Master Therion and this noble, nocturnal entity, and you will unleash the arcane virtues of your grandmother's legacy."

The girl hesitated. But she knew she didn't have a choice. She had promised the white bat. She had promised herself.

The Beast yanked the hair on the back of her head and forced her to gaze into his eyes. Then he channeled the rivulets of mingled blood into the girl's less-than-eager mouth.

At first she tasted nothing but salt and copper. She fought hard not to gag. But as the elixir trickled down her throat, something happened. It was as though senses that had been dormant her entire life had suddenly sprung to life. She could taste the variation in the blood. Her tongue could sense the different textures. Even the Beast's blood had two distinct elements—one decidedly human and one that she could only describe as...*power.*

She reached up and snatched Master Therion's hand. She drew it to her mouth and leeched as much as she could from his slashed wrist.

Then the Beast yelled, "Enough!"

He heaved her back with all his might. Wrapping the belt of his robe tightly around his wrist to staunch the blood, he staggered behind the fire to shield himself from his new ward.

The girl was already on her feet. Something like a hiss escaped her lips. Her mind was whirling with new sensations, new emotions. But one desire outweighed them all—the desire for blood. *Human* blood. And there was only one human on the island.

She crouched like a leopard, poised to strike. The Beast held up his uninjured hand.

"Stop this at once!"

And to her surprise, the girl did just that. Clarity returned to her head. Dignity returned to her poise.

She stared at the Beast in confusion. His shoulders dropped and he let out an audible breath. It was obvious to her that he was never certain about the outcome of his little experiment.

"You will call me 'Master,'" he said finally, with as much authority as his high pitch would allow. "If your grandmother had shared her blood with you, your fealty would belong to her. But I have withdrawn that prospect. Forever."

Somehow the girl knew this to be true. She wasn't confused. She wasn't angry. She wasn't even hungry anymore. Like a bride walking down the aisle to exchange vows with a man she knows she will never love, the reawakened Flapper held her head high and accepted her destiny with something that resembled pride.

And for the next year, Flapper accompanied Master Therion on all his nocturnal adventures. In return for keeping her safe during the day, she helped him complete his esoteric workings at night. They even traveled to Boston together to attend the arcane wedding ritual of a prominent Boston physician.

Flapper never regretted the decision she made that fateful evening. In the back of her mind, she remembered a young girl yearning for independence. Each day in this new incarnation she grew bolder and more headstrong. But her uncompromising allegiance to her Master never wavered. Somehow, it felt *right*. He protected her. He had *created* her. Her loyalty was as natural as a hatchling's devotion to the first thing that moved.

But when the time came for Master Therion to return to his homeland, Flapper experienced a horrifying reminder that nothing in life—or even in living death—is permanent. When their vessel had carried them four leagues from the mainland, Flapper felt a feeling of nausea overcome her. And then, even though the pestilent sun was ten hours distant, she began to wither.

As it turns out, that Bram Stoker fella had been right about a few things in his famous novel, including the fact that dewdroppers couldn't forsake their native soil. With no other recourse, Master Therion hurled the shriveled form of his minion overboard into the tumultuous sea. The swift current carried Flapper back to the shores of her inception where her supernatural strength and vitality were ultimately restored.

Ironically, her Master's act of valor meant that Flapper no longer had to depend on anyone for her feelings of self-worth. She would be responsible for her own happiness. Her own fun. Finally, she would be free.

That had been more than seven years ago. Since then, she had never strayed beyond the confines of New York City and its boroughs. And her appearance never strayed from that of a bright-eyed sixteen-year-old girl.

In all that time, she never found the hatchet-faced man.

The maggot that currently blocked her path somewhat resembled ol' Hatchet-Face. But taking vengeance on this man's flesh and blood would make her feel somewhat empty. Besides, she had promised the others that she would try to keep a low profile. They were already concerned that being without a master had made her somewhat reckless.

Ignoring her yearning to drain the cur, Flapper sheathed her eyeteeth (though she couldn't remember extending them). Instead, she grabbed the man between his legs, hoisted him over her head, and squeezed.

"Sorry, Mac, bank's closed," she said, hurling the man into a dumpster. He landed amidst the debris like a marionette whose strings had been cut.

"Who's the doll now?" Flapper asked, brushing her hands together to wipe off the filth. Other thugs had begun to circle like vultures but quickly scattered under her ferocious serenity.

Flapper continued her stroll down the sidewalk, twirling her black sequined purse, until she came upon a faded sign for Sugar Kane's Confectionary Shop. Across the street was an unmarked, two-story brick building between a tobacco shop and a funeral parlor. The bottom floor was painted black and the top floor was yellow.

Though it was early in the evening, a line of hopefuls had already formed along the black wall.

The Eighteenth Amendment had been ratified six years earlier, making it illegal to sell or transport liquor. But for many, Prohibition glamorized alcohol and in some places even increased its abuse. The Adonis Social Club was one of those places.

There were thirty-two thousand speakeasies in New York City, but the Adonis Club was the only one that Flapper knew of with a special room that catered to dewdroppers like her. "Speaks" were immensely popular, but not just anyone was allowed in. Customers knocked on an ordinary dull door where a lookout scrutinized them through a peephole. If they spoke the right code words to the eye in the peephole, they were invited inside. Since the drinking was usually done from a back room, customers were asked to "speak easy" so as not to be heard from nearby establishments.

Flapper skipped by the line of annoyed patrons, walked down

several stairs, and knocked exactly two times on the boarded-up door. A tiny panel slid open and a bloodshot eye glared through it. "What's the word, sweetcheeks?"

"Shaddup, Joe! You know who I am."

"You know the routine, Flap," the man called Joe replied.

Flapper always said that the Adonis Club should have been called "Joe's Place," but not just because Joey Adonis was its owner. The bouncer at the door was an up-and-coming middleweight known as "Italian Joe" Gans. In the back of the club, Flapper could hear Joe Browning tearing up a two-step on the grand piano while Joe Howard bellowed "Come on and Baby Me." There were also some Josephs on the club committee and at least one Josepe.

"Alright, alright already," Flapper sighed. *"Sugar daddy."*

Flapper heard Joe Gans fumble with the deadbolt and then the door opened to admit her.

"You're a sweetheart, Joe." Flapper blew him a kiss and the slugger's face pinkened.

The nightclub was mostly empty as she made her way across the floor toward the red door on the far wall. Waitresses and cigarette girls chattered back and forth, pausing uncomfortably as she flitted by. Flapper was just about to greet the two Joes on the bandstand when something distracted her.

A fair-haired girl in her late teens was standing alone by the stage. She was wearing a short fringed kneeduster with sequins, feathers, gold lamé, and a headband that nestled perfectly over her blond bob. It was a little tight on her head, but Flapper knew it would fit her own head just perfectly.

She looked at the girl's swanlike neck and the long string of white beads that wound twice around it. She couldn't help but think how the necklace would really complete her outfit.

Flapper floated toward the blonde, the unmistakable scent of Chanel No. 5 luring her like savory bait. Just then, an arm as strong as hers...maybe stronger...snatched her around the waist and shunted her to the side.

Her vision was briefly obscured by a veil of crimson but cleared as soon as Flapper realized that the man who grabbed her was another dewdropper—or night person, as most of the killjoys referred to themselves. And Flapper knew this night person quite well.

"Frankie Lamiano, as I live and breathe." She chortled at the inside joke. "What brings you outside the red door tonight?"

Frankie Lamiano owned the speakeasy in the basement beneath this one. Among their kind he was known as the *capo dei vampiri*— the godfather of dewdroppers. It was Frankie's goal to unite all the clans of *vampiri* under him. But Flapper was in a clan all by herself.

"Flapper, I've been asked to convey a message to you..." Frankie began in a voice not much louder than a whisper. Then his eyes grew wide and dark when he saw what she was wearing. He grabbed her shoulders in a vice-like grip.

"Wasn't there a girl here last night who had on that same getup?" he demanded. His cheeks and jaw were incredibly angular, and his face bore no trace of stubble.

"Not anymore," Flapper replied, casting her eyes toward the ceiling.

Frankie removed his hands from her body and ran them through his sleek dark hair.

"Flapper. What have I told you about...?"

"Aww, Frankie—lighten up. I made sure she was an orphan. No one's gonna come lookin' for her."

She took out her cigarette holder. "Now give me a ciggy." Flapper had never gotten over the embarrassment of her first attempt at smoking.

"What possible pleasure would you derive from a cigarette?" asked Frankie. "You actually have to make an effort to inhale and the nicotine has no effect on you. So what's the point?"

"It makes me look cool," she said, sticking her tongue out at him.

Frankie shook his head and closed his eyes. But he didn't get her a cigarette.

"What's your beef?" Flapper asked, popping the empty holder in her mouth. "You said you got a message for me?"

"The Beast is back in town. Your, *ahem,* master."

His mock cough was punctuated with a wry grin.

"He wishes to speak with you and has sent word that you would know where to meet him."

Flapper opened her mouth and the cigarette holder fell to the floor. The downside of having a human maker was that she didn't have the same telepathic bond that other dewdroppers shared with theirs. Even though Flapper instinctively knew whenever her master was in trouble, the Beast had to rely on conventional means to summon her for any other reason.

The band played the first notes of "Muskrat Ramble." Couples leaped to the dance floor. Hips jiggled, elbows flexed, heels stomped, and bodies quivered like gelatin. One couple was doing a knock-kneed crossover step.

Flapper was usually the first one to climb on stage and scream, "Everyone dance the Charleston!" But Frankie's announcement had put a damper on her mood. Even the blonde's pearls no longer appealed to her.

"He's back?" she asked, slumping her shoulders.

Frankie nodded.

"*Arrivederci,* Flapper," he said, waving his fingers in her face. "Or as you modern girls like to say, 'Toodle-oo!'"

Flapper turned and walked quietly to the exit. On the way out she snatched some cigarettes and a book of matches from Joe Gans while he was grilling someone for the password.

The journey from Brooklyn to the small island on the Hudson took far less time than it had on that fateful night long ago. That's because Flapper no longer had to rely on mass transit. One of the many benefits of her new form was that she possessed all the abilities of the creature whose blood she had consumed, including flight.

Other dewdroppers could actually transform into whatever nocturnal rodent had been sacrificed to "revamp" them, as Flapper called it. But she was able to avoid the icky metamorphosis thing and still enjoy the gifts of her alabaster benefactor.

Yes, the snow bat had been a beautiful animal. But that didn't mean she wanted to become one. For one thing, despite what they showed in the flickers, when dewdroppers changed back into their human forms, their clothes didn't magically reappear. And she had worked way too hard to have her wardrobe compromised by a rodent!

The moonlight caused the sequins on Flapper's dress to glitter like stars as she glided over the river's surface. Her galoshes flapped in the wind and the fringe on her dress and purse fluttered like miniature wings.

Crimson letters graffitied on the stony outcrop of the island's western bank welcomed her back with their familiar messages:

EVERY MAN AND WOMAN IS A STAR!
DO WHAT THOU WILT SHALL BE THE WHOLE
OF THE LAW

Earlier in his life, Flapper's master had acquired several world records in mountain climbing. So it had been a simple matter for him to move over these jutting rocks and paint his favorite slogans in enormous letters, upsetting the locals and annoying the passing day boats.

The proclamations also had the effect of capturing the attention of certain locals, particularly young women. They would giggle with delight as they made their daily deliveries of fresh produce and dairy to this so-called priest of profanity.

Flapper touched down on a terrace of mossy stone among the dappled woods of the island. A strange murmur mingled with the sound of the river's current as it sloshed against the rocky shores. The sound grew louder as she made her way through the trees to a rocky outcrop that walled a creek lined with dead lilies on its banks. She followed the creek to a familiar cave.

Firelight once again illuminated the gaping maw of the cave's skull-like façade. But this time the blaze was contained in a large ceremonial brazier. The murmur had grown to a monotonous chant that emanated from a group of black-hooded figures circling the brazier and swaying hand-in-hand.

Flapper took one step into the clearing and suddenly there was a dagger at her throat. One of the black-robed figures had somehow slipped behind her. A deep voice resonated from the shadowy depths of his hood.

"The Master doesn't like people crashing his party."

"I know," Flapper said, astonishing her assailant by shoving her hand under the dagger's hilt and plunging the blade into her own neck. Thick liquid the color of cabernet flowed from the gash and bubbled in her mouth.

She threw the acolyte to the ground. Her next words sounded as though she were gargling. "I crashed his party once. And I paid for it with my soul!"

Bicuspids descended from her upper mouth. The robed man clawed the ground, desperately trying to break free of the garish tramp's impossible hold. He turned his eyes from the demoness's fierce gaze, unwittingly exposing his throat.

Flapper caressed the man's jugular with her black fingernail. But before she could sink her teeth into his succulent flesh, a voice reached inside her skull and seized her mind.

"Flapper. Stop this at once!"

She felt the familiar sensation of a chain tightening around her brain. Her bloodlust subsided, her fangs receded, and she rose to a standing position.

She kept a foot on her intended victim's chest to keep him from scampering off to join the other robed celebrants. The throng had parted to admit a massive figure into their midst. Flapper stood sideways and yanked the dagger from her throat, barely turning her head to acknowledge the newcomer. The wound quickly sealed, but blood still pooled at the site.

"Seven years in merry England and still a big ol' party-pooper," she sneered.

The Beast stepped into the light of the fire. "I haven't summoned you for a party, my dear Flapper. I have returned to these shores for a much more pressing concern."

The shiny whiteness of his naked head contrasted oddly with the redness of his face. He was rounder since she had last seen him. Fat hung in heavy folds under his chin. He had grown oddly hideous in appearance, as though he wore a wrinkled suit of flesh that had swallowed his features into its horrid obesity.

There was something else different about him too. Like the thing that was inside him, the thing that had energized the very blood she had once drained from him, was now struggling to get out.

The Beast peered at Flapper through swollen lids. He was sweating freely and beads of perspiration stood on his forehead and upper lip. When he spoke again she noticed that his front teeth had been filed into two sharp spikes.

"You're looking old, Master. And fat." She pressed her teeth to her wrist. "I can't help you with the fat thing, but one sip of my blood will keep you from getting any older."

Master Therion thrust out his scarlet lips in contempt. His strange blue eyes grew cold with fury.

"You would have me feed on your essence? You would have the master exchange places with his servant? You have grown bold indeed, my dear Flapper. But your behavior has matured no more that your physical appearance."

Flapper started to giggle. Then she paused.

"Wait a minute! Did you just call me a dumbdora?"

"That remains to be seen."

The Beast exhaled loudly and stepped closer to her.

"I have a mission for you, Flapper. One I'm certain you will enjoy because it involves a figure of known celebrity."

"Valentino?" the dewdropper asked, licking her lips.

"No!" roared the Beast, and Flapper lowered her head in disappointment. "The celebrity in question is Harry Houdini."

Flapper perked up.

"Oboy! Can I turn him? Can I make him spill all his secrets?"

"You will turn no one, Flapper."

Again the vamp sulked as Therion continued.

"It has come to my attention that the great Houdini is fostering a child in his household. It will be your duty to keep a close watch on the young red-haired girl and report to me any bizarre occurrences you observe as a direct or indirect result of her actions."

"That's ducky, Master T," Flapper replied sarcastically. "But who's gonna watch the kid when the sun's raining poison on my parade?"

"If I'm right about this girl, nothing unusual will transpire during the day."

"Oh, yeah?" Flapper rubbed her chin. "And what about night? What if nothin' happens then?"

A smile crossed the Beast's swollen face.

"Then I will allow you to force the issue." He raised a finger in warning. "But the girl shall come to no harm without my express permission!"

Master Therion shooed her away with his fingers.

"Now off with you! And don't return until you have something to report."

The dewdropper's features softened as she looked at him.

"Master, it's a long way back to Brooklyn."

Therion cocked an eyebrow. Flapper directed her gaze at the hooded figure beneath her heel. Her fangs extended further from her mouth.

"I could use a juicy snack before blowing outta here."

"I see," Master Therion nodded. "Very well, my servant. You may feed."

The acolyte flailed violently on the ground.

"Master! I too am a loyal servant! I sacrificed my entire life in preparation for your exalted return!"

"Of course you have. And now you shall learn the *true* meaning of sacrifice," the big man mused. "Carry on, Flapper."

The robed man let out a petrifying scream that was immediately quelled when Flapper's teeth perforated his larynx. She could sense her Master's satisfaction as the flailing man's life emptied into her, restoring her and validating her at the same time.

She could smell the fear of the other acolytes as they recoiled from her. She could hear the blood coursing through her victim's veins, matching the intensity of the nearby creek. And she could feel her victim's body grow warmer as his heart fought to replenish its precious supply of blood, and then cool down as it ultimately surrendered.

With a final spasm, the figure went limp in her lap.

Flapper licked her lips. She stood and exhaled slowly like a glutton at Thanksgiving.

A cold breeze swept across the island, dithering her moonlit sequins and lifting her into the air. The hooded assemblage on the ground gasped in unison because she must have looked like a pyrotechnic star.

Flapper smiled down upon them. Master Therion was an old fop. Her mind and her free will were bound to him. But unlike these poor souls, he'd never take her boop-oop-a-doop away.

As she rose into the sky, she noticed splotches of blood on the purple fabric of her newly acquired garment.

Rhatz! she thought. *I hope teeny Houdini has a nifty taste in duds.*

A BOY AND HIS CORPSE

The sun's rays peeked over the high-rises that flanked the Loew's King. Sal brushed sawdust over the side of the theater's marquee so he could clear a space for this morning's edition of the *Daily Eagle*. He settled into the clearing with a big smile, anticipating a few thrills from the latest exploits of Mutt and Jeff, Walt and Skeezix, and the Bungle Family.

But before his eyes could focus on the first caption of "Gasoline Alley," something pounced on him. Sal fell onto his back and felt the stabbing pain of bony knees driving once more into his ribcage.

"Rand, if you want the pendant, you'll have to pry it from my dead corpse!" Sal shouted.

"What other types of corpses are there?"

The reply came from a voice that was much higher than Rand's, tinged with rage and sarcasm.

When he was able to focus, Sal realized that his assailant wasn't Alan Rand at all.

"Piper?" he asked, choking on his own astonishment.

The fiery redhead grabbed him by the collar and drew his face an inch away from hers.

"Was that question too hard for you? Then maybe you can answer this one...*What happened to me yesterday?*"

"At school?" Sal stammered.

"You know what I mean, Sal!" The heated fury of her breath was visible in the cold air. "What happened in *detention?*"

Sal blanched.

"That's not possible!" he exclaimed. "No one can beat an Imperatrix memory charm!"

Piper grabbed the amulet and threatened to yank it off its cord.

"Okay, okay!" Sal cried out. "Tell me what you remember!"

Piper relaxed her grip without releasing the charm.

"I remember you said the detention room was in England but it's also somewhere outside time and space. And I remember the woman, Miss Fortune, saying that the last Imperatrix punished kids who abused magick—with a 'k'—even if they did so by accident. She's trying to teach all of you how to use it responsibly."

Sal nodded slowly. "Sounds like you remember everything. So what do you want from me?"

"I want you to make sense of it all! There's no such thing as magic—or magic*k!*" she emphasized the k-sound. "What did you do to my head? Is this some sort of ploy by Conan Doyle?"

Sal looked insulted. "I assure you not. Sir Arthur Conan Doyle is an honorable man. A bit misguided, perhaps. But honorable. And I assure you, Piper, that magick is real!"

"Then prove it to me! What kind of thamaturkey did you do to get detention?"

"Thaumaturgy," Sal corrected.

"Whatever!" Piper growled, tightening her hold on the amulet.

"Alright, alright already!" Sal relented. "Remember how I told you that my brother is in a coma?"

"I'm listening," Piper urged him.

"Well, it's because of me."

Piper waited for Sal to continue.

"I'm the middle child. The dependable son. I keep an eye on my little sister. I put the bikes away at night.

"I also looked out for my older brother, Henri. He was a magician, like your uncle. Called himself Black Henry. But unfortunately, he was also a drinking man.

"One time Henri performed at a town near our home. He went to the local cemetery to gather names and dates from headstones to provide him with material for his 'mind reading' act later that night. But he never showed up. I went to look for him in the cemetery, but four roughnecks blocked my way. They were carrying large sticks and told me, 'This is our turf. You cross it, you gotta pay a tax.'

"'I'm exempt from any such tax,' I said, brushing right past them.

"But they didn't back down like I hoped they would. They just smiled at each other and tightened their grips on their clubs.

"Now ruffians like this are usually a superstitious lot. So I turned back to them and raised my hand.

"'My friends,' I said, 'I don't deal with materialistic matters such as money. I do, however, occasionally practice the necromantic art of waking the dead.'

"Before the confused idiots could say anything, I screamed, 'Baron Samedi, I command you to raise the body of Washington Reeves.'

"The punks heard leaves rustling off to the left and spotted a figure rising behind a tombstone. And the tombstone was marked with the name *Washington Reeves*."

"Applesauce!" Piper said, pointing her finger at Sal. "You expect me to believe you raised a dead guy? Just like that? You must think I'm not hitting on all sixes or something."

"No, of course I don't expect you to believe it," said Sal. "But like I said, superstitions run deep in the south. I gambled that the thieves probably weren't 'hitting on all sixes.' And the gamble paid off! They dropped their sticks and ran off, screaming like little girls."

"And the undead 'Washington Reeves'?" Piper asked.

"He stumbled closer to me. Reaching out. Moaning incoherently. In his hand he was clutching something. Holding it to his chest like it was more precious than air itself. Then I saw what it for what it was… an empty pint of whiskey."

"Henri," Piper said, letting out a long breath as though she had been holding it the whole time.

Sal's face broke into a huge grin. "My brother was notorious for disappearing for a quick drink before shows. I always knew where to find him."

"So how did he wind up in a coma?"

Sal stopped smiling.

"The graveyard is Baron Samedi's domain. I didn't realize it at the time, but it was midnight when I spoke those words. I had stood at the crossroads of the Baron's domain and taken his name in vain."

He looked away from Piper. "I was brought up Catholic, like my *papa*. But my *manman*—my mother—she was a *vodun* priestess."

"*Vodun?*" Piper asked.

"You probably call it *Voodoo*," Sal said with a sneer. "The slaves of West Africa, stripped of all they had, still carried with them their faith in their *loa*—their gods. *Manman* used to tell me stories of Baron Samedi, the *loa* of death who controls the passageway between the world of the living and the world of the dead."

Sal tapped the forged pendant that Piper clutched in her hand. "This is his sign—his *veve*."

Piper scrunched her nose.

"So, you're telling me that just because you insulted an African god in the middle of a cemetery you cursed your brother to a life as a vegetable?"

Sal exhaled.

"It's not as simple as that. Henri was a gambler as well as a drunk. He made enemies with the wrong people in New Orleans and owed them a lot of money.

"At one of his shows, Henri was doing a variation of your uncle's Milk Can Escape—which I'm sure you know is pretty basic, even for novice escape artists."

Piper nodded. She knew the milk can had a second lid outside the first one that was attached to the can by two fake rivets. Once it had been filled to the brim, Houdini would hop inside, remove the rivets from the inside, and lift the top of the can without disturbing the locks.

"Henri was handcuffed and padlocked inside the filled container," Sal continued. "But when he didn't free himself after three minutes, I knew something was wrong. I smashed the locks with an axe, but it was already too late. Black Henry—my brother—was dead. Someone had tampered with the rivets on the false lid so he couldn't unscrew them."

Piper gulped. "But I thought you said he was in a coma..."

Sal held up a finger.

"His death was confirmed by two doctors. And his burial was witnessed by my whole family and our closest friends."

A tear trickled down Sal's cheek. "My father blamed me for not trying to rescue him sooner."

"That's a bit harsh..." Piper began. But Sal went on as though he hadn't heard her.

"Remembering how well the scam in the cemetery had worked, I wondered what would happen if I really invoked the Baron. In Haiti there are stories about people being identified years after their deaths. Usually an evil sorcerer had taken their souls and had offered it to the Baron."

Sal stroked the silver pendant. "I bought this from a local Voodoo priestess. It's called a *wanga*. It can imprison shadow-matter entities, like spirits or souls. A *wanga* can be anything—a small statue, a sack, a shell, a vase..."

"An Egyptian jar?" Piper interrupted.

Sal nodded. "So I dug up my brother's body, forced some Jimson weed down his throat, and performed the soul spell that the priestess had also sold me. But I had no idea what I was doing. Only a fraction of Henri's soul still lingered in his body. I sucked it from his mouth and blew it into the *wanga,* where it remains trapped to this day."

"So he came back to life, but he was a vegetable?" Piper asked. "Sounds to me like he was buried prematurely and the lack of oxygen turned his brain to mush."

"Two doctors confirmed his death, Piper. And his body shows no vital signs. It continues to decompose in the hospital as we speak."

"Then what makes the docs think he's still alive?" Piper asked.

"Because when I'm close to Henri, he obeys my every command. Through the amulet." Sal lowered his head. "That's why I'm in detention, Piper. I turned my brother into a zombie."

Piper released the cord and gave her friend a shove. "Horsefeathers!" she exclaimed.

"*Verite!*" Sal replied in Creole. "It's true! Every last word of it!"

"Prove it!" Piper challenged. "Take me to your brother. I want to see you make a dead guy walk. Show me or I swear I'll tell everyone about detention...including Houdini."

"I was afraid you'd say something like that," Sal said, tucking the talisman into the collar of his shirt.

"Fine. Today after school. I haven't visited him for a couple of days, so he's probably starting to get ripe."

Piper looked at him with a puzzled expression.

"It helps when I walk him around a bit to keep the blood circulating," he explained.

Piper picked up her book bag and glared at him.

"Don't you dare think of ditching me at school, Salvador. I'll be watching you. In class, at lunch, during recess—I'll be sticking to you like glue."

Sal found Piper to be true to her word. In Miss Hine's class, he could feel the redhead's eyes boring into the back of his skull. Instead of sitting with him at lunch, she sat with the annoying pigtailed girls at the table across from him so she could watch him like a hawk.

She didn't speak with him at recess either. Instead, she sat in the bleachers while Sal pretended to play basketball with some of the other boys. And during the film strip lesson, Piper nailed Sal in the head with a spitball when he stood for a split second to shift his position.

When the dismissal bell rang, Piper was standing at Sal's desk before he even had a chance to pack up his satchel.

"I first have to get something from the market," he said. "So why don't we just meet outside the hospital?"

Piper placed the back of her hand to her forehead to feign insult.

"You'd let a poor, innocent girl ride the treacherous subway into the big, bad city all by herself? Not on your life, buster. I'm sticking to you like glue."

Sal led Piper out of the school, shaking his head the whole time. After they had hiked two miles up Bedford Avenue, Sal stopped at a butcher shop on Fulton.

A burly man with red hair and a redder beard beamed at Sal from behind the counter. Clasping a meat cleaver in his hairy hands, the butcher continued to trim perfectly symmetrical steaks while maintaining eye contact with his customer.

"G'day, laddie!" he bellowed, chomping on an old cigar that was burnt down to a stub.

"Hello, Mr. Laydon," Sal replied. "The usual, please."

The butcher wiped the cleaver on his once-white apron and then disappeared into the back room. He returned carrying a burlap sack that he handed to Sal. Out of the corner of his eye, Sal could see Piper's eyebrow rise inquisitively—especially when the contents of the sack started to wriggle in his grasp.

Sal thanked the butcher and plopped thirty-nine cents on the counter. As he and Piper turned to leave, Mr. Laydon called after them.

"Laddie, I could make things a whole lot simpler if ye jist let me do mah job! No extra charge!"

Sal waved goodbye. He and Piper walked a few blocks east and boarded the Fulton Street elevated train to Manhattan. Though he sat as far from the other passengers as possible, he couldn't hide the thrashing sack from Piper.

"You gonna tell me what's in the bag?" she asked.

"No," replied Sal, staring straight ahead and trying his best to ignore the flailing mass in his lap.

Once it had settled down a bit, the bag began making clucking noises.

"Is this some sort of hoodoo ritual where you sacrifice a chicken to your hoodoo gods?" asked Piper.

Sal sat up indignantly and shrieked, *"Hoodoo? Hoodoo?!"* The other passengers shifted uncomfortably in their seats, prompting Sal to lower his voice. "How'd you like it if I called your religion *jewdoo?*"

Piper shrugged almost imperceptibly.

"Do you think *hoodoo* is the only religion that sacrifices animals?" Sal hissed. "In Judaism, Miss *Weiss*," he emphasized her last name by poking her in the chest, "a rooster is sacrificed on the afternoon before Yom Kippur as a sacred vessel to receive man's sins. In Christianity, Joseph and Mary sacrificed two turtledoves after Jesus was born. So don't be so quick to judge!"

"Go chase yourself! I wasn't judging you!" Piper shouted defensively. "You always this touchy?"

Sal and Piper endured the rest of the ride in silence, save for the squawking burlap. Forty-five minutes later, they were standing on a sprawling campus overlooking the ominous gray stones and ivy-brick walls of Bellevue Hospital.

Sal placed a hand on his new friend's shoulder and pleaded with her.

"Listen, you'll have to trust me and wait here. The hospital only lets family members visit. I always take Henri outside in a wheelchair. Then we go for a walk in the fresh air. The doctors think it helps him."

Piper put her hands defiantly on her hips, but Sal knew she couldn't argue. After all, rules were rules. Enjoying his temporary victory, he asked her to hold the rustling bag.

She snatched the sack with one hand and wagged a finger at him with the other.

"Okay, Sal. But don't do a disappearing act through any mirrors. I'll follow you. You know I can!"

Ahh, so that's why she hasn't let me out of her sight all day, he thought.

Sal turned his back on her, threw his hands in the air, and proceeded to the entrance of the southernmost building.

After exchanging a few words with the guard, he registered with a blue-haired woman behind a large reception desk. Then he climbed a vast staircase, steered through some winding corridors, and walked toward a special section of the neurology wing where natural lighting provided a feeling of openness.

Sal turned into a room that afforded a magnificent view of the East River. An attractive bobbed-hair blonde clad in white leaned over the inert body of Sal's brother. She seemed to be listening for some sign of life.

"He doesn't breathe," Sal stated flatly.

The nurse jumped up and placed a hand to her chest.

"Jeepers creepers! You gave me the screaming meemies!"

Wonderful. A flapper, Sal thought.

Composing herself, the nurse said, "You must be the brother."

"At your service," Sal said, taking a dramatic bow.

The nurse gave him a curious look.

"You're the one he listens to?"

"In a manner of speaking," Sal replied.

"Can I watch?" she asked hesitantly.

She was obviously new. Henri's condition was on a need-to-know basis, but if flappers were being hired as nurses then the hospital must be pretty desperate for help. It wasn't as if Henri was difficult to care for. Hell, he rarely needed his bedpan changed—and Sal took care of all his meals!

"I guess so," Sal said finally.

He approached his brother and stood beside him. Pretending to scratch his upper chest, he groped the talisman beneath his shirt.

He directed the nurse's attention away from amulet by gesturing wildly with his other hand. If it became public knowledge that the *wanga* held magical properties that could wake the dead, people would stop at nothing to get a hold of it.

People like Rand.

Bowing his head discreetly to speak into the talisman, Sal uttered a single word in Creole.

"Reveye."

Henri's eyes shot open. The nurse almost tripped in her haste to put distance between them. Screaming meemies indeed.

"It's okay, it's okay," Sal assured her. "Would you please get me a wheelchair? We'd like to go for our walk now."

The nurse backed out of the room as though Henri might grab her if she took her eye off him. Sal half-expected her not to return.

When she did, in addition to the wheelchair she brought a group of nurses, interns, and orderlies. They all stood in the hall behind her, craning their necks to catch a peek. So much for secrecy, Sal thought. No wonder word about Henri had reached the ears of Rand's stepfather all the way up in Boston.

Sal uttered several more commands in Creole and Henri obeyed, stiffly rising from the hospital bed and then collapsing into the wheelchair like a bear shot with a hunting rifle.

Sal wheeled his older brother past the nurse and her entourage, through the corridors, and out the front door. Piper was standing where he had left her, holding the burlap sack impatiently and squinting her eyes even though the sun was behind her.

"I was getting worried," she said, tapping her foot.

"I had an audience," Sal replied, wondering why he had to defend himself at all. "Nurses and orderlies."

"No doctors?" Piper asked.

"The doctors gave up on him long ago," Sal confessed. "They don't like not having answers. It's easier for them to ignore the problem."

Piper leaned over to get a look at Henri, examining him as though he were a side of rotting beef.

"Sure looks dead to me," she said, crinkling her nose. "Smells dead too."

She was right, the smell of decay was unmistakable. Sal would have to do something about that. Soon.

He motioned for Piper to follow as he wheeled Henri past putrid barrels of garbage along the south wall of the hospital. They came to the back of the building where several of the hospital's wings converged to form a narrow entrance that led to an enclosed courtyard.

The rooms at the ends of each wing were the wards in which the mental patients were locked away. The grounds within the wards were attractive, with several trees, benches, and a fountain that was shut down till spring.

"This is where Henri and I take our walks. He can roam about freely in here without looking out of place when the loonies are out for recess."

Piper surveyed the grass perimeter. "No one's here now."

"It's late. Most of the orderlies have gone home and there's no one here to babysit."

"So this is where you perform your *Paligenesia* bit?" she asked.

"Pali-*what?*" asked Sal.

Piper smirked. "Sorry. That's what my uncle calls his resurrection act."

"I assure you, Piper, this is no act," he said, sounding slightly indignant. But obviously the girl needed more convincing.

From beneath his collar Sal produced the amulet. Holding it between his thumbs he blew on it and said, *"Leve,* Henri."

Sal heard Piper gasp as Henri raised his head and opened his eyes, revealing a milky white gaze that glistened in the setting sun. There was no life in those eyes, just a catatonic, docile stare.

Something thicker and darker than saliva dripped from the corners of Henri's slack mouth. The flaccid skin that hung on his face showed no emotion at all—as though someone had draped damp cheesecloth over the head of a Henry Moore sculpture.

Sal's brother lumbered out of the wheelchair and stood before Piper. Even though his gaunt yet towering frame blocked the sun, her eyes narrowed when she looked up at him. She opened and closed her jaw, but no sound escaped her lips. Sal hid a smirk, amused that there was something in this world that could make her speechless.

"Hello, Henri," Piper finally stammered. "My, aren't you a big boy?"

"He doesn't respond to outside stimuli," Sal informed her. "Not even his own name."

Piper walked around the brutish figure and inspected him closely. "Everything sure looks on the level. What's the trick?"

"There is no trick!" Sal said through gritted teeth. "It's all in the amulet. Don't you get it?"

"Well then, why doesn't everyone get themselves a voodoo coin so we can all have a party playing Lazarus?" Piper said with a mocking tone.

Sal sighed. "You're the only one I've told about the amulet. Only you, Rand, Miss Fortune, and the last Imperatrix know about it."

"Why not tell the doctors?" asked Piper.

"Because they'll lock me up in here with all the psychos! And even if I could get them to believe me, they'd just take the *wanga* for scientific research and I'd lose any hope of getting my brother back."

Sal paused to catch his breath. Then, trying to avoid eye contact with Piper, he continued more calmly, "It's not just the amulet. If it were, then maybe I *could* play Jesus. Back in New Orleans, word got out about me rescuing my brother from the Baron's eternal clutches. I became something of a celebrity.

"Then one day a woman from my neighborhood arrived at our door, wailing and pleading for me while clutching the limp form of an infant to her bosom. She begged me to bring back her *ti bebe*. But I told her I couldn't make her *bebe* whole—that it might wind up like Henri...or worse."

Sal took another deep breath and faced Piper, his eyes swimming in remorse. "My papa led the raving woman out the door and she spat at me. She called upon Baron Samedi and the other *loa* to curse me that I would share the same fate as my brother.

"That's when Papa decided it would be best for us to move to New York. And even though he never believed Henri's condition to be the result of black magic, we all agreed it would be best to never mention the *wanga* again."

Sal wiped the corners of his eyes with the cuff of his sleeve. Piper raised the bag in her hands.

"Well, if the *wanga* is all you need to wake the dead, then I take it we don't have to sacrifice our fine feathered friend?" she said with a look of relief.

"Not exactly," Sal replied, snatching the bag from her. Henri's glazed eyes followed it almost imperceptibly.

"Then what's it for?" Piper seemed almost reluctant to ask.

"Dinner," Sal said flatly.

"Umm, no thanks," Piper waved her hands. "Aunt Bess is making goulash tonight."

Sal wasn't sure how serious she was being.

"Not for us! For *him!*" he said, pointing to Henri.

Piper's eyes went wide.

"Is the hospital food that bad?"

Sal loosened the bag's drawstring and bit the corners of his mouth to suppress a grin.

"You're the one who said that he smelled bad. The doctors say his tissue is necrotic. It's decaying. And the only thing that makes him somewhat whole again," he said, pulling a fluttering white chanticleer from the bag, "is the flesh and blood of fresh game."

Piper bit her lower lip.

"You're gonna kill it? Just like that?"

"No," he said, setting the rooster free to race around the hospital grounds. "That honor belongs to Henri."

Pressing the amulet between his fingers in a prayer-like pose, Sal brought it to his lips and said, *"Manje."*

Faster than a jack rabbit on a hot stove, Henri darted after his quarry. The bird eluded its assailant at every turn. Sal blocked the egress between the buildings so that neither the chicken nor his brother could escape the courtyard.

"He prefers living prey. It helps him heal faster," he said, watching Henri make another clumsy attempt to seize the frantic fowl. "It always begins like this, but the chicken tires quickly. Henri never tires. Henri doesn't feel pain."

Piper shifted uncomfortably in her shoes.

"I don't get it," she said. "If the amulet holds just a piece of your brother's soul, where's the rest of it?"

Sal was grateful for a question that he could answer competently. Using his foot like a goalie to block the chicken's escape, he said, "In *vodun*, human nature is made up of three parts—a visible body called the *corp-cadavre*, a spiritual body called the *Gros Bon Ange*, and a soul body called the *Ti Bon Ange*."

Henri leaped at the bird by Sal's feet and missed, grabbing Sal's shoe instead. Piper jumped nervously.

"Don't worry, he won't hurt us," Sal reassured her as Henri released his foot to dash after his elusive prize. "He doesn't even know we're here.

"Anyway, all living things share a cosmic life force, which connects us in a great web of energy," he said, interlacing his fingers. "When we're born, part of this cosmic life force passes into us and becomes our *Ti Bon Ange.* It is the source of human conscience, morality, and emotion, symbolized by the reflection we see in a mirror. The *Ti Bon Ange* is what returns to the Creator after death.

"The *Gros Bon Ange,* on the other hand, is the source of each person's unique personality and will. It's represented not by our reflections but by our shadows."

Henri made another lunge at the weary bird and Sal pointed to the ground at his brother's feet. Piper's eyes widened and Sal knew that she understood. The late afternoon sun had projected long shadows on the lawn for him and Piper—but Henri failed to cast a shadow of his own.

"The *Gros Bon Ange* is the source of our thoughts, the wellspring of our ideas and creative impulses. It is the sum total of a person's knowledge and experience throughout a lifetime. It leaves the body only under specific circumstances—while dreaming, during spirit possession, and after death, when it becomes an immortal spirit. It's very important after death to ensure that the *Gros Bon Ange* separates from the body and is properly dispatched on its journey to the afterlife."

Sal paused, allowing Piper a moment to absorb everything she heard. Twirling a strand of her unkempt hair, she said, "So Henri is missing the thing that gives him his free will and personality? But there's still something inside him keeping him alive?"

Sal touched his amulet and nodded. "I think the *wanga* captured Henri's *Gros Bon Ange* and I'm somehow the link between it and his *Ti Bon Ange.*"

Stark white plumes now littered the dull green of the dormant grass as the frenzied chicken narrowly escaped another of Henri's attacks. Piper wound her hair more tightly around her finger, and Sal could tell that she was trying her best to ignore the situation.

"I've never heard of people having two souls," she said.

Sal rocked on the tips of his toes. "There's a difference between soul and spirit. By 'soul' I mean the inner world of subjective feelings, sensations, and perceptions—like pain or pleasure or the green of grass. The soul lives in its feelings and acts upon the world through the will.

"And by 'spirit' I mean will power, which is the essence of thought. Thought isn't subjective like the soul. It belongs to the world. People don't usually experience someone else's sensations and feelings. But they can grasp the same thought and through that they experience the same objective reality."

The chicken squawked with exhaustion. A thick length of sludge dripped from Henri's mouth and splashed onto the lawn.

"You wouldn't want to be grasping my thoughts right now," Piper said, almost inaudibly. In a louder voice she said, "So Voodoo says there's two souls. That doesn't make it so."

Sal raised his index finger. "Of course not. But it's not just a Voodoo thing. The concept of multiple souls is shared by many civilizations that grew up around the Nile and the Sahara.

"Take the Egyptians. In addition to the physical mortal body they believed that each human was made up of two other elements, the corporeal soul called *ba,* which goes on to dwell in the land of the blessed, and the larger *ka* or immortal life-principle. The *ka* is the spirit that wanders around the upper and lower worlds. It stays in the mummified body where it can do unpleasant things if it comes back to life without first reconnecting with the *ba.*

"Sound familiar?"

He didn't wait for Piper's response.

"Like the *Ti Bon Ange,* the *ba* is an aspect of a person that the Egyptians believed would live after the body died. Priests would conduct funeral rites to release the *ba* and unite it with the *ka* in the afterlife, creating an entity known as the *akh.* The resurrection of the *akh* was only possible if the proper spells and offerings were made.

"Hawaiian kahunas, Buddhist monks, Indian gurus—they all believe that in addition to a physical body we each have at least two unseen components."

Sal pointed to Piper. "Even the Jewish mystics say that there are two souls inside us—a Wind Spirit and a Breath Spirit. When a person dreams, the Wind Spirit journeys from one end of the universe to the other, and the Breath Spirit stays in the body."

"Well, I don't dream," said Piper, sounding slightly annoyed. "So what's that say about me?"

But before Sal could respond, she added, "And why do you always point at me when you mention Jewish stuff?"

Sal straightened. "I—I just thought…" he stammered. "I mean, Houdini's Jewish, right? I know he doesn't advertise it, but he doesn't deny it either. So I just figured…"

"I'm not anything, okay?" Piper declared. "I grew up in lots of different houses with families who had lots of different beliefs. And each one was just as plausible as the next. And just as farfetched."

Slowly backing away from Sal, Piper said, "One thing all of those beliefs shared was a mutual respect for others. That's why I can't let this go on…"

Before Sal could figure out what she was doing, Piper leaped into the middle of the courtyard where the exhausted chicken had been dodging Henri by zipping around the garden fountain. The desperate bird was so intent on keeping its eyes on Henri that it failed to notice Piper jump in front of it and snatch it into her arms all in one motion.

"Piper, no!" Sal shouted as Henri drew closer. Then, fumbling with his amulet, he cried, "Henri, *sispann!*"

Piper shielded the fluttering animal in her houndstooth jacket, closed her eyes, and braced herself for the full brunt of Henri's collision. It never came.

She opened her eyes again and saw Henri looming over her like a stuffed panther posed in mid-leap. The only thing that moved was the black bile oozing from the corner of his mouth, which splattered on the cuff of the girl's jacket.

"Gross," Piper groaned.

She flung her arm to shake the discharge from her sleeve, relaxing her hold on the agitated fowl within its folds. The rooster took one look at Henri's form hovering above them and began to squawk and flutter. It raked its claws across the back of Piper's hand in its desperation to flee.

"Zowie!" Piper exclaimed, tossing the fluttering bird in the air and sucking the three bloody slashes that stretched from her knuckles to her wrist.

Sal ran up to Piper. "What'd you go and do that for? You could've been hurt!" he scolded, huffing from the effort of his short sprint. "That bird would have ended up on someone's plate tonight anyway!"

"Better the butcher's knife than the horror you put it through!" she argued, using her lips to staunch the wound on her hand. But a tiny stream of blood trickled down her wrist and splashed onto the ground at Henri's feet.

Henri twitched his nose and subtly cocked his head.

"Henri?" Sal inspected his brother's face, still clutching the amulet.

Henri's blank eyes fixated on Piper's wounded hand. He leaned his decomposing face closer to it.

"I should have worn gloves like Aunt Bess told me," Piper grumbled, sucking on her skin and paying no attention to the living cadaver.

Henri opened his mouth to expose a dark hollow of yellow, gray, or missing teeth. Another wad of black goop fell from his mouth and splashed on Piper's new boots.

She glared at the creature and pointed in his chalky face, "You keep doing that, mister, and I won't have any clothes to wear!"

A grunt escaped through Henri's flared nostrils.

Piper straightened her back. She tilted her head toward Sal's ear and whispered from the corner of her mouth, "I thought you said he doesn't know we're here."

Wasting no time, Sal jumped between Piper and his brother. He held out the *wanga* and bellowed, "Henri, *sispann! Sispann!*"

Henri struck Sal's arm with a backhanded blow, sending the amulet flying. Sal glanced about wildly to see where it had landed. When he could find no trace of it on the ground, he looked up. Sure enough, even though there weren't many trees in the courtyard, the amulet dangled from the branch of a maple high over the fountain.

He looked at Piper but no words came. Henri's gaunt hand was reaching for hers.

She looked back at Sal, her desperate green eyes urging him for help.

Sal wracked his brain, trying to consider every option. But only one came to mind.

"Piper, run!"

THE AWAKENING

z z z z z z z z z z z z z z z z z z z z z z z z z z z z z z z z z z z z z z z.
  z z z z z brother z z.
  z z z z z z z z z z z z z z z z z z z z z.
  z z *awaken* . .
  . . . .
  Stand. . . *sit*.
  z z.
  z z z z z z z z z z z z z z z z z z z z z. z z z z z z z.
  z z z z z z z. *Rise*. . . . .
  feed?
  . . . . fluffy . . cluck cluck . . . .
  Feed. . . Feed!
  . . . . Catch.
  . . . . CATCH . . . .
  Fix . . . . Fix me.
  . . . .
  . . feed?
  . . . . *stop!*
  z z z. z z.
  sniff.

z z . . bleed . .

feed . . . .

Fix me! . .

. . *stop! Stop!* z z

. . NOT STOP! . . . .

BLOOD.

. . . .

HEAL ME!!!

11

THE FINAL STRETCH

Not again.

Those were the first words that came to Piper's mind as she barely dodged the swipe of Henri's massive hand. It was the second time in a month that a monster had tried to bushwhack her for her blood.

Would Houdini tell her that this walking pile of putrescence was just a figment of her imagination? No. But he'd probably say that Henri was simply a deranged lunatic suffering from some horrible flesh-eating disease. Why else would he be at Bellevue?

For a brief moment, Piper wondered if Sal had led her here on purpose so that Henri would keep her from revealing the truth about Miss Fortune's detention. But that wasn't likely. Even now the overweight boy lunged at his brother's ankles, trying to take the lumbering brute down. It was like Tom Thumb trying to take down Jack Dempsey, but it bought her a few precious seconds.

Henri stood between Piper and the only exit to the courtyard. He continued to amble toward her, dragging Sal with every stride. His face remained emotionless, but his blank eyes were riveted on Piper's scratched hand.

She ran to the far end of the pavilion where the dusky ivy on the wall of the administration building gave it a moist, velvety appearance. Black bars lined the hospital windows on the first floor to keep the patients inside, but they also served to keep Piper out.

The patient rooms on the second floor had balconies but she couldn't make out any bars. Henri didn't strike her as much of a climber so she took hold of the ivy and scrambled up it.

Just as Piper reached out for the stone rail on the balcony, Henri grabbed the vines and yanked them from their stubborn grip on the wall. She crashed to the ground just a few feet from the frenzied creature.

She had underestimated her pursuer's determination. If he hadn't gotten tangled in the same vines that he had ripped from the wall, it would have been dinnertime for Henri.

He still stood between her and the exit, shredding the strands of ivy like they were threads. Piper looked around for Sal and spotted him struggling to climb a tree.

"So much for my knight in shining armor," she mused.

"Okay then. If I can't go sideways, and if I can't go up, that leaves me with one choice." She glanced at the granite foundation of the building and spotted a ground-level window that she assumed would lead to the hospital's basement.

Pulling herself to a standing position, Piper took a step toward her goal. But as soon as she put weight on her right foot, she buckled under intense pain. The fall had twisted her ankle.

She heard a spit-clogged grunt. The vines were merely an annoyance for Henri now and he would be on her at any moment. Piper crawled to the window and tried to push it open.

The window held fast.

On any given day, she would able to jimmy the lock with one of Houdini's tools. But there was no time. She spun around on her backside and kicked the window with both feet. The glass shattered like a caramelized sheet of sugar.

Using her jacket sleeve to brush away the shards on the lower pane, Piper slid through the opening head first. She had almost gotten completely inside when something seized her injured ankle.

"Aaaghhh!"

Her scream was a mix of alarm and agony. Henri was tugging at her boot. Piper was dangling just a few feet above the basement floor, but Sal's undead brother was pulling her back through the window. She felt stabs of pain where shards of glass bit into her skin from the sides of the window frame that she hadn't cleared away. And she could feel Henri's teeth gnawing on her boot.

Despite the tortuous throb in her ankle, Piper tried to free herself by jerking it back and forth. Instead, she managed to wiggle out of her boot, which resulted in a harsh landing on the concrete floor.

Shaking the fog from her head, she climbed to her feet. Piper looked around and noticed that she was in some sort of store room.

She glanced up expecting to see Henri's colossal form clawing at her through the narrow window. To her dismay, he had already slid halfway through the meager opening like a serpent through a skull. Henri may have been a giant in height, but his body was almost as skinny as hers.

Paying no heed to the fragments of glass that skewered him like shish kebab, the ravenous brute dropped to the floor. Piper tried to scream, but nothing came out. Sal had told her that the hospital was understaffed. She knew that there would be no one down here to help.

Limping across the room on one stocking foot, Piper heaved the supplies off the shelves and scattered them on the floor behind her— anything that would impede Henri. She made her way to the entrance of the supply room and heaved a gurney across it before escaping down the darkened corridor of the hospital's lowest level.

She could hear Henri stumbling behind her, but she refused to look. She stopped at every door she could find, struggling with each knob to find one that was unlocked. She tried a hairpin in one. It dropped out of her trembling hands. This would be a piece of cake for her uncle. But it was no time for amateur hour.

Finally, Piper's hand settled on a doorknob that turned. The sign on the door read "City Morgue."

Piper slipped into the room and slammed the door behind her. The room was cold, but she didn't care as much about that as she did that the door had no lock. It buckled against her back as Henri slammed it with the full mass of his body. Then she heard the knob click.

But it didn't turn.

Maybe the simple mechanics of operating a doorknob were as challenging for Henri as those wire tavern puzzles were for her.

Piper took a step back from the door. Something snagged her hair and she stiffened. Wheeling around to see who it was, Piper found herself staring into the empty eye sockets of a human skeleton dangling on a metal stand.

Slowly she stepped away from the door and the skeleton, only to upset a crash cart that carried an assortment of beakers and test tubes. Glass shattered on the floor like pieces of ice. Before Piper could regain her balance her unshod foot came down hard on one of the broken fragments.

"Rhatz!" she hissed through gritted teeth as she pulled out the shard.

She could hear Henri's agitation mounting on the other side of the door. Could he smell the fresh wound?

The knob started clicking again and then there was a loud thump. She knew it wouldn't be long before he found his way in.

"Think, Piper, think!"

She looked around and gasped. In the center of the windowless room were four Allegheny metal tables, each one lit by a hanging electric bulb. The first three tables were empty. But the light over the fourth table exposed a naked corpse of a tall, thin man. Its head was propped up by a wooden block and a hospital sheet concealed its lower half.

Piper dragged her bloodied foot along the side of the room, passing shelves of linens, scalpels, saws, chisels, and some sort of hammer with a hook. Next to the body was a porcelain slop sink with two basins.

Piper grabbed the hammer and stepped closer to the dead man on the table. She covered her nose with the collar of her jacket so the stench wouldn't gag her. A tag on the corpse's toe read:

Clarence H. Alexander
(a.k.a. Elastic Skin Joe)
Property of Dr. Crandon
Transport after sunset only

At the base of the table, blood and other bodily fluids were escaping down a drain. A black hose connected to the drain expelled the blood into one of the catch basins.

A tube had been inserted into the left side of the cadaver's neck and a vat was pumping something into the main artery.

A peculiar sensation came over Piper, not unlike the dizziness she had experienced during Houdini's performance. The freckles on her face grew hot the closer she got to the vat. It was as though its contents were calling out to her and pushing her away at the same time.

It wasn't formaldehyde or embalming fluid, Piper was certain about that. But the stuff was replacing Clarence's blood, forcing it out through an incision in the other side of his neck and flushing it out the hose leading to the sink.

An obnoxious clang made Piper jump. The motor of the refrigerated vaults hummed to life. The vibration rattled the clipboards hanging on the metal doors of each unit.

Piper briefly considered rolling out one of the steel platforms to hide in one of the freezers. But she knew that her claustrophobia would immediately kick in, making her easy prey.

She heard another bang. This time it wasn't a motor. Henri's relentless assault against the door had created a huge lightning-shaped rift down its center. Piper's hand tightened on the hammer's wooden shaft. It wouldn't be long now, she thought.

She glanced at the pale body before her and she started to formulate a plan. Balancing on her uninjured foot, Piper lifted the wounded one above Clarence Alexander's naked torso. Dragging her foot along his rubbery gray skin, she smeared her blood from his neck to his belly. Then she draped a hospital sheet over the corpse so that it almost touched the floor on both sides.

Piper snatched the hose out the sink and slipped under the table where she was hidden by the sheet. Clenching the hammer in one hand and cupping the mouth of the hose in the other, Piper waited.

A moment later she heard a loud crash and a familiar grunt. Henri had smashed through the door.

Piper held her breath. Though her view was impeded by the sheet, she could hear the crunch of glass as her pursuer's bare feet trampled over the shattered test tubes and beakers. It didn't slow him down at all.

Henri doesn't feel pain.

The creature shambled across the room. Piper could hear a distinct click with each step, the result of tiny glass shards embedded in the soles of Henri's feet.

The clicking stopped. Piper pressed her cheek to the floor to peer under the left side of the sheet. Nothing. She peeked under the right side and bit her lip to keep from crying out.

Henri's bloated purple feet and mangled toenails stood mere inches from where she was sitting. She could hear Henri sniffing. Had he taken the bait? Did the smeared blood fool him into thinking that it was her body lying on the cold table above?

The feet moved out of Piper's view. She heard the click-click of undead feet and wondered if Henri was trying to decide which end to bite into first. Then Sal's words came back to haunt her:

He prefers to stalk living prey.

Piper reeled her head to the other side, but she was a second too late. The sheet flew away from the table. Piper stifled a whimper as she stared into the zombie's open mouth, inches away from its brown teeth and a swollen gray tongue. Henri groaned in victory and a drop of dark saliva as thick as pudding dripped onto Piper's scratched arm.

She raised the hammer. When Henri leaned in close enough, Piper closed her eyes and smashed the hooked end into his face.

"I'm sorry, Sal!" she cried.

She opened her eyes to see that she had lodged the hook in Henri's mouth. But the undead monster was still undead—and still intent on making a meal out of Piper. She grabbed the head of the hammer and gave it a strong yank. The jaw made a horrible crunching sound.

"You want blood, you walking pile of filth?" she screamed, wrenching out the hook and shoving the open end of the hose into Henri's gaping maw. "You got it!"

Clarence Alexander's blood flowed freely into creature's mouth. It mingled with black slobber as it spurted from the corners of his mouth. Piper wasn't sure if Henri even needed to breathe, but she could hear him cough and sputter as the crimson elixir clogged the airways of his throat.

Henri glared at the girl with a distorted face. Did Piper detect surprise? Desperation? She gazed into his eyes. The cloudy film that covered them seemed to diminish ever so slightly. There was something behind those eyes. Something that resembled…consciousness?

Henri stumbled toward her, grabbing the hose and fighting to pull it out. If he succeeded, Piper was out of options.

"Henri, *dòmi!*"

The voice came from the other end of the room. Henri stiffened, wobbled for two seconds, and then collapsed motionless on the floor.

"*Mwen regrete,* Piper! I am so sorry!"

Across the room she saw a pair of boys' shoes stomping through broken glass as they rushed toward her. Sal leaned over the metal table holding his silver amulet in one hand and a girl's boot covered in zombie drool in the other.

"Henri has never done that before! I swear! He's never disobeyed the *wanga.*"

Snatching the slimy boot from his grasp, Piper gave Sal a wry smile and said, "I seem to have that effect on men."

She tried to ignore the pain as she pulled the slimy boot over her injured foot.

Sal knelt beside his inert brother. Before Piper could warn him, he took the hose out Henri's mouth. Blood splattered everywhere and Sal fell backwards.

"*Bondye mwen!* What did you do to him?"

"I was hoping he'd lose his craving for Piper once he got a taste of Clarence."

"Clarence?" Sal cocked his head.

Piper lifted the corpse's hand to make it wave.

"Sal, meet Clarence. Clarence, Sal."

Sal's face tightened.

"He's never had human blood before. What if he won't go back to animal blood?"

"Then I guess I'll be a hero to downtrodden chickens every-where!" Piper said with a wry smile.

"It's not funny!" Sal berated. "He needs blood to keep him from rotting away!"

Piper planted her fists on her hips.

"Well excuse me for trying to stay alive! Maybe if you'd gotten here with your lucky charm a bit sooner instead of hiding in a tree I wouldn't have done something so drastic!"

"I wasn't hiding in a tree. My 'lucky charm' was hanging from one of its branches. Do you know how difficult it is for someone my size to climb a tree? Let alone squeeze through a basement window."

Piper looked down at Henri. "What are you complaining about? He doesn't look quite so dead anymore."

It was true. The patches of decayed flesh on Henri's body had already started to clear up and his skin looked a bit pinker. Even the jaw that Piper had broken seemed to be mending itself.

"That's what I was afraid of. It works too well!" Sal lowered his head. "How am I supposed to feed him human blood every day? He likes living prey, remember?"

Piper gulped. "Oh, right."

"Whose blood was it?" Sal asked, plucking the tag from the ca-daver's toe. When he read it, his eyes went wide. "Piper, do you know who this is?"

"I told you, his name is Clarence."

Sal ignored her. "It's Elastic Skin Joe, one of my favorite acts at Coney! He could pull the skin of his neck all the way up over his nose. And look, his nose was a fun toy too…!"

Sal stepped to the head of the table and grabbed the dead man's nose, stretching it so that it looked like an elephant's trunk. "I heard him say that he could stretch his skin eighteen inches from his body without any pain at all!"

Piper scowled. "That's kind of disrespectful, isn't it?"

"Who's gonna know?" Sal scoffed. Then he glanced at the tag he had taken from Elastic Joe's toe and his jaw dropped. "*Modi*. This is not good."

"What's wrong?" asked Piper.

Sal pointed to the tag. "It says here that our friend is the property of Dr. Crandon. That's Alan Rand's stepfather!"

Piper wrinkled her brow. "Why would Rand's dad want a side-show freak's dead body?"

"I have no idea," Sal said, lifting the black hose off the floor and placing it into the sink where it continued to expel its crimson payload. "But I'm sure that whoever started the autopsy will be back any minute, and he won't be pleased to see couple of kids messing around with the good doctor's piece of meat. Wait here, I'll be right back."

Before Piper could protest, Sal slipped through the broken doorway and out into the dark corridor. He reappeared a moment later pushing the mobile cart that Piper had foolishly tried to use as a barrier outside the supply room.

"Help me lift Henri onto this gurney," Sal said. Piper wrapped her arms around Henri's knees while Sal hooked a hand under each shoulder. "One, two, three!"

They both heaved on three and lifted Henri into the gurney. Sal grabbed the sheet from the floor, threw it over Henri's body, and shoved the gurney through the busted doorway.

"*Allons!*" he said. "Let's get out of here! Dr. Crandon must have some influence at this hospital and I don't want to give him any excuse to discharge my brother."

If anyone found it odd that two kids were whisking a body through the open corridors of the neurology wing, nobody said a word. When they reached Henri's room, Sal wheeled the stretcher next to the bed where he and Piper rolled the listless figure onto his belly. They didn't waste time trying to arrange his limbs to fit properly on the bed.

The two youths then scampered out of Bellevue's front doors and made their way back to the elevated train station. They spent most of the forty-five minute ride in uncomfortable silence.

Piper used the time to think up a story for her uncle about why she was so late. To hide her injuries, she would have to scuttle past him and Bess like she had the day before. But Houdini was very perceptive. How would she hide the smell of death and decay on her clothes and in her hair?

When the train finally arrived at Sal's stop, he stepped silently onto the platform. Before the doors snapped shut he turned and asked, "So, do you believe me now?"

Piper lowered her head. But she couldn't hide her smile.

"Sal," she said, "I'll never doubt you again."

A SYMPHONY OF HORROR

The days grew longer but also got colder. Piper could hardly believe that she'd been living with Houdini and Aunt Bess for almost two months. So far it had been a brutal winter. Over ten inches of snow had fallen during the second week of February—the heaviest since the blizzard of 1921. On top of what had already fallen, Piper had to slog through a foot-and-a-half of snow to get to school and back.

One day after the dismissal bell rang, Piper and Sal were plodding single-file along the dirty white footpath when she noticed that her companion was unusually silent.

"What's eating you?" she asked.

After her disastrous visit to the hospital, Sal had continued to visit his brother almost every day after school. He hadn't asked Piper to accompany him again, and that was fine with her.

Their worst fears had not come to pass; Henri had not developed an exclusive taste for human blood, which was both a blessing and a curse. While Henri may not have been chasing down orderlies in the courtyard, his complexion wasn't improving much either according to Sal.

"Nothing," the boy replied, wiping his brow with his glove.

"Then why are you sweating when it's ten degrees outside?" she asked.

"It's a lot of work for husky guys like me to slosh through this kind of mess," he snipped.

"Really? Because you weren't sweating this much yesterday when the snow was fresh and we were the first ones to make a path."

Sal turned to look at his friend, but he couldn't meet her gaze completely.

"Okay. Fine," he said. "Listen, I was just wondering if you were busy on Sunday. There's a couple of matinees going on at the Loew's by the boardwalk. Would you like to go with me?"

"For Valentine's Day? And how!" came her quick response. Then she paused for a moment so as not to appear desperate. "I mean, that would be very nice, Sal."

A baffled look came over Sal's face.

"Valentine's Day? I-I didn't know it was Valentine's Day," he stammered. "I just wanted to see *Nosferatu* with somebody."

"*Nosferatu?* Isn't that about some creepy old bloodsucker who likes rats?"

"Yeah!" Sal beamed with delight.

"I thought that film was banned."

"*Se vre.* But the guy who manages the Loew's got his hands on a copy—and he invited me to come see it!" Sal said with bluster.

"I can't believe you'd ask a girl to see a horrible disgusting thing like that on Valentine's Day," Piper said. "How about something with a dreamy star like Valentino? Or Douglas Fairbanks! Isn't he in some new pirate flicker? Romance *and* action! What more could a couple ask for on a date?"

She batted her eyelashes in jest.

"It's not a date!" Sal said, crinkling his nose at the word. "*Silvouple,* Piper! They're not even putting it up on the marquee. It's by invitation only! This could be the last time I ever get a chance to see it!"

Piper threw her hands up.

"Fine! I guess any movie is better than watching Collins clean the basement."

Sal ran up and hugged her.

"*Mèsi poutèt ou,* Piper! Thank you so much!"

Then he took a step back and gave her a gentle shove.

"But it's not a date," he repeated. "Meet me outside Nedick's at two o'clock. It's on the ground floor of the theater. Don't be late. You girls are always late."

Sal loved the flickers. He said it was like seeing your dreams in the middle of the day. But for Piper, it was the *only* way to see a dream. So when the time came to meet Sal at the theater, she ran the whole way so she wouldn't miss a thing.

She had told Houdini that she'd be going to the movies with Sal and he had asked, "Isn't that the boy you were with the last two times you were late?"

Piper blushed and promised that she would be home before dark. "After all, how much trouble could I get into at a movie theater?"

At seven stories tall, the Loew's Coney Island Theater was the tallest building in Coney Island. It stood across from the construction site of the Half Moon Hotel, which would be taller. So it was difficult for Piper to lose her way.

Storm clouds had gathered in the sky, but at least it wasn't cold enough for more snow. Piper made it to Nedick's just as the skies opened up. Sal was waiting there beneath an umbrella and staring at his pocket watch.

"I knew you'd be late," he scowled.

The smell of the butter-toasted buns drifted from the orange and white lobby of the fast-food restaurant, luring the two companions in for a taste. Sal fished out a couple of dimes and gave them to the boy behind the counter who handed them two hot dogs and two orange drinks in return.

"Nathan's may be a New York institution, but Nedick's is far better," he said, biting into his frank.

Piper looked at the hot dog and gave him a skeptical look.

"What's the difference? A hot dog is a hot dog."

But when she sank her teeth into the bun and its tasty contents,

Piper's mouth exploded with glee. She savored it for a few seconds and then with a full mouth she declared, "If they served Grape Nehi, this place would be heaven."

When they finished their hot dogs, they made their way to the movie palace. A glass display in back of the lobby showed black and white photographs for upcoming films.

"I hear they're gonna start making talking pictures," Sal announced.

Piper scoffed. "Talking pictures? How awful!"

"It's gonna be swell," Sal said with a self-assured nod.

Piper spotted a snapshot for *The Son of the Sheik*.

"Coming in July!" she gasped.

"Valentino?" Sal said, rolling his eyes. "He's such a cake eater."

Then he bought a bucket of popcorn, grabbed Piper by the wrist, and dragged her away from the display case. An usher in white gloves and a red suit led them down the aisle to their seats.

"Ninth row, please," Sal directed the usher.

Piper could tell by the usher's body language that he was annoyed by Sal's request.

"Why the ninth row?" she whispered.

"The ninth row is the best seat in the house!" he said, counting the rows as he led her down the aisle.

"Says who?" asked Piper.

"Says *me!*" replied Sal, pointing to the center of his chest. "Seven, eight...*nine!* Here!"

Though the theater lights were still on, the usher shined his flashlight down the row. Sal and Piper slipped into the first two red-velvet seats and waited for the movie to start.

Piper was suddenly aware that everyone in the theater was looking at her. No, looking at *them*. Whenever she lifted her head to glance around, they quickly looked away. She had no idea why until Sal passed the bucket of popcorn. His hand accidentally brushed hers. The contrast in their skin tones had never been more apparent.

It didn't matter that Sal and Piper weren't even teenagers yet. All anybody saw was a black boy and a white girl alone together. In a movie theater. On Valentine's Day.

When the house lights dimmed, Piper felt a sense of relief. Then she was ashamed of her relief.

Sal had been oblivious to the whole affair. Piper could sense his excitement as the movie projector flickered to life and its white light beamed through the haze of cigarette smoke.

The first thing that popped up on the screen was a newsreel that showed a horse named Crusader winning a race, a woman in Italy breaking a bottle against a ship, and a monkey with pants riding a bicycle.

The final news segment's title card announced in big white letters, "Harry Houdini to testify before Congress. World-famous magician proposes law that would make fortunetelling illegal."

The film footage showed a Congressman prodding Houdini for his opinion on astrology. Houdini's response flashed on the last title card:

"I do not believe in astrology. They cannot tell from a chunk of mud millions of miles away what is going to happen to me."

The theater broke out in laughter and Sal nudged Piper in the ribs.

The projectionist changed reels and the cartoons began. The first one was a Felix the Cat short and then there was a Krazy Kat short.

"That was a complete rip-off of the Felix cartoon!" Sal complained.

"SHHH! Be quiet!" someone shouted behind them. Piper felt herself sinking in her seat.

The main feature began and Piper knew right away that it wasn't going to be her cup of tea. She yawned during the very first scene and almost fell asleep when the hero took a weird ghostly carriage ride to a seemingly abandoned castle.

Only when the ominous doors of the rundown castle inched open did Piper sit upright up in her chair. A tall, pale figure clad in black ambled through the gate to greet the hero. The audience booed and hissed when the villain came on screen.

This was Count Orlok, and his appearance sent shivers down Piper's spine. Clutching Sal's arm, she whispered, "Holy horsefeathers, Sal—he looks just like my..."

But Sal didn't hear her. He was joining the others in jeering at the film's rat-like antagonist.

When the catcalls had died down, Piper decided to wait until the movie was over to tell Sal. She didn't want to risk annoying the people behind them again.

So she remained silent when Count Orlok tried to suck the hero's blood from a wound on his thumb, even though the scene was virtually identical to the night when her father attempted to do the same to her.

"Owww!" Sal squealed as Piper's nails dug so deep into his forearm that they almost pierced the skin.

The sudden commotion earned Sal another sharp hush from the tenth row. Sal glared at Piper irately when somebody threw popcorn in his woolly hair.

The storm outside was raging so fiercely that Piper could hear the crashing thunder over the harmonious sound of the mighty Wurlitzer organ. The melody started building to a crescendo, indicating that the movie was racing to its climax.

Piper chewed her fingernails as an eerie shadow crept ever closer to the hero's wife, cowering in bed. Count Orlok sank his teeth into the woman's throat. Then the film cut to a rooster crowing outside the house. In his obsession to drink the heroine's blood, the Nosferatu had mistakenly stayed out until dawn.

The audience applauded as the villain, attempting to escape the rays of the rising sun, vanished in a fiery puff of smoke. But this time Sal didn't join them, which Piper found odd.

She had little time to dwell on it, however. Before the audience could learn the fate of the hero's wife, a huge boom shook the theater. The projector went dead and the lobby lights blinked out. The freak storm had caused a power failure and the terrified movie patrons fell over each other trying to escape the inky darkness.

"Stick close to me," Piper said, taking Sal's hand. "I was always a ringer in Flashlight Tag."

"Okay, I'll hold onto you," Sal replied, "but I can see you just fine. Your freckles are glowing!"

"What are you talking about?" Piper touched her cheeks. She could feel heat radiating from them—the same sensation she had felt in the morgue.

A strange feeling compelled her to raise her head. She thought she spied someone looking at her from the balcony. She couldn't tell whether it was a boy or a girl, but whoever it was seemed to be floating in the air.

No, not floating. Flapping.

"Let's get out of here," Piper urged Sal.

Her keen eyes guided them through the crowd of panic-stricken movie-goers whose paranoia had already been inflamed by their cinematic encounter with vermin and vampires. The youths made it to the lobby where the usher brandished his flashlight as a staunch beacon for the frenzied mob of horror fanatics.

Sal and Piper fell out onto the wet sidewalk in front of the theater. It was raining pitchforks and the sky was black with thunderclouds. But at least the storm had cleared the streets of any remaining snow.

"Well, that was disappointing," Sal declared, opening his umbrella.

"Because you missed the end?" Piper asked, huddling against him to avert the downpour.

"No. Because the ending made no sense!" he grumbled.

Piper gave him a blank stare.

"When Count Orlok turns to ash, it all happens in front of a big mirror!"

"So?" She didn't understand his point.

"Everyone knows that vampires don't cast reflections!"

"You mean everyone named Sal Gamache," Piper replied.

Sal ignored her.

"Why was there even a mirror there in the first place? The director should have caught that. What's he saying, that a dying vampire suddenly gets a reflection?"

"Are you always this annoying or is Valentine's Day just special?"

Piper looked at him with a hint of irritation on her face. But she didn't wait for his response. "All I know is that Orlocks, or whatever his name was, gave me the heebie-jeebies."

"Orlok. He's a vampire. He's supposed to give you the heebie-jeebies."

"No, that's not why."

She turned her head so that they faced each other under the umbrella.

"The night my father brought me to Houdini I pricked my finger. And he attacked me. Just like Orlok attacked the guy in the movie."

"Houdini attacked you?"

"No, moron! My father! And he kind of looked like Orlok too."

"So, you think your father is a vampire?"

"I wasn't sure till now. But it's the only thing that makes sense. The only reason Aunt Bess and everybody else think he's dead!" The only reason he can't take care of me.

"Are you on the level? Are you trying to trump my zombie brother with a vampire *papa?*"

She stiffened at Sal's accusation.

"You calling me a liar?"

Then she shook her head, recalling how she had refused to accept Sal's story about detention.

"Sal, I said I'd never doubt you again. Now I need you to believe me."

She heard him take a sharp breath through his nose and watched him tug at his lower lip.

"You say your father looked like Count Orlok? So his fangs were in front?"

"Yeah. Why does that matter?"

"Because it means they're proteroglyphous."

"You speaking Creole again?" Piper asked.

"No, no. *Proteroglyphous.* It means he's got short fangs at the front of his mouth, like a rat...or a cobra. Traditional vampires have *solenoglyphous* fangs—long, folding ones like a rattlesnake."

"So?" Piper asked impatiently.

"Well, it sounds to me like your father's vampirism may be the result of a spell, not a vampire bite. And whoever cast the spell is a lousy cheapskate who skimped on the potion's main ingredients."

Piper tried to absorb what he was saying. "You mean someone stole his hot cross buns? Like they did to your brother?"

"*Gros Bon Ange.*" Sal corrected. "No. The *Gros Bon Ange* is the source of a person's willpower. But only a strong force of will would inspire a walking dead man to give his daughter the comforts of a life that he can't share."

Piper stared at him blankly.

"Think about it," he continued. "In the movie, you always knew when Count Orlok was about to appear by his long, creepy shadow. But a vampire casts no *reflection*. So what part of his soul is he missing?"

"The *Ti Bon Ange*," Piper shouted, impressed at herself for remembering what it was called.

Sal nodded.

"But who would steal a piece of his soul? And why?" Piper asked.

"Maybe he messed with the wrong people. Like my brother."

Piper rubbed her jaw and remained silent for a moment. Then she said, "Sal, remember those old urns I told you about in my uncle's library?"

"The canopic jars? What about them?"

"Houdini got awfully touchy when I went near them. What if they're the real McCoys? Could they be used to restore your brother's soul—and maybe my dad's?"

Sal shook his head. "You said he owns the falcon and jackal jars. But the Egyptians stored the *Ti Bon Ange*, what they called the *ba*, in the one that also holds the liver. It's the jar with a human head."

Piper slumped against Sal under the umbrella. She could feel his uneasiness as she huddled closer to protect herself from raindrops that were pelting the boardwalk like a jackpot of coins.

"Something's not right here." She spoke softly, as though she didn't mean for Sal to hear her. "He said Houdini owed him. For what?"

"W-what are you talking about?" Sal asked timidly.

She raised her voice so he could hear her over the downpour. "In a couple of weeks my aunt and uncle are going to Washington to push that anti-fortune bill through Congress. They're leaving me home with Collins so I won't miss any school."

"And?" It was Sal's turn to be impatient.

"He's been lying to me and I want to find out why."

"Who?" Sal asked, his voice edgy and shrill.

Lightning ripped the sky above the boardwalk. Piper and Sal jumped as the silhouette of a man appeared before them.

"I thought I told you to be home before dark," the shadow said with a familiar voice.

"Houdini!" Piper cried, running to him and hugging her face to his chest. The magician placed a hesitant hand on his niece's back. Even though he had an ample umbrella, a bowler hat, and a velvet-collared coat, Houdini was drenched from head to toe.

"You had us worried sick, young lady," he said sternly, though his stance relaxed considerably as she hugged him.

"Us?" she repeated.

Houdini stepped aside and Piper could make out the broad outline of Jim Collins standing vigilantly beneath a broken old umbrella. Flecks of icy rain assaulted his body and he looked miserable.

Piper folded her arms over her chest and huffed. "What's with the Irish brigade? It's not even nighttime yet!"

"They travel even when the sun's rays are merely shielded," Houdini answered, scouting the skies with his piercing blue eyes.

"They who?" Piper asked.

"I'm afraid it's my fault, sir." Sal said, stepping out from behind Piper. He tucked his shirt into the front of his pants and fumbled with his umbrella handle so he could offer his hand to Houdini. "I'm Sal. Salvador Gamache. It's an honor to meet you, sir. I'm a big fan! So's my brother!"

Houdini gave the boy's hand a limp shake while turning his gaze to Piper. "This is your friend? You didn't tell me he was..."

There was an uncomfortable silence. Piper narrowed her eyes at Houdini as if daring him to complete his thought.

"Plump?" Sal finished the sentence with a nervous chuckle.

The magician let Sal's hand slip from his and shifted his attention to the darkened movie theater. "Why did the power outage affect only this b—?"

"Piper?" Sal gasped, cutting him off. "Your freckles are glowing again."

Houdini seized his niece's shoulder and reeled her around to face him. She could feel her cheeks growing hot again under her uncle's intense scrutiny.

"We have to leave here at once," the magician said.

Then he motioned to his assistant. "Jim! Take the boy in the car and return him to his family. I'll escort my errant niece back to the house."

Without allowing time for even a quick goodbye, Houdini snatched Piper by the wrist and pulled her along the wet planks of the boardwalk. Struggling pathetically in her uncle's grip, Piper looked back and saw Collins hauling Sal off the boardwalk to the street where the car was presumably waiting.

She was about to protest when a strange sight caught her eye outside the dime museum. Someone dressed in a muumuu huddled under its sparse outcrop to shelter herself from the storm. Her pointed head looked way too small for her body so it was hard for Piper to tell whether she was a girl or a woman. The figure clenched a tiny naked doll to her breast and rocked it back and forth.

The pinheaded girl looked at Piper and her thin lips broke into a huge grin. She extended her hand but Piper couldn't tell if she was waving or trying to summon her. That's when Piper realized the doll was moving. It heaved with a continuous, steady motion and mewed in protest because the girl's sudden movement had disturbed its breastfeeding ritual.

There were a few short hairs irregularly placed on one side of the baby's head. Its skull was enormous, smooth and distended like its mother's. Even in the dark Piper could tell that its skin was colored a livid terra-cotta.

The infant turned its horribly misshapen head toward Piper. She saw something that looked like a small face, no more than two inches wide, ghastly and fiendish. The forehead protruded grotesquely over its eyes, which opened slowly and stared at her with an odd, unseeing glance. Like the eyes of a lab rat, they had no pigment.

The infant licked its crimson lips and Piper realized that there were two red puncture marks on the little woman's chest. The creature had not been nursing after all. It had been feeding on something else.

Piper continued to squirm in her uncle's grasp. Houdini led her past a horrid satanic figure that leered over the entry to Hell Gate. A sign next to the haunted attraction announced a new Hall of Mirrors would be opening in the summer.

At one point Piper thought she saw another pink eye peering up at her through a knothole in the boardwalk. And she could have sworn she heard a fiendish whisper on the wind. Although she didn't hear it very clearly, it sounded very much like "star child."

Houdini wasn't looking at the boardwalk. His eyes were fixed on the sky. So neither of them noticed as a woman in a hooded raincoat stepped out of the downpour and blocked their path. When he finally spotted the stranger, Houdini took a defensive stance between her and Piper.

"Where are you taking this child?" the woman asked through a thin scarf that concealed the lower part of her face.

Then she leaned in to give Piper's uncle a closer look and her posture softened at once.

"Houdini, is that you?"

Houdini pinched the hem of the woman's scarf and peeled the silky material over her chin. He smiled as a lush set of whiskers escaped their confinement and danced gleefully in the cold, wet breeze.

Piper stifled a gasp.

"I do believe I've discovered the Missing Link," Houdini beamed. "Piper, I'd like you to meet Krao Farini, the Ape Woman of Borneo. Krao, this is my niece, Piper."

Piper never knew what to do when meeting people for the first time. She hated to curtsy and a handshake was considered "unladylike." But she didn't want the bearded woman to think she was being rude. So she raised her hand and wiggled her fingers in greeting.

"Pleased to meet you, Miss Farini."

The woman gave the girl an intense look. Piper's hand sprung to her cheeks and she realized her freckles were still glowing.

"Call me Krao, child. Farini was the name of the man who 'discovered' me. I took it out of respect for him."

Houdini turned to his niece. "Piper, I worked with Krao in the sideshow circuit back when I was just getting started."

"You were a better wild person than I could ever hope to be," Krao teased. "So what brings the two of you out on a dreadful night like this?"

"Not fit for man *nor* beast?" the magician winked at Krao. "My niece was taking in a movie and I'm here to escort her back home."

"Always the gentleman," Krao's lips curled into a grin beneath her beard. "I'm sure that Mrs. Houdini has something enticing waiting for you on the table, so I won't keep you. It was a pleasure bumping into you, Houdini. And very nice meeting you, Piper."

She took a step away from them, but her eyes lingered on Piper for an uncomfortable moment.

"Goodbye, Krao." The magician waved. "Tell the others that Bess and I are looking forward to our annual pilgrimage in June."

They hadn't gone five steps when Krao called out, "Houdini! Why didn't you ever grow a beard?"

"Because I could never grow one as luxurious as yours, my dear!" The magician laughed and urged his niece onward.

When Piper was sure they were out of earshot, she asked, "Was she for real? The beard, I mean."

"Oh, more than just the beard, my dear. The woman's whole body is covered in black hair. The tresses between her shoulder blades are so thick that it could pass for a mane."

Piper didn't want to know how Houdini knew such intimate details about the bearded woman.

"And you worked with her? In the freak show?"

"Yes," her uncle admitted. "But I was a fake. Krao is as real as they come. A sensitive soul as well. Never married, at least as far as I know. Too bad. She would have made someone an excellent wife."

Houdini led Piper the rest of the way home without incident. But the magician never stopped scouring the sky. He tried to fill the void in conversation with snippets of dialogue, but Piper's replies were short and pithy. She kept thinking about Houdini's statement that he had begun his career as a fake. If that were true, then why had he started his zealous crusade against fake Spiritualists? What made their actions any more deplorable than his own?

And what about the way he reacted to Sal? It was no better than the behavior of the people in the movie theater.

Houdini promoted himself as some great humanitarian that was open to all walks of life. He was no stranger to bigotry. Piper knew that Aunt Bess's mother didn't speak with her for ten years because she had married a Jew. Why was her relationship with Sal any different?

Was Houdini just a big phony? Now more than ever, she was convinced that he had lied about her father. But what was he hiding?

Piper was determined to find out.

ASSAULT ON THE APE WOMAN

Krao Farini navigated a path around the puddles as she made her way from the subway station to the house she shared with a "normal" German couple on Manhattan's Upper East Side. She was brimming to tell the others about whom she had seen earlier. Unfortunately, most of them stayed in Gravesend during the winter unless they were travelling on the circuit. So the news would have to keep until she saw them all again in April or May.

All, that is, save Clarence. Poor Clarence. She would miss the way his arm slithered around her like an eel and how his tongue pushed aside the stray hairs on his forehead. Krao snickered at the memory of him telling her to kiss his butt and then bending over to demonstrate how to do it. She refused to believe that a man so full of life would have taken his own.

The bearded woman lived on the second floor where she enjoyed cooking and entertaining guests. She hadn't yet decided whether to prepare a nice Russian *palov* or if she was in the mood for something closer to her own native cuisine, maybe *kaeng pa* or *phat thai*.

Despite her appearance to the contrary, Krao's travels with the sideshow had turned her into a cultured woman. As the fabled "Ape Woman," she covered her face with a scarf in public—not to hide her appearance but to hide her identity.

The previous summer, Krao had been hyped as Darwin's Missing Link. That was the same year a high school teacher in Tennessee had been accused of unlawfully teaching evolution. Promoters capitalized on the "Scopes Monkey Trial," offering Krao as proof of Charles Darwin's controversial theory that man had descended from the apes.

Ads hailed Krao as belonging to a race of people who lived in trees and survived on roots, nuts, and grass. Some researchers took this "missing link" claim seriously and wrote articles about Krao for respected science journals. One doctor had even given her three hundred dollars in exchange for exclusive rights to her body after she died.

But the joke was on them. This supposed tree dweller was well-read, multilingual, and probably more intelligent than most of the so-called scientists.

The publicity had generated a huge surge in popularity for the bearded lady. Fans from all over the country would write to her or come to Coney Island just to get an autograph or touch her beard.

But Krao's rise to stardom brought with it as many detractors as it had admirers. For every autograph seeker waiting for a chance to chat with her after a performance there were just as many psychopaths lurking in the audience—and it was difficult to tell one type of fanatic from another. Rotten fruit and cat calls had become commonplace on her stage even when Travis the Strongman was by her side.

Krao finally reached the foot of the stairs to her house without getting sprayed by the tires of passing motorcars. She fumbled through her purse looking for her keys when she noticed a man in a dark raincoat and trilby hat approaching her with purpose in his step.

"Krao Farini?" he asked with an accent that Americans might confuse with her own. He was a strange looking man, but who was she to judge?

"Who wants to know?" she asked, furtively inserting a key between each knuckle.

"Anata wa kami no me ni shūtaidearu," was his reply.

It wasn't her native tongue, but Krao knew enough of the language to realize that this man was neither a fan nor an autograph seeker. Something about "abomination" and "God's eyes."

Because her instincts had never let her down, Krao's fist exploded from her purse and she thrust it keys-first at the stranger's face. The man sidestepped the blow with poise and skill. She was surprised at how easily her swift maneuver had been foiled.

The man whirled around and responded with a punch of his own. Krao tightened her abdomen and squeezed her eyes tightly. But the pain she anticipated never materialized. The blow was a light, seemingly harmless jab delivered just below her navel—a short prod with not enough force behind it to leave even a bruise.

The stranger looked much stronger than the punch to her midsection suggested, so when Krao opened her eyes she gave him a puzzled look. He simply tipped his hat to her, turned, and walked away.

"How odd," she mused.

★★★★

TOADS AND TOADIES

Eighty miles to the north, robed acolytes looked up from their festive ritual to behold the fearsome yet delicate contours of the Master's pet as she descended on their tiny island. But this time they neither gawked nor cowered.

One of the hooded figures approached the pale woman with a brash confidence in his step.

"Welcome, Miss Flapper. I am the Patriarch," he said with a voice that was strong and resonant. He swept his hood back to reveal the face of a handsome young black man whose head was shorn as smooth as the Beast's. "Master Therion has been anticipating your arrival. This way, please."

With a gentle touch to her elbow, the Patriarch ushered Flapper toward the mouth of the cave. But the vamp shook his hand off and bared her fangs.

"I can ankle it all by my lonesome, bozo," she sneered.

The Patriarch didn't flinch, which made Flapper more annoyed. He simply bowed his head and took a step backwards.

Flapper heard the melodious echo of many voices chanting in unison as she wandered into the cave. She followed the earthen walls to the source of the music. In the middle of the cave was a huge clearing where a circle of twelve figures, men and women, swayed to the otherworldly mantra while shedding their black robes. They were surrounded by another group of disciples who were still in their robes, their faces hidden behind golden masks.

In the center of the circle, a man in a red cloak and hood stood on a dais with his back to the celebrants. His beefy contours bulged at the crimson material like a walrus in a sausage casing.

Master Therion stamped the ground with his walking stick and brandished a censer that exhaled clouds of smoky incense. Without glancing at his fanged minion, he extended a pudgy hand through his draped sleeve and motioned for her to join him.

The throng parted. Flapper could sense that, like the Patriarch, these men and women no longer feared her. They adored her. Any one of them would have jumped at the chance to feed her if the Master had commanded it.

Flapper was impressed at how her Master's ranks had grown in both size and devotion. His disciples were just like she used to be— loners on the fringe of society, young people who had a need to belong to something greater than themselves.

Isolated from interaction with people on the mainland, these undernourished souls were fed a steady supply of dogma, ritual, and mind-altering substances to create a total dependence on their Master for belief, behavior, and practice. They had lost their personal freedom and the ability to choose for themselves.

But unlike her, they venerated the Beast for relieving them of that onerous burden called free will.

She stepped up to the platform and immediately noticed a huge toad pinned to a crucifix. She looked closer and realized that the animal had three legs on either side of its body and a third eye in the middle of its head. It was writhing on the cross, still alive.

From the depths of his shadowed hood, the Beast intoned, "I assume unto myself and take into my service the elemental spirit of this animal, to be about me as a lying spirit, to go forth upon the earth as a guardian to me in my work for mankind. And this shall be its reward, to stand beside me and hear the truth that I utter, the falsehood whereof shall deceive men."

Removing his dagger from its sheath, Master Therion pierced the toad's heart with the wavy blade, immediately stilling its convulsive movements.

"Into my hands I receive thy spirit."

Flapper looked away. Despite her elevated rank in the food chain, she had no stomach for killing animals. Humans? That was another matter entirely.

The clothed members of the congregation bowed their heads in unison while the naked celebrants performed acts that even Flapper considered decadent. Finally, the acolytes formed a line and retreated one by one. Only when their chanting had diminished to a dull murmur did the Beast lift his head to acknowledge his servant.

"Sorry to crash your petting party, Master T, but I got some dirty laundry to air about your little tomato."

"*Master T?*" the Beast repeated with derision.

He lowered his hood and peered at her through the folds in his eyes.

"I have given you a long leash, Flapper. Be sure not to abuse the privilege."

The words came as a hiss through his filed teeth and Flapper didn't need heightened senses to catch a whiff of his breath. It was nastier than the stench of the docks on the Gowanus. She pinched her nose and waved the air in front of her.

"Master, what have you been eating?"

The Beast's eyes widened in outrage. Then they darted sideways as though she had shamed him.

"It's this body," he sighed. "I am outgrowing it. Or rather, I should say, it is outgrowing me."

Flapper had heard him say schizoid things like this before but she never knew what the heck he meant.

The Beast inhaled and straightened his back. "Tell me, my thrall, what news do you bring?"

"I don't know if this means anything, Master *Therion*," she made sure to say his full name, "but I'm pretty sure teeny-Houdini saw me roosting in the love nest of a movie house."

"I told you to keep a low profile."

"I did! But she saw me *after* I cut the lights."

"Hmm. That *is* interesting." The Beast tapped his sharpened nails on the metal cobra tip of his walking stick.

"What gives, Master?" Flapper asked. "I thought dewdroppers had the exclusive rights to night peepers."

Master Therion leaned his massive bulk on the stick. He pondered his servant as though trying to decide how much the guileless vamp needed to know.

"The age of the slave gods is over, my dear Flapper. And while your Master is the gatekeeper of the coming Apocalypse, a crowned and conquering child shall be its progenitor. There are those who believe the Houdini girl might be that child."

"I guess I shoulda' saddled up to her a bit more snuggly then, huh?" Flapper said with a smirk. "S'too bad Harry Butt-inski pulled his knight in shining armor act."

Master Therion slammed the end of his stick against the podium floor. Flapper fought the urge to recoil.

"You are *not* to make yourself known to her, do you understand me?" the Beast roared. "No saddling, no snuggling! Not until Houdini is out of the picture."

He took a deep breath through his nose. In a calmer voice he continued, "The girl is, after all, almost a teenager. There will come a time when her uncle's custodianship becomes so overbearing that she will sever it of her own volition."

"And then I can act?" asked Flapper.

"And then you can act," the Beast affirmed with a nod. "Now off with you," he said, dismissing her with a wave of his hand.

There was a time when Flapper would have bowed before stepping off the dais. But Master Therion had not commanded her to bow, so there was no need for the histrionics. Let the hooded sycophants lick his boots.

There was a reason the Beast had chosen a toad for his sacrifice.

But Flapper refused to be just another toady. Yes, like them, she had to obey the Master. But that didn't mean she couldn't have a little fun along the way.

The Houdini brat had put a crimp in her style. But a crowned and conquering chaos-bringer? What a wad of chewing gum! Why was Master T really obsessed with the little redhead?

Flapper aimed to find out.

REQUIEM FOR A MOTHER

Beyond the sober colonnade of Doric columns that marked the entrance to New York's Pennsylvania Station, Piper bid farewell to Houdini and Bess as they boarded the *Capitol Limited* for Washington, D.C. It was the last week of February and her aunt and uncle would be gone for the better part of it.

Amidst the obligatory farewell hugs and kisses, Houdini warned Piper not to invite anyone inside the house.

"Particularly the man who brought you to us," he cautioned. "In fact, if he ever shows up again, anywhere, don't listen to a single word spewed by his forked tongue."

"What about Sal?" she asked with as much hesitation in her voice as there was defiance. "Can he come over?"

"Your little friend?" Houdini said.

He glanced at his wife who gave him a cross look. The magician rolled his eyes.

"He can visit...under one condition! When you're together, the two of you will stay on the first floor at all times. No closed doors! And only when Mr. Collins is around to chaperone. Understood?"

He slapped his hand on the shoulder of his well-dressed assistant to emphasize his sincerity. Piper replied with an enthusiastic nod.

Collins then helped Houdini haul a large trunk aboard the coach, giving Bess a chance to speak with Piper alone.

"Don't mind him, dear. He's a big old windbag," she smiled. "But a windbag who loves you. So please take care of yourself; we'll be home soon."

Piper and Collins stood on the platform and waved until the train vanished from the station. Collins was not much of a chatterbox. Neither was Piper for that matter. So they spent most of the ride home in silence. And that was fine with her.

Piper was determined to get her hands on the Egyptian jars in Houdini's library, but over the next few days Collins thwarted her every move. From the moment she came home from school until she went to bed, he was on her like a hobo on a ham sandwich. When she went to her room and pretended to do homework, the faithful assistant checked in so often that even going to the bathroom became an uncomfortable ordeal.

To make matters worse, Collins was sleeping in a room that had belonged to Houdini's librarian. It was on the fourth floor at the top of the stairs—between her bedroom and the library, which made it impossible for her to sneak in at night.

So when Piper came home from school on Friday afternoon, she practically jumped for joy when she found Collins in the basement working on one of Houdini's contraptions. Sal was supposed to meet her after taking care of a few things at home. But when 4:00 rolled around and her friend hadn't shown up, Piper decided to take matters into her own hands before Collins packed it up for the night.

She crept up the stairs, stepped into the top-floor nook, and ducked into the larger workroom, careful not to disturb any creaky loose boards. Edgar Allan Poe's desk was even more cluttered than the last time she'd seen it, littered with papers and photographs. Piper guessed that Houdini had been trying to organize his pictures into photo albums.

The wooden heads of the jars beckoned Piper from their glass abode at the end of the library. The lock was a crude thing. She didn't even need one of her special picks. Taking a bobby pin from her hair and ignoring the foreboding stares of the jackal and falcon, Piper jim-mied the lock and opened the glass doors.

With a quick "eenie, meenie, miney, mo," Piper selected the jack-al-headed vessel and carefully removed it from the cabinet. She ran her fingers along its surface hoping to find something that might help her decipher its secrets. But the smooth calcite pottery showed no signs of ever having displayed any sort of inscription. Piper turned it over hoping she wouldn't find a "Made in Japan" label on its base. Without warning, the wooden lid slipped off and fell to the floor.

With a muffled grunt, Piper inspected the jackal head for dam-age. When she was satisfied that nothing had been chipped, dented, or broken, she lifted the second container from the cabinet and gen-tly removed its bird-headed lid so she wouldn't accidentally drop it as well.

She looked into the open neck of the falcon's jar and a strange sen-sation overcame her. It was similar to the feeling that had overcome her at Houdini's performance. Or the odd sensation she encountered every time she climbed the stairs to her room. Or the way she felt when she went through the *Kefitzat Haderech*.

But if she had to compare it to something in the real world, she would say that it felt like someone had stuck a huge vacuum cleaner hose in her face and had turned it on. Because, as impossible as it seemed, Piper was being sucked into the jar!

She fought against the unseen force, pushing against the ancient object while trying to stay mindful of how fragile it was. With a final lurch, Piper broke the vessel's hold on her and fell onto the hardwood floor beside the other jar.

But before she could recover from the falcon jar's attack, she was assaulted by another invisible force, this one coming from the second vessel. It took hold of the silver padlock around her neck and dragged Piper across the floor by it. The padlock plunged into the jar's open-ing but stopped abruptly when the back of Piper's head slammed into its sharp edge.

The energy that pulled at the lock was different from the suc-tion-like one that had seized her before. The force from jackal jar was like a magnet. Unlike the falcon-headed jar, it wanted nothing to do with Piper. She was just the unfortunate bearer of the object it desired.

The force kept pulling on the padlock, slamming Piper's head against the lip of the jar in a desperate crusade to win its prize. The lock craned against the chain hanging from Piper's throat.

Gasping for air, she reached for the jackal head and clawed her hand up its whittled face trying to purchase a fingerhold. She managed to pinch the snout of the wooden animal and tried lifting it off the floor.

But she lost her grip and the lid fell from her grasp.

Struggling blindly to grab it again, Piper felt herself losing consciousness. Her fingers finally found their mark. If she dropped it this time, there would be no third chance.

Slowly, carefully, she lifted the lid to her face. Then she plunged her free hand into the stoneware jug, scooped out the padlock, and immediately slammed the jackal head on the container.

The momentum hurled Piper across the crowded room headlong into the side of Edgar Allan Poe's desk.

"Ow," she groaned, collapsing onto the cold floor.

A heavy photo album fell from the messy desk, striking Piper on her injured noggin before landing in her lap.

"Ow," she groaned again.

Rubbing her head, Piper sat upright on the floor and glanced at the volume. It had opened to a full-length portrait of Houdini who was standing in the middle of a line with four other men. Piper didn't recognize three of the men, but she was certain that she knew the one standing to her uncle's right.

"Jaysus and Janey Mac! Are you off your nut, lass?" The thunderous fury in Jim Collins's voice made her jump. "I leave you alone for one minute and you're up here acting the maggot!"

"They started it!" Piper shouted back at him, pointing at the jars. As soon as the words left her mouth, she realized how ridiculous she sounded.

"Did they now?" Walking in a slow arc around Piper, Collins squinted at the thick portfolio in her lap. "Whatcha got there?"

"Photo album," Piper replied. She pointed to the man standing next to Houdini. "Collins, do you know who this is?"

His run up the stairs had made him perspire like the devil in a church. Collins leaned in to take a closer look. A meldrop of sweat hung from his nose and Piper shifted the album sideways to avoid it.

"Why, it's a picture of Mr. Houdini and his brothers!" Collins said, trying not to sound winded. He pointed to a bespectacled man with a pointed beard on the left and then continued to slide his finger across the page as he identified each one.

"That's Leo, the doctor. And Theo, the family's other magic man. Your uncle, of course. And…"

Realization hit Collins like a storm. He gazed intently into Piper's green eyes.

"Lobster Bill. Your dad."

"I knew it! I knew it was him!" she shouted. Fuller in the face and a lot less creepy looking without his bucktooth fangs. But the man in the picture was definitely the same person who had brought her here!

"Why'd you call him 'Lobster Bill'?"

Collins flashed a toothy grin.

"'Cuz your dad was fond of wettin' his throat till he was red in the face and full as a gypsy's bra."

He held up a hand so Piper wouldn't misconstrue his words.

"He was a good man, your father. Tossed back a few pints with him myself when he was alive."

As if he had already said too much, Collins turned away from her to examine the stoneware containers on the floor.

"Look at this place! You made a right bags of it!"

"Sorry about that," Piper said sheepishly.

Jim Collins picked up the falcon head with one hand and its lid-less ceramic vessel with the other. Piper took a sharp breath.

"Don't…" she said, reaching out to warn him.

But Collins had already returned the falcon head to its proper place on the jar and placed it back in the cabinet. Piper scratched her head. Why was he able to touch it without it sucking him up like an Elektrolux?

"I wouldn't bother my arse about these pots if I were you, young lady. You have no call to them."

"Who does?"

Collins placed the other canopic jar on its shelf in the cabinet.

"Mr. Houdini kept his mam in them when she went to her final reward."

"Her ashes?" Piper asked.

The Irishman locked the glass door, returned the keys to his pocket, and looked at her through narrow eyes.

"Jewish folk don't cremate their dead. I said he kept *her* in them."

Piper waited for an explanation. The tension between them grew like a thundercloud until Collins finally broke.

"Ahhh, fine then. Mr. Houdini wasn't around when your grandmother died, a fact that will haunt him till the end of his days. He was in Copenhagen with me and the missus performing for the royal family."

"So when did he find out?" Piper asked.

"Leo sent him a cable. Poor Mr. Houdini, he burst into tears and passed out right on the stage floor. When he came to, I says, 'Mr. Houdini, can't you do anything for your mother?'

"He looks at me and says, 'What do you mean, Jim?'

"And I says, 'You know what I mean. Can't you do anything for her?'

"There was a long hush and then he says, 'Do I understand you, Jim, that you think I really possess some kinda' power to help my mother?'

"And I says, 'Yes.'

"So the boss gives me a wave of his hand and says, 'No. No, Jim, this is the will of the Almighty, and God's will be done. It cannot be undone.'

"But I knew that Mr. Houdini adored his mam. He always said, 'If God in His infinite wisdom ever sent an angel upon Earth in human form, it was my mother.'"

Piper scowled. "So? Lots of people adore their mothers like that."

"Yes, but he's a driven man, your uncle," Collins replied. "On stage he defies death every day. But do you think that's enough for a man like him? If there was a way to defy death for real, wouldn't the great Houdini be the one to find out how to do it?"

Piper found herself nodding. But she wasn't sure if she was humoring Collins or if she actually agreed with him.

"What if Mr. Houdini could immortalize his mam by turning her earthly body into a divine vessel where the angel in her could go on living?" he asked.

Piper gasped. "Like a mummy!"

"Ahh, you know something about it then?" Collins smiled, indicating the jars behind the glass doors. "A couple of years before his mam's death, Mr. Houdini was in Egypt and got his hands on those freaky pots."

"What did he do with them?" asked Piper.

"You're getting ahead of me, lass."

Piper tightened her lips ruefully.

"Your uncle sent a cable back to Leo and Theo telling them to delay the funeral," Collins continued. "Then he sent another cable to Lobster Bill with strict instructions to leave the clay pots next to their mam's body with their lids open."

"Why him? Why my father?" Piper asked.

"Who knows? That's a secret your dad took with him to the grave," he said, shaking his head.

"Anyways, after that, we hopped a train to Hamburg and booked passage on the next steamer to the States. Six days later, the boss stormed into his house with me and the missus. He went straight to the parlor where his mam was laid out.

"The open pots were next to her like he asked. She looked so dainty and restful lying there. Mr. Houdini kneels beside her and says, 'The face which haunted me with love all my life is still and quiet.'

"Then Theo put a hand on his shoulder and says, 'Mama died asking for you.'

"The boss wanted to know exactly what she said, but Theo couldn't say for sure. So brother Doc tells him that their mam had a stroke and her face was paralyzed and all, so they couldn't understand her.

"Then he says something that sends Mr. Houdini through the roof!

"'She's a rabbi's wife, Harry—you should've let us bury her the next day. Not even you, the great mystifier, can bring her back.'

"If Mrs. Houdini hadn't held him back, the boss might've slugged him right there.

"He looks at his brother with those magical eyes of his and says, 'If I could contact her, she would at least be able to speak to me those final words locked within her paralyzed face as she lay here dying under *your* care!'

"Then he looks all around the room and asks, 'Where's Willie?'

"They tell him that Bill rushed out of the house in a fit of fury after he'd done Mr. Houdini's bidding, mumbling something about getting it right this time.

"When the boss heard this, he ordered everyone out of the house...except me and the missus, of course. The brothers all left cussing and griping.

"As soon as I closed the door behind them, Mr. Houdini stroked his wife's pretty face. He tells her, 'You look tired and should go to bed.' She obliged him even though she knew he was up to something. I remember her walking up the stairs to her room and Mr. Houdini's eyes following her with utter devotion."

Collins paused and sighed with the goofy smile of a lovesick teenager.

"What happened next?" Piper asked impulsively.

Collins shook his head. A look came over his face like he was frightened to go on. Then he drew a deep breath and continued his tale.

"Once he heard the bedroom doors shut, the boss drags a wooden lounge chair from his mam's room and props it next to her body. He tells me to stay in the foyer to make sure nobody disturbs him. He closes the door and tells me to ignore whatever I hear coming from the room.

"So I stay in the foyer all night, like Mr. Houdini said. And he stays by his mam. I was tired from the long trip and must've dozed off 'cuz when the horrible moan came I nearly fell outta my seat."

Piper realized that she was leaning closer to Collins, like a child listening to a ghost story.

"The moan came from behind the door and it was followed by a long wail like a banshee's. Sounded a bit like laughter but it weren't a happy laugh. Then I hear Mr. Houdini whispering. Not in English or in any other language I ever heard him speak.

"After that, there was dead quiet. I press my ear to the door hoping to hear something. The banshee's laugh would've been preferable to that awful stillness.

"I was about to knock on the door when I heard someone crying. Might've been Mr. Houdini, but the only time I ever heard him weep was in Copenhagen. Sounded nothing like that.

"All of a sudden, Mrs. Houdini runs down the stairs in her nightgown and makes a mad dash for the parlor doors. I hold her back and she pleads with me to let her go.

"I says, 'I'm sorry, Mrs. Houdini. I can't let you go in! I promised him.'

"She looks at me with those sleepy eyes of hers and says, 'But something's going on in there! Something dreadful! Can't you hear it, Jim?'

"I think there was more worry in her eyes than fear. So I take her hand and says, 'Mrs. Houdini, please calm down. You've been behind the curtain with him. You know if anyone can come through this, it's the Great Houdini. Just keep him in your heart like always and he'll come out unhurt like always.'

"Then there was this voice coming from the room, high-pitched and loud. A woman's voice, and I recognized it. We both did. We also recognized the language but I couldn't understand it. It was German—the language Houdini's mam spoke.

"The missus translated it for me: *'Don't do this, Ehrie. In God's name.'*

"Then she broke down in my arms.

185

"'Oh, Jim,' she says, 'even in death she comes first. She'll always have a hold over his heart. His dear sainted mother. I'll never be able to replace her. Not in this life or the next.'

"We sat together the rest of the night. Morning couldn't come fast enough. When it did, Mr. Houdini pushed open the doors and stumbled onto the floor. His face was pale, his lips were cracked, and his shirt was dripping with sweat.

"The missus ran into his arms.

"'Oh Houdini,' she says. 'You need a shower in the worst way.'

"He just brushes her aside and says, 'No time for shower. Gotta find Bill. Get to Esopus.'

Then he boxed up the clay pots and headed off by himself. Didn't come home till the wee hours of the next morning."

Piper sat back against the desk, trying to absorb everything she'd heard.

"Where did he go? Who or what is Esopus?"

Collins shook his head.

"Dunno. But whatever happened, I'm thinking it didn't work out. The boss never learned what his mam tried to tell him. He buried her next to his dad in a Jewish cemetery up there in Cypress Hills.

"Ever since he's been trying to find a ball-gazer who's not full of beans. But so far they've all been shams. All except that Margery bird. No luck exposing her. Yet."

Piper resisted the urge to ask about this Margery person. Instead she chewed her lower lip and said, "Collins, when did this all happen?"

"Thirteen years come July. Why...?"

Two rich chimes rang throughout the house.

"The door," Collins announced needlessly.

"I'll get it!" Piper exclaimed, darting out of the room.

"Remember, lass," Collins called after her. "Don't be stickin' your nose where it don't belong. I'll have my eye on you like a stinkin' eel."

Piper was already dismissing the warning as she raced down the stairs. She had a fire in her belly and couldn't wait to tell Sal all she had learned.

But when she opened the front door, her excitement faded. Sal's face held a gloom that was grayer than the late afternoon sky behind him.

"Piper, it's Henri!" he choked, tears streaming down his cheeks. "Dr. Crandon signed his death certificate. He's going to perform an autopsy!"

★★★★

FIDDLES IN THE DARK

Alan Rand stepped out of the cheval mirror's mahogany frame onto the hard wood of his bedroom floor. The only good thing about Miss Fortune's detention was that she allowed him to use the *Kefitzat Haderech* to get home. His mother would typically have Nokouchi make the 10-mile drive to Dedham in the rain to pick him up from school. But today, Margery and Dr. Crandon had more urgent tasks for their Japanese valet, so the mirror was a godsend.

Loosening the knot at his throat, Alan slid the blue-and-white necktie through the collar of his prep-school uniform and let it spiral onto the plush duvet that padded his bed. He then pulled aside the leather and suede curtains to peer down the four-story drop outside his window.

Standing outside the front steps with their shoulders hunched against the downpour, seven men waited as an eighth rang the doorbell. Alan heard the chimes sound throughout the house.

Nokouchi would greet the men and, after they exchanged pleasantries with their hostess, he would lead them up the stairs. The party would then proceed to the parlor at the end of the hall where Alan's mother conducted her séances—free from the prying eyes on Lime Street.

That gave Alan a very small window of opportunity to raid the refrigerator for an after-school snack. Slipping out his bedroom door, he darted down the stairs at the far end of the hallway.

When he reached the bottom, he could hear his mother bantering with her visitors. He peered around the corner to check them out. The light in the foyer silhouetted his mother's figure beneath her thin dressing gown and Alan rolled his eyes. He knew she was wearing nothing under the sheer fabric but silk stockings and a pair of slippers.

Suddenly, two large fingers clamped Alan's earlobe like a vice and pulled him back up the stairs.

"Ow, ow, ow!" the boy whimpered.

"How many times have I told you to make yourself scarce when your mother is performing?" Crandon's hiss was so close to his step-son's tormented ear that Alan could feel the bristles of his mustache.

"B-but, it's raining outside!" Alan protested as he cleared the top stair and was dragged down the corridor toward his room.

"Then you know the routine," Dr. Crandon said, tossing him into his bedroom. "You'll stay in here for the rest of the afternoon. We don't want to invite rumors that your mother has a secret accomplice roaming the house, do we?"

Crandon pulled the door shut with slightly less than a slam. Alan heard the jingle of keys and the latch of a deadbolt sealing him in from the other side.

He sat on the edge of the bed and gazed at his doleful image in the mirror. Then he leaned closer; something wasn't right. Almost ten minutes had elapsed since he'd stepped from the framed glass. So why was it still rocking?

✟✟✟✟

The first thing that had struck Piper was how neat the room was. Then she remembered that Alan Rand's family was one of Boston's elite Brahmins and probably had servants who cleaned up after him every day. Certainly no teenage boy she ever met could be this tidy.

She imagined how messy Sal's room must be, with books and soda cans strewn all over the place.

Where was Sal, anyway? Piper looked back at the full-length mirror. Her emergence had made it teeter on its ringed brass hinges.

"Come on, come on!" she breathed.

Piper and Sal had planned to follow Rand through the *Kefitzat Haderech* so they could get into his house and find out what Dr. Crandon was up to. Crandon had convinced Sal's family that Henri was legally dead by arguing that there was no brain activity. He demonstrated how a dead frog twitches its legs when struck by a spark.

"Therefore, it is my conclusion, and the conclusion of this hospital," he had said with finality, "that your son is simply receiving some sort of stimulation from an external electrical source. There is no conscious activity."

Crandon offered the family three hundred dollars for his son's body. Sal's father said that they didn't need the money. So the physician instead appealed to his humanitarian side and convinced the grieving father to donate Henri's body to science by insisting that it would help cure others with brain damage.

Piper and Sal knew that was a load of hooey. They had seen the property tag on the toe of Elastic Skin Joe and as far as they knew, malleable skin wasn't a condition that science was knocking down doors trying to cure. So what was Crandon's deal?

Up until now, everything had been going as planned. Aunt Bess had returned home over the weekend and Houdini had gone to Chicago to scout the next location for his show. So Piper wouldn't have to worry about another scolding from him if she got home after dark.

She stayed after school and met Sal in Room 117B where the opulent mirror still stood among the collection of wretched brooms and stiff mops. Sal muttered some sort of Creole incantation and touched the mirror. Its surface shimmered and then opened on a scene in the faraway detention hall. Sal and Piper watched and waited in the silent darkness as Miss Fortune grabbed some books from a shelf and led Alan Rand through a set of the doors in the candlelit hall.

Once the headmistress and her pupil were out of sight, Sal gave Piper a shove through the mirror. The startled girl had to suppress a yelp as she tumbled onto the hall's stone floor. When Sal stepped through a few seconds later, she gave him a firm punch in the arm.

"Next time a warning maybe?" Piper breathed through clenched teeth.

"No time," Sal whispered, rubbing his bicep. "I had to cast another spell so I could get through."

She scowled at him. "Why didn't we just leap together?"

"Oh no," Sal wagged his finger at her. "Not a good idea. Last time two folks like us tried to jaunt together, he wound up with her girl parts and she got his boy parts."

Piper got to her feet and brushed off her khaki twill skirt. "I think you just have intimacy issues," she huffed, remembering his discomfort at sharing an umbrella.

"No, I'm serious!" Sal said a bit too loudly. He ducked his head, looked around, then continued in hushed tones. "The *Kefitzat Haderech* has a failsafe spell so people can't use it to send armies all over the world..."

A commotion in the other room cut their discussion short and sent them scurrying for a hiding place. The first place they both considered was behind the *Kefitzat Haderech*. But the bottom of the mirror was raised several inches off the floor and their feet would easily have been spotted.

The two friends made a dash for the medieval tapestry that hung from ceiling to floor on the far wall. Piper slipped behind one side of the colorful display and was able to conceal her slender body behind the fine wool fabric with hardly a wrinkle. But when she glanced at Sal's belly and the bulge it created, she shook her head and sighed. Piper could only hope that no one would be paying attention to the rotund wall hanging.

Rand's detention had ended early. The noise they heard was the sound of Miss Fortune escorting him back to the *Kefitzat Haderech*.

Piper heard the headmistress recite the familiar invocation that would send Rand home. There was a *whoosh* followed by a long silence. Piper and Sal stared at each other with their backs pressed to the wall, daring not to breathe.

Finally they heard the clip-clop of Miss Fortune's heels as they echoed down the stone corridor and faded from the room. Piper and Sal hesitated a bit longer to make sure that she had gone. Then Sal whispered, "Now!"

The tapestry fluttered as they bolted toward the *Kefitzat Haderech*. Alan Rand was still visible on the other side of the glass. Piper and Sal had to stand on either side of the mirror until they saw him leave his room. Sal then repeated his personal incantation to activate the magic glass.

He turned to Piper and smiled. "Here's your warning," he said with a wink. Before Piper could react, he launched her through the mirror's misty glass. Once again she felt as though her body were being squeezed between two elephants. When she emerged on the other side, she fell into a heap on the floor.

That was almost two minutes ago. Where was Sal?

Piper sprung to the bedroom door and peered out. She heard a disturbance coming from the stairwell at the end of the hall. She looked back at the mirror. She couldn't wait. If she stayed here, Rand would certainly find her. Sal was on his own.

Moving as silently as she could, Piper slipped down the corridor in the opposite direction of the stairs. She fled into a large room at the end of the hall that was as dismal as a mausoleum. The ceilings were at least nine feet high and bookcases adorned each corner of the room and a part of one wall. Chintz curtains were drawn tightly over each window so that not a single ray of sunshine could penetrate the room.

Piper noticed that the doorway she had come through was the only way in or out. On the far side of the room, between a large sofa and a fireplace made of tapestry bricks, she could hear the recorded melody of a violin trilling its sentimental tones through the tapered horn of a Victrola.

In the center of the room stood a large round Crawford-table around which ten chairs had been placed. They were ordinary fold-ing chairs except for one: a black comb-back Windsor that was clearly reserved as a place of distinction.

At the end of the hallway, Piper heard voices approaching the top of the stairs. She vaulted over the sofa and ducked behind it. Hopefully nobody would be lighting the fireplace, despite the chill in the room.

A group of eight men filed into the room. They were led by a woman wearing a straight-lined robe that looked like a kimono. Piper assumed that this was Alan Rand's mother. But who were the others?

Rand's mother settled comfortably into the Windsor and bid her guest to take their seats as well. A tall, rather thin man hustled into the room, nodded to the other guests, and sat to the woman's right.

Piper's lip curled because she instinctively knew that the late-comer was the enigmatic Dr. Crandon. He was a grim looking man of about sixty whose glasses and peppered mustache gave him an intellectual bearing that was entirely in keeping with the book-lined walls of his study.

Taking his wife's hand, Crandon said in a low voice, "My dear Psyche, so sorry to delay the proceedings." Then he turned his at-tention to his guests.

"Gentlemen. All of you know J. Malcolm Bird, associate editor of *Scientific American,* our nation's most popular science journal." He clapped the shoulder of the slim, beak-nosed man to his right. "Over a year ago, the journal offered five thousand dollars for proof of psychic phenomena. They put together a committee led by Mr. Bird here to study our esteemed Margery."

Piper perked up at the name *Margery.* Was this the same woman that Collins had mentioned in Houdini's study? And if so, what was her connection to Sal's brother and Elastic Skin Joe? Piper felt as though someone had given her a puzzle to solve but hadn't provided all the pieces.

The mention of another familiar name brought her attention back to the table. "One member of that original committee made a mock-ery of these proceedings. The culprit, Harry Houdini, may have sabotaged at least one of them so that our dear Margery was denied the prize.

"That is why I have asked Mr. Bird to find the right people to serve as members of a new committee." Crandon continued, nodding to the lanky editor and then to the other seven. "That honor has been bestowed upon all of you. Birdie, I do believe introductions are in order?"

As Bird rose, a lock of wavy brown hair flopped onto his forehead. He acknowledged each of his new team members with cool eyes.

"Although I have not met all of you in person before today, your reputations in your chosen fields precede you. It is my privilege to welcome you to this commission, which will determine once and for all if the dead can speak through the living."

Beginning with the man to his right, Bird moved in a counter-clockwise rotation and introduced each of his colleagues. They were an assortment of psychology professors, scientists, psychic researchers, authors, and another stage magician. Piper's mind started to wander. But when Bird announced the final delegate who was sitting to Margery's left, something made her take note.

"This is Dr. Edward Saint," Bird announced proudly, "a practitioner of both the medical *and* spiritual arts from Rye, New York." Piper dared to pop her head above the back of the sofa to get a better look.

Saint was a distinguished-looking gentleman with a waxed handlebar mustache and an immaculately trimmed white goatee. He acknowledged the introduction with a brisk nod, causing his thatch of white hair to flutter wildly. There was something about the way he moved that struck a familiar chord in Piper, but she couldn't put her finger on what it was.

When the introductions were finished, Dr. Crandon barked orders to a well-dressed Japanese man that had been standing beside the entrance.

"Nokouchi, douse the lights and shut the door on your way out."

"Very good, Sir," the servant replied.

As he walked out, his hand clicked the wall switch and the séance room was suddenly bathed in unearthly red. Piper, of course, could see perfectly fine. But she noticed that several of the sitters were fidgeting uncomfortably in the near-total darkness.

Margery leaned back in her chair.

"People often ask why séances are held in the dark," she began, with an accent as distinct as her son's. "The reasons are twofold. The first is that darkness helps to dull the awareness of our external environment, making it easier for me to enhance my extrasensory awareness."

Margery touched the sides of her face in a bizarre way, as though she were trying on new skin. Then she took a deep breath.

"The second reason is a bit more esoteric. Psychic structures are photosensitive—they prefer red light to bright white. That's because ectoplasm originates in a dark dimension outside our own. Should white light strike any structure formed by ectoplasm, the material would withdraw back into my body and I could suffer grievous harm."

Piper had no idea what the woman was talking about. But she suddenly felt a cold breeze blowing from the table and the temperature of the room dropped several degrees.

"Take the hand of the person next to you," Margery instructed, grasping her husband's left hand and Edward Saint's right. Then she closed her eyes and began swaying in her chair.

Piper suddenly heard a whistle and the table jumped a foot off the floor. Several of the men shrieked like children. Margery's head lolled to the side and the cantankerous voice of a man emanated from her lips.

"I said I could put this through," the voice announced.

"Hello, Walter." It was Margery's voice now. "Where have you been?"

"Oh, I had to take my girl to a strawberry festival," Walter's baritone voice replied with a chuckle. Piper could see that the voice was clearly coming from Margery's mouth.

"I never saw such a bunch of stiffs in all my life!" the entity known as Walter announced. "Talk about dead people! My God!"

One of the sitters overcame his dread and stammered, "Can you read my mind?"

"Yes, but you wouldn't want me to tell that!"

All of the participants laughed. It was obvious that these modern scientists and professors, engaged in the ancient rite of the séance, had not expected to be amused while attempting to speak with the dead.

A mist had begun to gather in the room that carried with it the smell of carrion. Despite the frigid air around her, Piper felt a bead of sweat dripping down her lower back.

"There's something in my mouth," Margery said, addressing both her husband and Edward Saint. "May I break the circle to remove it?" The two doctors released her hands, though Saint seemed a bit reluctant.

The medium held up both hands to show that they were empty. Then she opened her mouth and withdrew something slimy and rubbery that glowed in the red light. She disengaged it and showed it to the onlookers. Something about it seemed eerily familiar to Piper.

Without warning, Saint produced an electric torch from his pocket and shined it on the rubbery substance when poof! It vanished. Margery cried out and collapsed, smacking her head upon the table.

"That was a foolish gesture, Dr. Saint." Walter's voice resonated from the throat of the unconscious medium. "Ectoplasm is the material from which we in the spirit world draw our energy when manifesting. Through its power, we can materialize at least part of our earthly body. Why would you attempt to abort such a glorious, supernatural birth?"

As if in response to Walter's anger, a booming peal of thunder exploded outside the house. The ghostly red lights flickered and died. Even the beam from Dr. Saint's flashlight inexplicably died, pitching the room into complete darkness. A few of the participants gasped. Was this all part of the show?

Lightning flashed and Piper spotted something that made her blood run cold. There was a small shadowy figure that had been standing motionless in the corner of the study. It sprang to life and darted around the room, ringing bells and flipping over papers. Then it lifted an old fiddle and strummed it randomly.

The soles of the creature's feet had been painted with a luminous substance, creating the effect of flashing psychic lights as it leaped around the awestruck spectators. Then, with a blue flash, the strange shape lurched under the table and vanished beneath Margery's kimono.

Taking advantage of the impenetrable darkness, Piper scampered across the room to get a better look. Careful not to brush against the sitters, she squeezed between the chairs and squatted beneath the table at Margery's feet like a dog looking for scraps.

Before long, a crude, flaccid hand parted the folds of the dressing gown. Piper held her breath. Was this a spirit after all?

Something peered out of the flimsy gown and Piper instantly recognized its blind eyes and gossamer skin.

She had told her uncle about the girl with the strange-looking baby and the eyes that glared at her from under the boardwalk.

"Consider yourself lucky," was his reply. "The ugly things that lie below the surface of Coney are usually not seen until it's too late to avoid them."

And now the ugly thing, this twisted parody of human life, was reaching for her. Piper slapped a hand over her mouth, lurched backward, and bumped carelessly into a leg. Wondering what had nudged him, the sitter leaned over and announced, "I see glowing stars under the table. Two of them!"

Oh, no! thought Piper, pressing her fingers to her cheeks. *My freckles!*

"Stars?" Margery's woozy voice repeated in surprise. The creature halted at the hem of her kimono as if awaiting instructions.

Dr. Saint craned his neck under the table to investigate. Piper knew that he could see only her freckles, but it felt as though his eyes were boring into hers.

"Piper?" he whispered harshly.

Even though she had difficulty discerning color in complete darkness, the confused girl instantly realized whose eyes she was looking at.

Edward Saint was Harry Houdini in disguise!

But what was he doing here? Why hadn't he told anybody? Was he in league with the Crandons, involved in their dark plans for Henri and Elastic Skin Joe?

Margery shouted something. To the others it might have sounded like she was trying to conjure the great Julius Caesar. But Piper heard the words differently, and she knew they were meant for her.

"Seize her!"

The repulsive thing crawled and clawed after her. Piper had to crab-walk backwards to avoid its misshapen talons, and she no longer cared who she struck in the process. The creature raked at her ankles as she wedged herself between two chairs.

Once she freed herself from the confines of the table, Piper got to her feet and raced to the entrance. The last thing she saw as she threw open the door was the creepy baby-like thing leaping for her and then exploding into dust when the light from the hallway struck it.

Piper was stunned and bewildered, but she had no time to react. The people in the séance room would be blinded for only a few seconds. A long shadow bobbed on the wall of the stairwell down the hall, getting shorter with each jounce. Nokouchi must have heard the commotion or the Crandons had somehow summoned him.

Piper's only avenue of escape was the way she had come in. But when she reached Rand's bedroom, the door was locked. It was a simple deadbolt, but it would require something stronger than a hairpin. Fidgeting through her pocket, Piper retrieved the gizmo with Houdini's name on it and withdrew one of its steel picks.

There was a sound of stumbling in the séance room and the shadow had almost reached the top of the stairs. Piper's hand fumbled as she inserted the pick. The lock turned, but when she tried to jiggle the metal strip out again, the tool fell to the floor.

There was no time to recover it. Piper turned the knob, slipped into the room, and then eased the door shut with barely a click. Pressing her ear to the door, she heard a parade of aroused footsteps and a chorus of distracted voices.

"What did it all mean?"

"I distinctly saw a girl when the door flew open."

"Who do you think it was?"

"Perhaps it was my dear Caroline."

"Wonderful! Simply wonderful!"

Shadows promenaded along the crack at the bottom of the door. One of the shadows hesitated and Piper held her breath.

"Dr. Saint, this way, please," a voice with a Japanese accent instructed politely. The shadow moved on.

"Gentlemen, it was an honor," Piper heard Margery call from the opposite end of the hall. "The spirits were lively indeed. I do hope *Scientific American* will provide us with a positive evaluation of tonight's proceedings."

When Piper was certain that the last of the party had been ushered down the stairs, she leaned her forehead against the door, closed her eyes, and sighed.

Wait a minute! Piper opened her eyes and stood erect. *I'm in Rand's room. Where's...*

A soft ribbon of blue-and-white silk slipped around her neck and pulled her back hard before she could react. Thin lips touched her ear and jeered, "Didn't your father ever teach you that it's not polite to enter someone's house uninvited?"

Piper was annoyed, but more by the sound of the voice than her foolishness at being caught. The necktie had cut off her air supply. Otherwise, Piper would have enjoyed telling Alan Rand that the *r* in *father* wasn't silent.

CHILDREN OF THE MOON AND STARS

Mina Crandon was standing outside the parlor long after the party had disappeared down the stairs. The séance had confused and amazed them. And for the first time since becoming a Spiritualist, she shared their bewilderment.

I distinctly saw a girl when the door flew open.

As soon as Mina had gone into her trance, Walter had warned her that there was an intruder among them. She thought he'd meant one of the sitters.

I see glowing stars under the table. Two of them!

Could it be? After years of searching in vain, had the wormwood star been delivered virtually into her lap only to be lost once more?

Her thoughts were disrupted by a thumping noise coming from the door to her left. Mina sighed deeply. Once again Roy had locked her son in his room. He said it was to avoid accusations that Alan might be her accomplice. But Mina knew his real concern was that the world would find her less desirable if she was known to have a thirteen-year-old child from a previous marriage.

Mina knocked on the door. "Alan, I'll send Nokouchi right up with the key."

No answer. But she could still hear some sort of ruckus going on behind the door. Mina turned the knob and was surprised that the deadbolt hadn't been locked at all.

"Alan?" she said, peeking around the door.

What she saw next made her blood run cold. Her beloved son was maniacally squeezing the life from a helpless girl with his prep-school tie. The girl's face had turned purple and only the whites of her eyes showed, but she continued to struggle valiantly.

Mina burst into the room and slammed her willowy frame against her son with all the force she could muster. The boy released his quarry and fell onto the feathery haven of his down comforter.

"Mom, she's a spy!" Alan exclaimed, springing once more to his feet.

The medium turned to examine the stranger. As soon as she laid eyes on the girl's flushed cheeks a wave of emotion sent Mina staggering against the open door. Mina fought to regain her composure by gripping both sides of the doorframe.

The intruder unwrapped the tie from her neck and rubbed her throat. Mina extended one hand toward her in a gesture of comfort even though she felt unsteady without the doorframe's support.

"Are you all right?" The words came out as a loud gasp and Mina realized that she hadn't been breathing.

Instead of addressing her, the girl turned her attention to Alan.

"Are you loaded to the muzzle or something, Rand? You could've killed me!"

"That was the idea," Alan said, narrowing his eyes.

Mina shook her head, trying to make sense of what was happening.

"What's your name, dear?" She ran her thumb down the side of the redhead's starred face.

"What's it to you?" the girl replied, recoiling from Mina's touch. She folded her arms over her chest and looked up at the woman through cold, emerald eyes—eyes that reached out to her from some remote, forgotten darkness.

"It's Piper," Alan answered his mother. "Piper *Houdini*."

Mina grabbed her son's arm, perhaps a bit too roughly.

"You know this girl? Why didn't you tell me?"

"He's still balled up over my voodoo switcheroo," Piper said, sticking her tongue out at him.

Mina's son tried to lunge at the girl, but she held him back.

"Alan, stop this behavior at once!" She took a breath and then turned to Piper. "It seems that I'm the only person here in need of introduction."

"I know who you are." The redhead glared at her. "You're that Margery woman my uncle's been trying to expose for years."

"Your uncle?" Mina asked, shooting an inquiring look at her son.

"Says her uncle is Harry Houdini," he replied.

Mina paused to ponder her son's response.

"Uncle. How very interesting."

Dismissing the matter with a wave of her hand, she returned her attention to their uninvited guest.

"Yes, the press calls me Margery. I continue to use the name so my husband's standing in the medical community is not jeopardized. But you can call me M..."

She glanced at her son before finishing the sentence. Mina was shivering. Yet her skin was perspiring, pasting the thin material of her dressing gown to her chest. "You can call me Mina."

The medium smoothed her dressing gown.

"So what brings the niece of my most pigheaded foe to our humble abode on a menacing night like tonight?"

"Isn't it obvious?" Alan blurted. "Houdini sent her to snoop!"

"That's a load of bunk, Rand!" the girl shouted. "He knew something fishy was going on even before tonight!"

She stopped talking and covered her mouth with her hands.

"Tonight?" Mina shook her head, feeling like a damn fool.

"Of course. Edward Saint. Harry Houdini. I should have realized it as soon as I held his hand."

She inhaled deeply through her nose and held her breath for the count of two. Then she exhaled and continued, "So tell me, little one. Did you find anything in my dark parlor that would expose me as a fraud?"

Piper lowered her hands from her mouth.

"I don't know what was running around ringing bells and making the pretty light shows, but it didn't look like any kind of spirit I've ever heard of."

"How interesting. You can *see*." Mina replied, narrowing her eyes. "I suppose that would make sense."

Piper gave her a confused look. Mina's body temperature was still fluctuating between hot and cold. She wished that she had a shawl to warm her shoulders and a fan to cool her face.

She turned her left side to the freckled girl, measuring what she would and would not say.

"I've believed in Spiritualism since the time I was first called to it," she began. "Since then, I've had legions of followers pleading for physical proof to fortify a belief they could not otherwise maintain."

She looked Piper in the eye. "The truth is, little one, spirits have no more ability to float a trumpet across the room than a ray of light does. So I thought I'd be justified in helping them out a little. Justified in trickery because only through trickery could I get more converts to what I still believe is a good and beautiful religion."

The girl crossed her arms waiting for her to finish. Mina smiled in resignation.

"When I was younger and married to another man, I agreed to certain arcane alterations that were made to my body by a doctor with a special blade."

The girl stood up straight, her curiosity roused for the first time during the conversation.

"Dr. Crandon," she said.

Insightful girl, Mina thought, nodding evenly.

"The surgical modifications made me a living portal to another dimension—a conduit between our physical realm and the spiritual one."

Piper gave her an accusing look.

"That still doesn't explain what that creature was and why it exploded when I opened the door."

Mina sighed and it sounded almost like a lament.

"Four hundred years ago, an alchemist named Paracelsus claimed that the ultimate goal of alchemy was not the transmutation of elements into gold but rather the artificial creation of man. Paracelsus created such a life form and sustained it with human blood. He called it a homunculus. We call them pseudopods.

"Dr. Crandon has made it possible for me to bear my own pseudopods. The little demon you saw was molded out of spiritual secretions called ectoplasm. They are merely caricatures of living beings, soulless golems formed of extradimensional clay that turn to dust when exposed to the light that sustains our world."

"So what's the point?" Piper asked harshly, taking a small step backwards. "Babies without brains, without souls, running around causing all sorts of trouble until someone turns on the light?"

"My dear Piper, pseudopods are just the first step to something much bigger," Mina said, peering down at the girl who continued to shrink away from her.

"Imagine if the spirits could assume living flesh and bear living children of their own—children who, unlike your so-called father, could function within our universe day or night."

Piper stood up straight.

"What do you know about my father?"

"I know whose blood courses through your veins, my dear. I'm sure you've asked yourself, 'Did I get that blood before or *after* his... affliction?'"

The girl gave her a confused look. Mina leaned closer to clarify what she had said. "Did his mate receive him before or after he *turned?*"

She let out a little chuckle. Her body temperature had stabilized and she was now able to take joy in her guest's discomfort.

"Imagine a race of such beings, Piper. Creatures with unique material forms and independent souls. Their power would be beyond comprehension. Not only would they be immortal, they would be virtually indestructible. To such beings, we humans would be nothing more than playthings. They would bring about an air of chaos in which every living thing would be annihilated or enslaved."

"Sounds ducky," said the girl with a wince, like the word she just used somehow offended her. "But what's in it for you?"

Mina caressed her son's face.

"We're survivors, little one. The Spirits are in alignment and we are in the end times. God has ordained that a powerful light will shine into the souls of men through a great force that is slowly penetrating our atmosphere. Souls that are found unworthy will be expelled. We can choose to ignore it, or we can choose to become a part of it."

Piper pinched her bottom lip.

"You're saying God is like a school principal who's gonna expel people's souls from their bodies for being bad?" she asked.

"Interesting analogy," Mina nodded. "I see him more as a benevolent landlord forced into evicting his unruly tenants."

"Leaving a bunch of vacant bodies for your otherworldly spirits?" Piper looked like she was trying to suppress a laugh. "Lady, if you think that's going to happen, you're even flukier than Houdini thought!"

Mina saw that the girl was trying to maintain a safe distance from her in the tight space.

"Going to happen?" The medium lowered her head and leered at the girl through her bangs. "My dear girl, what makes you think it hasn't already begun?"

Piper froze.

"Henri. Elastic Skin Joe!" she exclaimed.

Alan made a menacing lurch toward the girl. "Mom! She knows about the freaks!"

Mina squeezed her son's arm to keep him from saying anything more.

"My, aren't you astute for one so young?" she said. "Rest assured, little one, the true Star Child has yet to make its presence known. Your zombie friend and that sideshow aberration are mere guinea pigs, nothing more."

Piper gave her a disparaging look.

"That goop your husband was replacing Joe's blood with—it was *ectoplasm,* wasn't it?"

Mina smiled. "You're asking me? You, the living ecto-detector?" She made the image of a star upon her own cheek.

Piper touched her fingertips to her face. Mina could see the bewilderment in her eyes.

"Oh, my dear girl. Hasn't your uncle explained anything to you? Like why they glow only at certain times?"

Piper staggered in the middle of the room like a lost soul. Mina had shaken her confidence to its very core. But why did the sensation of triumph elude her?

"Of course he hasn't," the medium conceded. "The fool refuses to relinquish his skepticism even in the presence of undeniable evidence."

She got to one knee and opened her arms. The flowing sleeves of her gown draped like the soft wings of an angel. "Don't go back to him, Piper. You can stay here. With me."

"Mom…" Alan began.

"Alan, shhh!" she said, holding up her hand. "Piper, I can't promise an answer to everything, at least not right away. But I can promise you a place alongside me during the Great Harvest."

"Mom, the mirror!"

Piper looked behind her. "No, Sal! Not now…!"

But it was too late. A pair of chubby brown hands reached through the looking glass and pulled the red-haired girl into its shimmering surface.

"No!" Mina screamed, leaping across the room in a frenzy. Beyond the glass she could see Piper and someone else falling into a chamber that looked like a medieval classroom. The image faded quickly, replaced by the lucid reflection of a gawking mother and her son.

Mina clenched her fists.

Damn Dion and her magic mirror.

FAMILY MATTERS

An old superstition states that one must hold one's breath when passing a cemetery. Even if the Great Houdini believed the legend, he wouldn't attempt it while passing the Queens Cemetery Belt. Despite his vast lung capacity, he knew he would collapse long before reaching the end of the three-mile stretch of headstones.

Machpelah Cemetery made up only a tiny part of this sprawling necropolis, but it was here that Houdini had purchased a burial plot for his family twenty years ago. The shrine's tidy, uncluttered grounds were a welcome distraction to the rows of cramped tombstones that littered Machpelah's rumpled terrace.

Houdini often came here to seek refuge from the real world. But today was different. Today was special. Today was the sixth of April.

Two weeks earlier, Houdini had turned fifty-two. But if his sainted mother had still been alive, today would be the day she'd celebrate with him.

"It hurts me to think that I can't talk it over with darling Mother," the magician had once said. "But since *she* always wrote me on April 6, then that will be my adopted birthdate."

Over a month had passed since his attempt to expose Margery

while disguised as the enigmatic Dr. Saint. From there Houdini had gone to Chicago's Princess Theatre where his show had been selling out every night. The obligations of that lengthy engagement had made it impossible for him to be with his family. He looked forward to making a surprise visit as soon as he was finished paying his respects.

The magician ascended three shallow steps leading to a pedestal that perched atop a bench of curved stone. The pedestal would remain empty until his death, at which point a bust carved in his likeness would grace its barren surface.

With a disparaging grunt, Houdini turned and nearly tripped over the figure of a woman carved in granite. She knelt upon the floor of the exedra, nuzzling her ashen face beside the name *WEISS* while deliberately ignoring the *HOUDINI* etched in more prominent letters above it.

Cursing his clumsiness, the magician regained his footing and shifted his attention to a plaque on the left side of the monument. It was difficult to read by the hazy light of dusk, but Houdini had memorized every word:

Here in eternal peace slumbers our darling mother, Cecelia Weiss, who entered her everlasting sleep July 17, 1913, as pure and as sweet as the day she was born, June 16, 1841.

"Does it bother you, Harry, that I was laid to rest alongside her before you?"

Despite its hollow tone, the voice failed to rattle the magician. To his right, a few feet past his father's extravagant headstone, was a simple rectangular tombstone marked *Willie 1872-1925.* Upon it stood the family plot's most recent denizen.

"Is that why you faked your death, my brother? So you could taunt me till the end of my days?" Houdini said to the man on the grave marker.

"I faked *nothing*," the man snarled. "I *am* dead, Ehrich! Why do you continue to refute the irrefutable?"

Houdini could always tell he had struck a nerve when his brother called him by his birth name.

"We've discussed this before, Willie," Houdini said with a scowl. "There's a rational explanation for the unusual course of your condition. If you hadn't taken the coward's way out, medical science would have…"

"Unusual course?!" Will's eyes blazed a lurid red. "My condition has nothing to do with science, Ehrich! You believe there's some ancient, forgotten science in those old texts of yours that's been diluted by generations of superstition. Why can't you accept the fact that the superstition itself might be real?"

Houdini faced the tomb again, struggling with his own doubts. "And why is it so much easier for you to believe that you're a dead man who walks and breathes?"

"For starters, the only reason I breathe is because it would be difficult to speak otherwise," Will said, making an exaggerated gasping sound. "I can exist indefinitely without air. Just as I can slow my pulse so that it's virtually undetectable. How else would I have convinced the medical examiner?"

"Many Egyptian fakirs can do the same trick," Houdini argued. "None claim to be anything but beings of living flesh and blood."

"Then why do I need to feed on that blood to sustain myself? Why does my skin smolder in sunlight?" Will demanded.

"There have been numerous cases reported where a person bursts into flame with no apparent source of ignition. Perhaps your condition makes you more susceptible to…"

"You dare!" Will screamed. The hairs on Houdini's neck stood up as his brother drew closer, his upper incisors extending into tiny daggers. "Because of you, I have exchanged an affliction of the flesh for an affliction of the soul. And you insult me by saying that I suffer from some sort of chronic spontaneous human combustion?"

Houdini refused to back away, despite the chill of his brother's cold breath on his neck.

"And why do you suppose it's an affliction of the soul?" he asked. "I was under the impression that the soul was immortal and therefore immune to illness."

Something like a growl escaped Will's throat. He pushed himself away from his brother, retracted his fangs, and gave an exasperated huff. "Do you remember four summers ago, Ehrich, when you insisted that I join you and Bess in Atlantic City?"

"How could I forget? It was the same weekend Sir Arthur and Lady Doyle invited me to their suite claiming to have contacted our dear mother in the Great Beyond." Houdini fixed his attention once more on the plaque. "I went along with it because the day happened to coincide with mama's birthday."

"Lady Doyle did not intend any malice," Will replied. "The Doyles are simple, trusting people. You've said so yourself."

"Gullible is more like it," Houdini sighed. "I once performed a particularly easy trick for them..."

The magician tucked his thumb behind the palm of one hand and placed his other thumb over it, making it look as though it was connected to the other hand. He then "removed" the first joint of his thumb, showed it to his brother, and replaced it.

"They believed you actually removed your thumb," Will said.

"Believed it? My dear brother, they almost fainted. A kindergartener could pull the wool over Lady Doyle's eyes. I have no doubt she believes that she can speak with the dead."

Will studied the ground. "What if I told you that Jean Doyle *did* make contact with the spirit world that day?"

"Nonsense!" Houdini barked. "She filled fifteen pages with so-called spirit writing—in *English.* You know as well as I do that mama spoke German, not English. And the words said nothing about it being mama's birthday."

"I'm not talking about *that* Jean Doyle," the gaunt man retorted. "Do you recall the daughter?"

Houdini gave him a puzzled look.

"Of course I do," he said, his lips turning upward in a smile. "A spirited young lady. Quite the tomboy. I believe she preferred to be called *Billy.*"

Will nodded.

"While you were in the Doyles' room where the elder Jean was distracting you with delusions of divination, I received a strange visit from the younger Jean."

Houdini gave his brother a discerning look. "You made it clear to us that you were not to be disturbed until the sun went down due to your...sensitive skin condition."

Will nodded again.

"Which is why I was so annoyed when I heard the knock at my door. At first I thought it was a juvenile prank because no one was visible through the peephole. But when I heard the knock again, I threw open the door, bared my fangs, and shouted, 'Are the words *do not disturb* too difficult for you to understand?'"

Willie smiled.

"Imagine my chagrin when I spotted those innocent blue eyes gazing at me through thick, horn-rimmed glasses."

"Despite my appearance, she neither feared nor pitied me, Ehrich. She just stood there stroking this beat-up old blanket and said, 'Mr. Wriggly has a message for you.'"

"Mr. Wriggly?" Houdini bit the inside of his cheek to keep from laughing.

"Go ahead, smile. But that is the name of her familiar—young Jean's direct contact in the great beyond." Will paused as though debating whether Houdini would poke fun at his next words. "Mr. Wriggly is a dead cat."

This time Houdini could not contain his laughter. "Oh, my dear brother!" he howled. "And here I thought your illness had robbed you of all sense of humor!"

Will shook his head, waiting for Houdini's laughter to subside.

"I don't blame you for laughing, Ehrich. I had the same reaction. I thought the girl was playing a game of fortune teller. But then she said the following words—words that I will never forget:

"'Mr. Wriggly says he has a message for you from Gottfried William Weiss.'"

"You mean a message *for* Gottfried William Weiss," Houdini corrected.

Will held up a hand. "I thought so too. So I crouched down,

looked her in the eye, and said, 'But little girl, I *am* Gottfried William Weiss.'

"Young Jean shook her head slowly. She just kept stroking her blanket and stroking her blanket." Will mimicked the action with his hands. "Then her eyes rolled up into her head and she said something in a voice that made my blood run colder than it already is:

"'Usurper, until you leave my body and reunite with me, I am stranded and cannot enjoy the fruits afforded us in the hereafter.'"

Will hesitated before speaking again. Then, speaking softly as though he were afraid someone would hear, he said, "The voice, dear brother, was my own."

Houdini stood in silence.

"Don't you understand, Ehrich?" Will pleaded. "The child *knew* I was but a shade of a man. She *knew* I was bereft of a soul because the soul of William Weiss is trapped between worlds until the day I forfeit this body. *His* body."

Houdini wagged his hand in a dismissive gesture. "Have you been feeding off the derelicts on skid row again? You're accepting the word of a child who was pretending at being her mother."

"I considered that," Will retorted. "But then why wouldn't she say *our* mother was reaching out to me? Or our father? Why would she claim that I was reaching out to myself when there was no way she could have known what I was? And how does a nine-year-old girl mimic the voice of a grown man?"

The magician ran his fingers through his thinning curls and studied his brother. Finally he threw up his hands and said, "What's your point, Willie? Why did you keep this to yourself until now?"

"Because until now my daughter was living in safety and obscurity, shuffled off from one foster home to the next."

Houdini gave his brother a look of pity.

"Just because you rescued a babe from the hands of a lunatic doesn't make you her father."

"Piper is my daughter!" William hissed, circling his brother like a wolf sizing up its prey. "It's my blood that runs through her veins!

Weiss blood!" He scraped his pointed fingernail across the word on the lower half of the tombstone.

Houdini shook his head. He was sorely disappointed at his brother's ignorance.

"There was nothing supernatural about Piper's birth! I've seen so-called faith healers employ the same sleight-of-hand by removing chicken livers through bloody incisions they claimed to have made with their bare hands."

He caressed his mother's plaque and felt a tear roll down his cheek.

"If the supernatural existed, Willie, then why is the corpse of our dear mama rotting beneath our feet? Why couldn't the supernatural bring her back?"

"Ah. The truth at last," Will sneered. "The Great Houdini failed to master the supernatural, so the supernatural must be a fraud like him!"

Houdini straightened his back. He turned slowly to look his brother in the face.

"Perhaps that's true, Will. But the difference between me and practitioners of the supernatural is that I've never claimed to be anything but a fraud."

Will flared his nostrils and snorted. Houdini wondered if he were sniffing him in consideration for a tasty snack.

"What if you're wrong, Ehrich?" Will said. "What if you're less of a fraud than you realize? What if, despite your arrogance, your little experiment to postpone mama's encounter with the Grim Reaper succeeded in ways you never imagined?"

"Nonsense!" Houdini boomed. "Despite the law of our faith, I made sure to keep mama from being laid to rest for a full four days. I watched as her body was lowered into its grave. I wept as the first trowel of earth made its sickening thud upon the thick pine of her coffin."

Will narrowed his eyes.

"I'm not talking about her body, dear brother. What if you succeeded in saving mama's *soul*?"

The words struck Houdini speechless for several seconds. Then he cocked his head and demanded, "What does all this have to do with Piper?"

"Ehrich," Will began, pacing the ground like an attorney in court. "Did Piper ever make anything happen? Anything when she was scared or excited that your rational mind couldn't explain? Particularly...after sunset?"

Houdini thought about the crystal decanter and the genuine flowers produced from the wand during Piper's New Year's performance. Had that been at night? Yes, it had.

But no, those were just tricks. He could easily duplicate them if he had taken the time to try.

Then he recalled the incident in Boston and his face dropped.

"Last month," he said in barely a whisper. "I made one last attempt to expose Margery. There were two glowing stars under the table. Someone said they saw a young girl..."

Will cut him off with a savage snarl.

"You brought her to the witch's lair? Why not just gift-wrap her and hand-deliver her to the Beast with a bouquet of roses?"

Froth flowed from his mouth and the flames in his eyes burned a deeper shade of crimson. He clutched and unclutched his fingers as though struggling to keep them from his brother's throat.

"No," Houdini said quietly, grappling with his own self-doubt. "No—it couldn't have been her. When I was finally able to reach a phone, I called Bess. Piper was sitting beside her doing homework. I even spoke with her!"

Will shook his head. "There are faster modes of travel than even Mr. Ford and the Wright Brothers ever dreamed of, Ehrich. Doorways in space that spirits use to travel between worlds. Until recently, the spirits always returned to their own realms, shutting the doors behind them and securing them tightly."

Houdini noticed his brother's lugubrious voice was tainted with an uncharacteristic vitality. He couldn't tell whether he was growing agitated or excited.

"If my theory is true," Will continued, "harvesting a soul like

Piper's could release enough energy to open a permanent rift between worlds, shattering the barriers that have kept the demonic hordes at bay since the creation of the physical universe."

Houdini clenched his teeth at the callous words William used in reference to his self-proclaimed daughter.

"It matters not whether I believe your theory to be true, dear brother," the magician said. "But there are factions who *do* believe it. And belief is a dangerous adversary."

"And that is why you must double your efforts to protect our child, *dear brother*," Will said, repeating Houdini's term of endearment with disdain. "No more jaunts across the country to ogle your name in lights above antiquated vaudeville camps and moth-eaten movie houses."

"Don't be absurd, Willie," Houdini said, dismissing the notion with a wave of his hand. "When I'm forced to travel on business, I entrust Piper's care to your old friend Jim. As a former boxer, he's better suited than anyone to protect the child.

"But with regard to the spiritual claims you've made," he added, taking a step toward his brother and looking him sharply in the eye, "I think it's time to put your 'daughter' to the test."

THERE'S A TRICK TO IT

As usual, Piper was up before the sun. And as usual, she climbed the stairs to her uncle's library where she could explore his vast collection of books without disturbing Aunt Bess.

She and Bess had grown even closer since Houdini had left to dazzle Chicago with his feats of daring and wonder. On Easter Sunday, Bess had taken her into Manhattan where she and two hundred-thousand other people flaunted their new spring clothing in the parade along Fifth Avenue.

So when Piper strolled into the kitchen for breakfast and spotted a familiar head of peppered curls poring over a newspaper, she hesitated.

Aunt Bess was removing a steaming flat-bottomed dish from the oven. When she saw Piper, she smiled and said, "Guess who decided to grace us with his presence?"

Seated in his customary chair as though he'd never been gone, Houdini lowered the paper and smiled. "Come give your uncle a big birthday hug," he said, opening his arms wide.

"I didn't know it was your birthday," Piper replied, making timid steps toward him.

When they embraced, she couldn't tell if she sensed tension between them or if it was just her imagination. After all, how could he have known for sure that it had been her in Margery's parlor? The only thing he could possibly have seen was a pair of glowing stars, which wouldn't be out of the ordinary in a weird room like that.

As much as she tried, Piper couldn't put the events of that day behind her. Miss Fortune's unexpected return to the detention hall had forced Sal to abort the teleportation spell. By the time he was able to reset the *Kefitzat Haderech,* Piper had already been collared by Rand and his mother.

She had seen him beckoning her through the mirror and had inched her way across the room. But the air of glamour surrounding Margery had so entranced her that she could barely take her eyes off the woman.

Sal had taken a huge risk by reaching his arms through the *Kefitzat Haderech* to rescue her. And though he successfully retrieved her with each of their boy parts and girl parts intact, Piper's gratitude had been anything but profound. Margery had been about to reveal something about her past when Sal's eager hands had snatched her away.

Piper wondered why Margery hadn't come crashing through the mirror to pursue her. Sal rejected the notion with a shake of his head.

"She can't use it," he said calmly. "Only kids can. Another fail-safe built into the mirror. Once you reach the age of eighteen, *pffft.* You have to wait in line at Grand Central along with everyone else."

That was over a month ago. Since then Piper had spent no time with Houdini. Maybe that's why his embrace felt so cold. With an impassive pat on the back, Piper stepped away and sat down across from Houdini.

"This morning, shirred eggs for the birthday boy," Aunt Bess said, placing a silver serving tray on the table in front of her husband, "oatmeal, fresh squeezed orange juice, toast, and a big glass of milk."

"And for you, young lady," Bess said, pouring Piper a bowl of Uncle Sam Cereal, "Uncle Sam wants you to eat right, be strong, and keep regular."

"Aunt Bess!" Piper groaned and rolled her eyes.

She caught Houdini trying to hide a smirk behind his newspaper. He took a sip of his juice and turned the page. Then he made a clucking sound with his tongue and stiffly set the paper down over his breakfast. His smile was gone.

"Remember that woman I bumped into on the boardwalk?" he asked Piper with a sullen look in his eyes.

"The nice lady with the, umm…" Piper caressed her jawline with her fingertips.

"Krao Farini," Houdini choked. "She passed away."

Piper gasped. "What? But she seemed so healthy, so full of life!"

Houdini shook his curled head. "Says here she died from influenza. Maybe she caught something that night in the rain."

Or maybe something caught her, Piper thought.

"Such a shame," Bess said, consoling her husband with a gentle pat on his shoulder.

"If anyone has gone to heaven, that woman has," Houdini said, laying his hand over his wife's.

"Right next to your mother?" Piper said, shoveling a spoonful of Uncle Sam flakes through her lips. As soon as the words left her mouth, she wished she had swallowed them instead of the cereal. She could see Bess holding her breath and staring at Piper with eyes as wide as saucers.

Houdini neatly folded his newspaper, leaned across the table, and looked his niece in the eye.

"So, my dear, have you been practicing your magic?" he said in a cheerful manner, clearly trying to change the subject.

"Her studies have been keeping her very busy," Bess said, the tension in her body visibly easing now that the conversation had shifted.

"Oh, I doubt homework would keep this one busy for long," Houdini said with a note of pride in his voice. "She's a fast learner."

Bess leaned in close and said, "Then maybe tonight she can help *you* with your spelling while I visit my mother. Poor soul hasn't been feeling well."

"What a splendid idea, my darling. It'll give Piper and me a chance to catch up—maybe teach her a new trick or two?"

Houdini smiled hopefully at his niece. But there was something about his request that made her uncomfortable.

"I gotta go. I'll miss the bell!" Piper grabbed her knapsack and rushed for the door.

"Tonight! My study! Six o'clock!" Houdini called after her. "Don't be late!"

At school that day, the boys kept poking and shoving Piper whenever they moved around her. She was annoyed that Miss Hine was being nice to them, making silly excuses for their behavior. She said that they all had "spring fever" and left it at that.

Sal's seat in the front row was empty again. He had been absent a lot lately, and Piper knew it had something to do with a last-ditch effort to save Henri.

She hadn't told him what Margery said about her being an *ecto-detector* because she still wasn't sure what that meant. But she did tell Sal how Margery had all but admitted that her husband was pumping dead freaks with ectoplasm and planned to do the same to Henri.

But Sal couldn't very well announce that to anyone. Who'd believe him? Henri would still be handed over to Dr. Crandon and Sal would be sent to Bellevue in his place.

When Sal wasn't around, school days always dragged. So when the four o'clock bell rang, Piper sprinted to catch the early trolley home. She considered dropping by Sal's house first, but she didn't want to bother his family if they were busy making final preparations for Henri.

When Piper got home, she heard some sort of commotion in the basement. She tiptoed downstairs to investigate and stopped halfway. Houdini and Collins had their backs to her and were standing over an unadorned gray box. The box was shaped like a coffin, but instead of wood it looked like it was made from galvanized iron. On each end of the lid there was a porthole covered with bronze discs.

Houdini slapped Collins on the back and said, "I assume you tested it then? Airtight? Watertight?"

"Absolutely, Mr. Houdini," Collins nodded. "I followed your instructions to the letter."

"And a fine job you did of it, Jim!" Houdini replied, inspecting his assistant's handiwork. "I said I could remain submerged in a coffin for the same length of time as those so-called Egyptians fakirs. And this is fine piece of craftsmanship is going to help me do just that."

Collins removed his fedora and scratched his head. "But I still don't get it, boss. There's no invention to it. No trick, no fake. You simply lie down in it and breathe."

Houdini gripped his assistant's shoulder. "I didn't ask you to make it for the submersion stunt. I wanted you to make it so I could be buried in it."

The two men looked at each other, but no more words passed between them.

Piper slipped back up the stairs before either of them could spot her. She stopped in her room to change into a pair of blue dungarees and then withdrew to Houdini's study on the top floor. Despite her incident with the Egyptian jars, it was still the one place in the house where she felt inspired to do her reading assignments.

She was just finishing Mark Twain's *The Innocents Abroad* when Houdini entered the room. Six o'clock on the dot.

"Ready to dazzle me with hocus-pocus?" he asked, rubbing his hands together in anticipation.

"I guess so," Piper said closing the book. She didn't know why she felt so nervous.

Her uncle opened his magic chest and sorted through its contents. At first they reviewed some basic card tricks. But Houdini quickly grew weary of these routines. He walked over to his closet and pulled out a canvas garment with long, dangling sleeves. Piper recalled seeing it the night of the show when her uncle wiggled out of it like a butterfly from a cocoon.

"You want me to escape from a straitjacket?" she asked warily. "Closed-in spaces kind of make me nervous."

"Nonsense," Houdini said, holding out the garment with its open back to her. "It's not like I'm locking you in a box. Just think of it as a sweater that's a few sizes too big."

Piper examined the uncomfortable fabric for almost a full minute before tentatively inserting one arm into the straitjacket's extra-long sleeves and then the other. Turning her so she faced the wall, Houdini crossed Piper's arms over her chest and pulled the loose ends of the sleeves tightly behind her.

"Some escapes use no tricks at all beyond uncommon strength and flexibility. So I want to be sure your arms can move as little as possible," he said, winding the sleeves and yanking them firmly.

"When I was your age, I worked in a tie factory. The work was uninspiring, but I learned how to make all sorts of knots. The Prusik knot, for example. Virtually inescapable."

"Oww!" Piper complained as Houdini pinned her arms against her chest with a sharp tug. "How am I supposed to do that thing you do with your shoulders if I can't move them?"

"Ha!" Houdini barked, tying a second knot in the sleeves. "You don't have to dislocate your shoulder. That's what I say to spice things up and frighten off the competition. You just have to be flexible enough to get your head under your arms in front of your body. Shouldn't be hard for a limber little sprite like you."

"Okay, I'll give it a shot," Piper said.

Despite feeling like a trussed turkey at Thanksgiving, Piper began a frantic attempt to escape the garment. She crouched, kneeled, twisted, and hopped, trying to bring in front of her the strap that connected the long arms of the jacket behind her back.

"I can't do it," she finally admitted, shrugging inside the thick fabric.

Houdini made no move to free her. "I won't allow any niece of mine to throw in the towel."

Still lying on the ground, Piper set forth both feet on the strap stirrup-style and pushed with all her might. When her strength gave out, she huffed in exasperation,

"Aren't you supposed to be giving me a few pointers?"

Houdini tilted his head and gave her a smug look. "It certainly can't be more difficult than pouring milk into a newspaper from your aunt's crystal or making a trick wand sprout real flowers, hmm?"

Piper stopped struggling and gave her uncle a blank stare.

"I'll make a deal with you, child. Tell me how you did those tricks and I'll release you."

"I don't know," Piper said, wiggling again because she knew her uncle wouldn't be satisfied with her answer. "I broke the pitcher you gave me, so I got one from the cupboard. It just sort of happened. Same with the flowers. Sometimes the tricks worked the way they were supposed to and sometimes they didn't."

She arched back and forth wildly like she was riding a lunatic rocking horse, trying to push the strap down with her legs at the same time.

"Please! Let me out!"

Houdini removed a pocket watch from his vest and studied it. "I have to keep you in the jacket until at least six-thirty."

"Why?" Piper demanded.

"To prove a point," he said flatly.

Piper pulled and hauled, jerked and jumped, rolled and wriggled. Perspiration from her forehead dripped into her eyes and her body felt like a loaf of bread in an oven. "Get it off me!" she screamed.

"I taught you well. A good magician never shares her tricks, no matter what." Houdini said with a smile. But as he leaned closer his smile turned into something that resembled a sneer. "Let's make a new deal. Tell me how you got into Margery's parlor and back here by dinner and I'll set you free."

Once more, Piper stopped thrashing. But this time her eyes couldn't meet Houdini's. "I don't know what you're talking about."

Clasping his hands behind his back, Houdini paced around the captive girl like a spider taunting its prey. "So you're saying it wasn't you under Mina Crandon's table a month ago?"

Piper shook her head but still couldn't meet her uncle's gaze. "Who's Mina Crandon?" she stammered.

Houdini thrust a hand in front of the girl's face. Piper closed her eyes thinking he was going to strike her. She opened them again and saw that he was holding something metallic in his outstretched palm. It wasn't his pocket watch.

"Tell me, girl, what was *this* doing in Margery's hallway?"

It took a second for Piper to focus. But when she did, she realized her uncle was holding the lock-pick gadget that she had dropped outside Rand's bedroom. The name *Houdini* was prominently etched across it, so there was no denying it was the same one he had given her.

Piper fumbled for words. She wanted to be truthful about how she had gotten there, but she had promised Miss Fortune that she would never reveal her secret—even though the headmistress had put a memory spell on her anyway.

"It's all done with mirrors!" she cried out finally, being as honest as possible.

"Ha! Next you'll be telling me there's a trick to it!" Houdini snorted, checking his watch. "My train to Chicago doesn't leave till tomorrow, little one. I can keep you tied up all night if need be."

At this, a feeling of nausea overcame Piper. The jacket seemed to constrict more tightly around her. Rolling on the floor in a frantic effort to escape, she managed to slip her head under one arm. But now it was lodged in that position and she felt more vulnerable, more desperate, than ever.

"Show me what you can do!" Houdini shouted in her ear.

Piper skated along the floor on one shoulder trying to get away from him. But she collapsed halfway to the door.

"Help me," she whimpered, gazing up at him with eyes widening in fear.

The sight held Houdini. He grabbed Piper by her trussed shoulders, stared deeply into her eyes, and shook her violently.

"*Mamaleh! Mamaleh! Sind Sie da drin? Es ist mir, Ehrie!*"

Was he speaking German?

Who was this man?

Maybe she didn't know him at all.

Maybe no one did.

Maybe the Spiritualists were right about him all along.

Or maybe he was some sort of German spy who'd gone insane when they lost the War.

Piper's head began to spin and her field of vision narrowed. But she refused to lose consciousness. She chewed at the sleeve of her madhouse trappings, trying to peel them off with her teeth.

Where was Aunt Bess?

For some reason she pictured Bess performing the Metamorphosis with Houdini, the trick where they exchanged places with each other. How had they done that?

Piper shook her head, trying to stay focused. Instead she started thinking about the spell Miss Fortune used to activate the mirror. It began as an imperceptible whisper. Then, like a child recalling the chorus to a forgotten song, she bellowed the last two lines:

"Carry this one from this place to that, without harm or folly!"

Suddenly Piper was standing in the spot where Houdini had just been standing and Houdini was at her feet, hogtied in the straitjacket. The pocket watch and lock picks were lying on the floor next to him.

At first the magician looked as stunned as Piper was. Then he beamed at her in wild-eyed glee and exclaimed, "Piper! You did it!" He craned his neck to look at the watch on the floor. "Six-thirty, on the nose."

She took a step backward.

"No! It's okay! I had to be sure." He began to shake and kick. "Just wait for me to get out of this thing and I'll explain."

Piper knew she had only seconds to spare. It would be a simple matter for Houdini to escape from an ordinary straitjacket, even if he had used a prosaic knot or whatever it was called. Hesitating only a moment to snatch the lock-pick device from the floor, she turned and bolted from the room.

"Piper, come back!" her uncle shouted, thumping wildly on the floor. But she had heard enough. She flew down the stairs and rushed out the door, almost forgetting about the trick knob in her haste.

It had all been too good to be true. The time had come for her to go. Again.

But where? Back to Hollygrove? No, that's the first place they'd look.

She needed a place where she could easily lose herself.

Pausing on the doorstep for no more than a second, she looked to the south. Then, without a glance back, Piper Houdini headed for the bright lights of Coney Island.

SMOKE AND MIRRORS

With its nightly music and rooftop dancing, Childs Restaurant was one of many establishments at Coney that offered reasonably priced food for people of average means. The building itself was designed to complement the surrounding fairytale environment of wild shapes, colors, and lights. But its unique nautical motif actually set it apart from the flimsy shacks that housed the neighboring entertainment venues.

The Childs' yellow exterior was adorned with arched windows and doors framed with terra-cotta moldings and swags. Each corner had a towering column crowned with an urn. Unfortunately, its rooftop garden would remain closed to the public until summer's official kickoff.

On this particular night, however, a pale individual chose to ignore that edict. Perched atop a column next to the Childs' huge cursive logo, Flapper scouted the passersby on the boardwalk below for a meal the restaurant didn't offer. A bib scrawled with the same logo was tied loosely about her neck to protect her garment from splatter. It was, after all, a Vionnet.

The boardwalk usually offered easy pickings this time of year. The crowds weren't large and there was always a straggler high on hooch or a jilted bearcat running away from her goof. But tonight the chill blowing in from the beach had kept the loners inland. The only people bold enough to defy the crisp ocean air were snuggle pups stuck on each other's arms.

Flapper was about to call it a night and return to the cloying duties of her stakeout when her keen eyes picked out a tiny figure running up the ramp across the way. She licked her lips and prepared to descend on her prey. Then she looked more closely and realized there was something familiar about the girl.

"Is this for real?" she asked out loud. "My little tabby cat is hoofing it all by her lonesome?"

Flapper watched as the redhead ascended the ramp to the boardwalk and then veered left at the Washington Baths. The dewdropper swanned over to the bath house and settled upon its rooftop.

Extending her body beyond the arch of its brick façade, she called out to her fleeing quarry.

"What's the trouble, seetie?" she called, using a term her fellow flappers applied to anyone they disliked. "You in Dutch with Houdini?"

The girl stopped and looked around, her fingertips brushing her cheeks. Flapper could see glowing dots on the girl's face, the same thing she had seen in the movie house.

"Up here, seetie. Remember me?"

The Houdini girl looked up and her face went flush at the sight of Flapper. She turned on her heel and sprinted up the boardwalk, wasting no time to look over her shoulder.

Flapper leaped over the brick parapet and floated down to the wooden planks below. "Aww, don't be a wet blanket!" she called after the girl. "The Master just wants to Edison you, and he don't want no klucks."

She remembered her Master's words. *You are not to make yourself known to her...No saddling, no snuggling! Not until Houdini is out of the picture.*

Well, Houdini was clearly out of the picture now, just as her Master had predicted. And even though Flapper's mission was still one of observation, she now had permission to have a little fun.

She kept a cool distance between herself and the redhead to give her the impression that she might stand a chance. A chance to exhibit whatever special talent her Master had expected.

So Flapper was a tad surprised when Teeny-Houdini dashed into the amusement area. Did she think this was playtime? Did she think that her stalker was someone who could be trifled with? Did she think that Flapper was just another pretty face? With renewed intensity, the vamp took to the air.

This part of the boardwalk wouldn't be open for another month and was steeped in darkness. All the amusements were closed. So why was her tabby cat heading toward Hell Gate, Steeplechase's chamber of horrors?

"Ain't gonna get rid of me that way, seetie," she called down to her prey. "My peepers work just as good as yours when the lights go down."

The redhead looked around, trying to locate the source of the voice. Then she looked skyward and her body tensed. The vamp smiled and bared her fangs. "That's right, tabby. I can fly. Now don't be no crepe hanger—show me what *you* can do."

The girl was holding some sort of pocket-knife doohickey and she used it to jimmy the lock to the haunted amusement. Then she pried open the electric panel box, seized the knife switch, and threw it upwards. A red light flashed inside the black entrance.

"You think a bunch of cheap props are gonna scare me?" Flapper asked with a sneer.

"You're right, it's not very scary," the girl shouted, pointing overhead to the titanic statue of Satan looming over them with outstretched wings. "It would've been a whole lot creepier if they used your face instead."

Then she disappeared into the flashing red light. Flapper's face scrunched in irritation. As she dove after her quarry, the smell of creosote assaulted her nostrils. A fresh layer of tar had been spread across the roof to repair winter's harsh treatment.

The dewdropper touched down at the entrance and snorted at the dripping red letters that spelled out "Enter at your own risk." A second sign announced "a bold new addition" called Mephisto's Mirror Maze. Next to the ticket booth stood a full-length mirror with a third sign that read, "So you won't forget how you really look."

Flapper studied the sign for a second. Then she smashed the mirror with her fist.

"I already have forgotten," she said, stepping into the pulsating light.

Hell Gate began with a boat ride into a whirling maelstrom then continued along an underground channel leading to the molten interior of the earth's core. But none of the boats had been put in the water yet and the tunnel's low ceiling made it impossible for Flapper to float above it. So she stepped into the knee-deep water and cursed.

"My Mary Janes! Do you know how hard it is to find these shoes on someone my size?"

The red strobe light made it difficult for even Flapper's night peepers to focus on anything, so she had to rely on her other heightened senses. At the end of the tunnel she could hear the pitter-patter of feet sloshing through the manmade waterway.

"Hey, Teeny Houdini! Here, kitty kitty!" Flapper's piercing voice echoed off the walls of the dripping corridor.

She continued to bait the girl in the hopes that it would rile her up and force her out in the open. "Don't worry, tabby. I ain't gonna blip you off or blow you down. I just want a little taste, you know? Let's see why the Master thinks you're such a choice bit of calico."

Flapper's long legs and a short hemline made it a simple matter for her to lurch through the waters of Hell Gate's cistern. The watercourse ended in a large room painted in bright oranges and reds to make it look like fire and lava. Flapper stepped onto the landing and looked down at her shoes.

"Ruined," she said flatly. Then she called out to the darkness, "You hear that, tabby? You owe me a pair of dog kennels!"

There was a hole in the wall marked "Barrel and Bridge Room," and through it Flapper heard the distant echo of a reply: "Dog kennels? And here I thought you lived in the zoo!"

The vamp gritted her teeth. The kid certainly knew how to push her buttons. But why was she letting her snappy comebacks get her in such a lather? After all, she was the one at the top of the food chain here, right?

Flapper kicked off her Mary Janes and marched into the Barrel and Bridge Room. She was immediately assailed by a barrage of colorful lights flashing inside a huge revolving cylinder. The vamp wasn't used to walking without heels, but her bare feet managed to get her through the Barrel of Fun and over the tilting "Billy Goat's Bridge" without falling. Once she made it to the other side of the bridge, she stepped lightly across a wooden surface that had been painted to look like stone.

"Gonna have to do better than that, tabby cat," Flapper called out, testing each "rock" with her big toe to make sure there were no more floor tricks.

She followed a tunnel of fake brick that led to a spiral slide made of polished hardwood. It was much taller and steeper than any slide Flapper had ever seen. The tower at the center of the spiral prevented Flapper from seeing what was at the bottom.

"You down there, seetie?" she hollered through cupped hands. "Fun time's over. Mama's comin' to get you!"

Sitting on the thin material of her skirt, the dewdropper launched herself down the slippery face of the helter skelter. The slide deposited her on a polished metal disk spinning in the middle of a large room surrounded by padded walls and doors. The huge disk rotated faster and faster, and as much as Flapper struggled, it was impossible to stand up.

Her prey knelt in the center of the disk. She maintained her balance with one hand and rubbed her chin with the other as she contemplated the blundering vamp.

"The Human Roulette Wheel was my favorite ride as a kid," the girl said as Flapper struggled against its centrifugal force. "The orphanage used to take us here and I was always the last one to get thrown off."

As soon as the girl said "thrown off," Flapper lost her hold on the slippery surface and was tossed against the padded wall. The enraged vamp jumped to her feet, brushed the dust off her Vionnet, and said with a grimace, "Poor little bunny. Always the orphan. Who's gonna be your butter and egg man now that you ain't got Houdini?"

The spinning redhead seemed to cringe at Flapper's vocabulary. But she never took her eyes off the vamp. "Why don't you climb over here so we can chat about it," she said, patting a spot next to her.

"I've got a better idea," Flapper replied, baring her fangs and rising softly into the air. "How about I fly over there for a little drink instead?"

Flapper thought the girl would be intimidated. Instead, she simply smiled and said, "I was hoping you'd do something like that."

She slid off the hub and streaked across the metal disk like she was wearing invisible roller skates. Using the wheel's momentum to gather speed, she launched herself into the air, directly at the vamp.

The blunt force took Flapper by surprise. It carried the two girls through a door marked "This way to Mephisto's Mirror Maze." The redhead mumbled something like, "Sal, you'd better be right," and then they crashed onto a wooden floor beyond the door.

Flapper's body absorbed most of the impact. The red-headed girl wasted no time somersaulting over the dazed dewdropper and taking off down the glass-walled corridor.

"Naughty, naughty!" Flapper called out, rolling to her feet and straightening her dress. "Keep jumping around like that and the doctor won't give you a lollypop!"

Once more, the ceiling was too low to get a bird's-eye vantage. So Flapper commenced her pursuit on bare feet. Irritation turned to anger as she bumped into various angled panes of glass. She would catch a glimpse of her quarry through a glass-walled dead end, but the girl would disappear deeper into the maze by the time she doubled back.

At last she spotted the redhead at the end of a corridor, hunched over and huffing to catch her breath. Flapper sprinted down the passageway and leaped at her like a ravenous cougar. The girl stood up and smiled cheekily. Flapper realized too late that a glass pane stood

between them. But did the teeny-tabby really think it would protect her?

Flapper made a throttling gesture with her hands and smashed
through the barrier. But instead of feeling the soft flesh of a teen's
neck, the vamp crashed to the floor with nothing but a few shards of
glass in her hands. The girl had disappeared.

For the third time that night, Flapper got off the floor and brushed
the panels of her skirt. But this time she noticed smeared blood on
its ruffled lace. Her blood. It trickled down her arm where shards of
glass had penetrated her skin.

The cuts would heal quickly.

The Vionnet would not.

"You little brat! Look what you did to my dress!" she screamed
in every direction. "And I bought it all by myself!"

"Doesn't count if you used someone else's money!" the girl's voice
echoed from somewhere deep in the maze.

Flapper's patience had worn as thin as the fabric of her gown. She
hadn't felt so chintzy since the hours leading up to her revamping.

The wind outside was whistling through Hell Gate's thin wooden
walls. She could hear it rattling a loose board somewhere. No, not
rattling. It was more like a creaking sound, like someone prying a
plank off the wall.

The sound of a *snap* confirmed her suspicion.

"My friend was right about the mirror thing," the girl's voice
bounced off the glass walls. "I wonder if he was also right about the
stake-in-the-heart thing?"

Flapper was suddenly surrounded by a host of freckled redheads
advancing on her with wooden spikes. Her first instinct was to cower.
But how would it look to the others if she was brought down by an
army of Orphan Annies?

Mustering her courage, Flapper lashed out with her obsidian fingernails against the nearest threat. A glass panel exploded, sending
fragments in every direction, and the legion of redheads vanished.

The mirror thing.

Of course! She was a dewdropper in a maze of mirrors. It was impossible for her to tell the difference between transparent glass and reflective glass. She had been duped and the egg on her face had been thrown by a twelve-year-old girl.

"You and I can play dodge ball all night," the redhead's taunts continued from the shadows. "But unlike you, I have only one target."

The brat was right. Flapper couldn't see her own reflection so there was no way to orient herself in this maddening maze. To her, every mirror was just another pane of glass. It would take some time to destroy them all, but her opponent only needed one lucky shot.

Flapper scowled. The tables had been turned against her and she had allowed it. To regain the upper hand, she would have to change the rules. She could try to track her prey by scent, but the cloying scent of tar from the rooftop overwhelmed her nostrils. So instead of going left or right, Flapper decided to go up. Crouching on her heels, the vamp catapulted skyward, smashing a hole in the flimsy ceiling and soaring through the rafters.

Flapper brushed splinters of wood from her hair that trickled down to the roof below. The fresh tar on the parapet gave her a nasty idea. If she couldn't get to the tabby then she'd make the tabby come to her.

Fumbling with the looped tassels of her beaded purse, Flapper plucked out the book of matches that she'd pocketed at the Adonis.

"You know, for what it's worth, I actually enjoyed our romp," she called through the hole in the roof. "But there comes a time when a gal needs more."

She lit the match and let it fall to the rooftop's glossy black surface. The sheet of tar ignited at once and the force of the blast propelled the vamp higher into the night's sky.

Flapper didn't dare approach the hole to see what her patsy was doing. Fire was as poison to dewdroppers as sunlight or a stake through the heart. Instead, she hovered above the exit ready to ambush the redhead whenever she fled the burning building.

Seconds turned to minutes. Flames assailed Hell Gate on every side. Flapper bit her lower lip and continued to wait.

But the girl never emerged.

When she heard the bells and whistles of the fire brigade, Flapper knew that she couldn't afford to hang around. She made one more desperate revolution around Satan's burning visage and then soared away.

Oboy, she thought. *Master T is gonna plotz when he hears about this.*

DISTORTION AND REALITY

Deep in the bowels of Hell Gate, flames were already licking the narrow support beams of the walls and ceiling. Piper could hear shouts of "fire" being yelled into the night. But her own screams of "help" were drowned out by the inferno raging around her.

A fallen rafter smashed one of the countless mirrors that reflected her image, paralyzing her with momentary fear. Patting her body to make sure she was okay, Piper scurried down the next length of the maze in a mad dash to escape the conflagration. Smoke and debris made it more difficult to navigate the glass labyrinth, but somehow she made all the correct turns without flaw.

The maze deposited Piper into a hall of mirrors, the final attraction in this seemingly endless pavilion of fun. Across the room, the funhouse exit was half-lit by leaping tongues of fire.

Piper knew that Clara Bow's crazy twin would be waiting for her outside with her flapping tassels and dripping fangs. She still had no idea why the vamp was after her. Was she in league with Houdini? Her father? Both?

Gripping the wooden stake more firmly in her hand, Piper scanned the room for another means of escape. The mirrors here were different from the ones in the maze. They were tilted and curved in a variety of ways to make her look thin, fat, short, tall, weird, crazy, scary, funny, or any sort of combination.

And then, like a slap in the face, Miss Fortune's words came back to Piper:

"In thaumaturgy, all mirrors lead to the Kefitzat Haderech.*"*

She turned to the nearest mirror. It had a three bends, making her look like a thick wet noodle. She gazed into it intently and chanted Ms. Fortune's incantation. This time she had no trouble remembering the words.

"I conjure thee, Qaphsiel, and thy host,
In the name of the three-times holy,
Carry this one from this place to that
Without harm or folly."

Piper touched the mirror. Nothing happened. It was still as solid as it looked.

There was a crash in the next room and Piper could hear the shattering of glass. It wouldn't be long before the mirrors in this room would suffer the same fate. Along with her.

She tried to remember Sal's incantation, but the Creole words meant nothing to her. Why had he used a different spell anyway?

Of course! Each person had to use their own personal method to get through the *Kefitzat Haderech.* And what was hers?

Miss Fortune had called it *sanguine* magic.

Piper looked at the jagged wooden post in her hand. A rusty, crooked nail protruded from one end. Holding her breath, Piper touched its pointed tip to her finger. She pressed a bit harder and winced as the nail punctured her soft flesh. A droplet of blood leaked from the tiny wound. She hoped it would be enough.

Tossing the wooden stake to the floor, Piper traced a huge oval around the mirror, smearing her blood along the edges of its wavy surface.

Another crash. The fire wouldn't be contained in Mephisto's Mirror Maze much longer.

Believe there's a way of getting through it, she told herself. Believe the glass isn't solid but soft like gauze.

Slowly, Piper's reflection dimmed and the mirror turned into a sort of mist. The glass faded away like silver dust.

It was hot and getting hotter. Piper's hand penetrated the icy veil. In another moment, she was through the glass. The last thing she saw before being sucked into its wavy blackness was a flaming beam crashing down where she had been standing.

As she faded from one existence to the next, Piper felt the imminent and the infinite come together. Her step into the mirror became a cosmic fall into light and darkness. She had made this round-trip journey twice before, but this time something didn't feel right.

The orange glow of the detention hall's lamps and candles snapped Piper back into existence. Her hands and knees fell harshly onto cold stone. It was a struggle to lift her head, but when she did she found it difficult to discriminate between this place and the funhouse.

Then, distinctly, she heard someone scream. A raven-haired girl stood over her, pointing while her mouth gaped in sheer terror. Piper's head kept bobbling forward. Why was it so hard to hold it up?

Three other kids about her age gathered around the shrieking brunette. The only one she recognized was the girl with the blanket. Billy's eyes looked bigger than normal through her thick lenses.

Why was everyone gawking at her?

Suddenly an obnoxious cackle pierced the air. Piper recognized it at once.

"Bwa-ha-ha!" Alan Rand laughed. "What happened, Houdini— you get into a scrap with a taffy puller? Serves you right for hitching a free ride on my last jaunt."

Piper wasn't sure what she found more irritating, Rand's Brahmin pompousness or the piercing Brooklyn patter of the vamp back at the funhouse.

Taffy puller? What the heck was he talking about?

She tried to stand only to fall flat on her face. Why was she so unsteady?

Rand was laughing uncontrollably. She looked around hoping to find Sal. But Sal hadn't gone to school that day, so there was no reason he would be in detention.

"Alan, it's not funny!" Billy said, laying her worn quilt delicately on the floor. "Here, let me help you." The bespectacled girl helped Piper wobble to her feet.

Why did she feel so much taller than everyone else?

Billy turned the redhead around so she could see her reflection in the magic looking glass. Piper gasped at what she saw. She looked exactly as she had in the funhouse mirror.

But the *Kefitzat Haderech* was not a funhouse mirror!

"Oh, my God," she muttered, putting two stubby fingers to her lips. Her face and head were stretched, making her look like an obscene jack-o-lantern. Her arms and torso were squashed like a dwarf's and her legs, like Rand said, looked like strands of pulled taffy.

The wooden door at the end of the room burst open and the rotund figure of Miss Fortune scuttled through it.

"I heard a scream. Is everyone...?"

She saw Piper standing in front of the mahogany frame and stopped. The color drained from her face.

Piper held her stunted arms out to the dismayed headmistress. "Please help?"

"Bright Lady in Heaven! Little one, what have you done?"

"IwasintheamusementparkchasedintothefunhousebyalunaticvampiredressedlikeClaraBow!" Piper blurted, trying to explain what she couldn't explain.

Miss Fortune's gleaming blue eyes flashed like a fire on the ocean.

"Slow down, child. Slow down. Did you say 'vampire dressed like Clara Bow'?"

Piper replied with an abrupt nod. The she waved to the mirror.

"I'm sorry. It was the only way I could escape."

Miss Fortune took several measured steps toward her, massaging her temple with the fingers of her right hand.

"It sounds to me like you were paid a visit by Flapper. Master Therion's personal guardian. But what, pray tell, did you do to raise her ire?"

"I have no idea!" Piper exclaimed. "Who's Master Therion?"

"An Englishman," the girl named Billy answered. "Not a fact my fellow countrymen are particularly proud of."

The raven-haired girl stepped forward and said, "To some he is known as 'the Beast.' To others he's known as 'the world's wickedest man.' But we all know him as Crowley. Aleister Crowley."

Miss Fortune looked at Piper to see if she recognized the name. Piper shook her elongated head and said, "Doesn't ring a bell."

"Hey, Houdini!" Rand exclaimed. "I hear the freak show needs a new Rubber Man! You should apply!"

His face was red from laughing so hard, making his serpentine birthmarks even more prominent.

"Rand, I'm gonna…"

Balling her stubby fingers into a fist, Piper took a step toward the snickering blueblood. But she lost her balance and would have fallen flat on her face if Billy hadn't caught her.

The sight sent Rand into another bout of hysterics.

"Nice gams, Red!"

"Mr. Rand, that will be quite enough!" Miss Fortune scolded.

The boy turned to the headmistress and his mirthful expression immediately soured.

"I beg your pardon, *Imperatrix*," he said, making no effort to hide his sarcasm. "But how many unsanctioned jaunts has she made now? Three? Maybe if you weren't so scared of her uncle, she could sit through one of your detentions and learn all about the Beast and all his stupid aliases—Frater Perdurabo, Prince Chioa Khan, Ankh-af-na-khonsu, the Prophet Baphomet…"

"Ankh-af-na-khonsu!" Piper shouted in sudden recognition. "Of course! I saw one of his books in my uncle's library. *Liber*-something."

"*Liber Legis*. The Book of the Law," Miss Fortune said, narrowing her eyes. "Crowley's proclamation of a new era in humanity's spiritual evolution. He calls it the New Aeon of the Child."

The distortion of Piper's face amplified her confused look. "What's that got to do with me?"

"That's what I was hoping you could tell me, child," the headmistress replied. "My initiates and I have been observing of late how easy it has become to work certain spells. Magick is becoming a simple matter, even for neophytes such as these."

She extended her hand to encompass all her students.

Rand scowled. He obviously didn't like to be grouped with these "neophytes."

"We suspect that a door to the other realms has been unlocked," Miss Fortune continued. "Various powers are already coming through. Some say a child will rise to open it fully, releasing humanity from its pretense of altruism, its obsession with fear, and its consciousness of sin."

"The Star Child," Piper whispered.

Miss Fortune raised an eyebrow in surprise. "You know of this?" she asked.

"Let's just say I know a few people who'd like to get a ringside seat to the debut performance."

She scowled at Rand whose burning eyes silently threatened her to not say another word.

Miss Fortune looked from Piper to Rand and back again. She obviously sensed the friction but chose to ignore it. The stout headmistress turned to her other students and addressed them as though she were teaching class.

"The Star Child will possess no consciousness of its purpose. On the one hand, it will be utterly cruel and without conscience. On the other, it will be helpless, affectionate and ambitious—without knowing why. The child will shun reason yet at the same time will be intuitively aware of the truth."

Miss Fortune then turned her attention to Piper and leaned closer.

"Make no mistake. The Star Child's ambition may appear to be virtuous and good. But the means by which it will attain such goals will be anything but."

A chill shot through Piper's gangly body as she recalled Margery's words:

God has ordained that a powerful light will shine into the souls of men through a great force that is slowly penetrating our atmosphere.

Souls that are found unworthy will be expelled. We can choose to ignore it, or we can choose to become a part of it.

She opened her mouth to say something that would expose Rand's mother. But the only thing that escaped her lips was a hair-raising shriek. Billy held her tightly, but all the other students jumped back.

"Piper! What's wrong?" Billy asked.

"Pain...everywhere," she grimaced, doubling over and clenching her stomach.

"Quickly! Place her before the *Kefitzat Haderech!*" Miss Fortune shouted, helping Billy move her. "She must return to her point of origin at once."

"No!" Piper protested, trying to wrest free. "Fire in the funhouse. Flapper outside."

The headmistress gripped her with two hands.

"But child, your body cannot sustain this form any longer. I don't know how you've survived this long, but the only way to reverse the spell is to send you back through the mirror from which you came!"

Addressing the *Kefitzat Haderech,* Miss Fortune recited the incantation that had become all-too familiar to Piper. Words she now wished she had never learned.

An image appeared in the dark glass that made the headmistress gasp. The others gathered around her and peered into the mirror. All they could see was smoke.

"The fire—it's everywhere," said the dark-haired girl who had screamed at Piper's unsettling arrival.

"But the mirror still appears to be intact," Miss Fortune replied with slight hesitation. "Enough time has passed. By now the fire has attracted an audience. Flapper wouldn't linger with so many witnesses."

She laid a reassuring hand on Piper's shoulder. "Do you know which direction the exit is, child?"

Piper nodded, wincing as another wave of agony shot through her.

"We can wait no longer," the headmistress said, nudging Piper's stooped, oblong body toward the mirror. "As soon as you reach the other side, run as quickly as you can toward the exit!"

Without so much as a farewell or a "good luck," Billy and Miss Fortune hurled Piper through the smoke-filled glass. Before she knew what was happening, the mirror had sucked her into its gray mist. She felt the same marginal grasp on reality that she had experienced on her previous journeys. But this time, the sickening feeling in her stomach only grew worse.

Piper crashed onto the wooden floor of the funhouse. She was surrounded by smoke and charred debris. The ceiling was collapsing in fiery embers all around her, littering the floor with soot and timber.

She felt woozy. The smoke was already making her cough. Piper pulled herself across the floor and tried to get to her feet. But she couldn't get her legs to work. Maybe they were still shaped like overgrown noodles?

Examining her arms and fingers, she observed with relief that everything had returned to normal. The spell had been reversed!

"Thank you, mirror!" Piper said, looking back at the warped glass.

Then she saw it.

The mirror was where she had left it, her drying blood defiling its scalloped edges. The fallen rafter had missed it by inches. But running straight across the mirror, dividing it into almost two equal parts, was a jagged cleft.

Piper lowered her eyes to inspect the base of the mirror. On the floor, several feet away from her, were a pair of legs in blue dungarees.

She craned her neck trying to see the lower half of her body. But she knew what she would find.

Nothing.

That explained why she was so dizzy. But she wondered why there wasn't any blood. And then she wondered why she cared.

Piper started to laugh.

"Well isn't this a fitting end?" she mused. "Half a person trapped in a room full of mirrors. This really is a gate to hell."

She inhaled a lungful of smoke and her laughter collapsed into a fit of coughing. Her vision began to blur.

"Hello?" she heard someone call out. "Is anyone in here?" It was a squeaky voice, and Piper wanted to laugh again.

Across the room she saw the silhouette of a man hopping and climbing over the charred rafters. But the figure wasn't moving like an ordinary person. He was walking on his hands.

And like her, he was snapped off at the waist.

How strange, she thought.

Then she passed out.

LIKE A PHOENIX...

Louise Recht walked around the Child Hatchery in a huff. It was the late-night feeding hour for the premature babies and there was some sort of commotion outside. But what did she expect? When she took this job as head nurse at Coney, she knew that there would be hooligans horsing around on the boardwalk all night long.

The newborns were lined up under heaters breathing filtered air. The nurse peered down at the most recent arrival, a wrinkled little tyke weighing less than two pounds. His parents had little money, but they were given free access to the incubators in exchange for allowing their untimely infant to be put on display.

Louise was about to assign the wet nurses their tasks when the outer door flung open. A man wearing a nightshirt and a straw boater on his head rushed into the room barking orders to the nursing staff.

"Open the incubators! Collect the babies!"

The incubators were experimental machines that hadn't been accepted by the local medical establishment. So years ago, the man in the straw boater had turned his clinic into a sideshow exhibit. During the summer, he was known as Dr. Incubator. But Nurse Recht and her staff always showed him the proper respect and addressed him by his proper name.

"Dr. Couney! What's wrong?" she asked.

"Hell Gate is on fire!"

Hell Gate! Louise's eyes grew larger. The wind was blowing off the ocean from the south. It would soon carry the fire to the next building north. And that building was the Child Hatchery!

Dr. Couney grabbed the new arrival and one other. He was a sturdy man with a gentle grasp, like someone who had spent a lifetime handling canaries. Louise snatched two of the babies and so did each of the four wet nurses.

To protect them from smoke, Nurse Recht covered the infants' heads with blankets. Then she and the wet nurses followed Dr. Couney out into the night with their precious bundles.

It would be another month before the amusements officially opened, so the darkness on the boardwalk was almost complete. The moon and stars were shielded by a veil of smoke. The only source of light was the flickering orange and yellow to the south.

Louise looked over her shoulder. Hell Gate was consumed by flames, the glowing embers laughing and twirling in a fiery dance. So distracted was she by the visage of Satan enveloped in a mantle of genuine hellfire that she failed to notice a lumbering figure coming toward her with a stack of baskets.

The nurse let out a little shriek when she collided with the brute, losing her grasp on one of the newborns. The figure dropped its cargo and caught the infant in its overgrown palm. Then it gently returned the babe to Louise's arms.

"Bouche bée!" she exclaimed in her native French. "Zip! You scared me half to death!"

Zip the What Is It? lowered his head in self-reproach. He was a large black man whose unusually small head made him appear even larger.

"It's all right, Zip." Louise softened her voice to mollify the gentle giant. "What are you doing here? You should get to where it's safe."

Zip crouched and patted the inside of a basket. It was lined with a soft blanket. He peeled it back to reveal a hot water bottle. Louise looked him in stunned silence.

Zip was often publicized as a creature from Africa that had lived with the apes. Louise knew that it was all just ballyhoo. But she sometimes wondered if there were more to Zip than meets the eye. Last year he had saved a child who had nearly drowned in the rough Coney Island surf. And now...

"Dr. Couney!" she called to her supervisor. "There's something here you should see."

Zip laid out the baskets in two neat rows as the Incubator Doctor doubled back with the other nurses in tow. When he saw that each basket was heated by a hot water bottle, he beamed at his head nurse.

"*Gute idee,* Madame Recht!"

Louise shook her head and then nodded to Zip. Dr. Couney shot the so-called pinhead a surprised look. Then he smiled warmly and Zip looked away bashfully.

The doctor and his nurses wasted no time tucking the babies into their baskets. With Zip's help they carried the infants across Surf Avenue to Luna Park where years ago Dr. Couney had set up his first incubator exhibit.

All eleven occupants of the Child Hatchery were saved by the dedicated nurses and Zip's quick thinking. Some infants had to double up for the evening, but not one was harmed.

The wet nurses stayed to feed the hungry newborns. But Louise accompanied Zip and the doctor back to the fire in case there were any medical emergencies.

Bells and sirens pierced the night as fire engines and hook-and-ladder trucks raced for Coney Island. The offbeat trio watched in mute sorrow as flames devoured the top floor of the Child Hatchery. Suddenly, Zip cocked his head to the south. Something had caught his attention. Louise gave him a puzzled look, and then she heard it too. It was a weak cry coming from the blazing inferno that had once been Hell Gate. But the words were unmistakable.

"Help! Somebody help!"

Zip raced toward the voice. Louise and Dr. Couney followed. There was a terrible rumble deep in the belly of the haunted attraction. Zip held out an arm, preventing the nurse and doctor from going any further. Just then, the exit to Hell Gate collapsed before them in a fiery heap.

The intense heat scorched Louise's eyes and she could only make out a mound of debris. But as the smoke and ash cleared, she saw a shadow haul itself to the top of the pile, dragging something behind it. The shadow kneeled among the flaming ruins and bellowed into the night with the same high-pitched squeal she had heard moments ago.

"Help us!"

When her eyes adjusted to the heat, Louise realized the figure wasn't kneeling at all. It was balancing itself on one hand because it had no legs to stand on.

"Johnny!" Zip roared, springing into action.

The What-Is-It? was a creature of few words. On those rare occasions that he did speak, it was usually because he was passionate about the matter at hand. Johnny Hart was a fifteen-year-old whose sideshow moniker was "the Half-Boy." He was born with a truncated torso and legs that were virtually nonexistent. Johnny was a mediocre magician, a capable acrobat, and talented artist. He was also Zip's friend.

The pinhead ripped through the wreckage like it was made of straw. He tossed the Half-Boy onto his shoulder and carried the other individual under his arm like a stack of schoolbooks. When he reached a safe distance, Zip handed Johnny to Dr. Couney. Then he laid the girl on her back.

"Johnny, what in heaven's name were you doing in there?" the doctor demanded.

"The girl!" he replied, gasping and coughing. "She was inside! Is she going to be okay?"

Louise put her ear to the girl's mouth. "She's not breathing!" She raised the girl's arms above her head and began pressing against her chest.

After a few seconds, the girl gasped and coughed. Her eyes fluttered open and Louise stopped the compressions.

"Stargirl missing something," Zip said, his eyes drifting below the girl's neck.

"Stargirl?" Dr. Couney repeated, setting Johnny down and nudging his way past the others. He knelt upon the ashen boardwalk and wiped the soot from the girl's cheeks with his thumbs.

"*Gott im Himmel!*" he exclaimed, revealing two perfect sets of star-shaped freckles. "Zip, you're right!"

"You know her, Doc?" Johnny asked, tottering toward them on the palms of his hands.

When the girl laid eyes on the Half-Boy, she scrambled backwards like a terrified crab. Her path, however, was blocked by a pair of thick legs. She looked up and was greeted by Zip's smiling face. Her wide eyes grew wider and she pressed her back into the boardwalk like she was trying to escape by seeping into it.

"Relax, *liebchen*. You're not in Hell Gate anymore," Dr. Couney said with a soothing chuckle in his voice. "I assure you, the monsters out here are quite harmless. You don't have to run from them."

"Run?" The word escaped the girl's throat like a grunt.

Louise watched her expression turn from fear to worry. The girl clutched Zip's trousers. Then she looked down at her own legs. Louise could see the tension in her face melt as she patted her shredded dungarees up and down. Her mouth spread into a huge grin, like she had just been reacquainted with a long-lost friend.

Louise extended a hand and helped the soot-covered girl to her feet.

"Is everything all right?" she asked.

The girl continued to slap her legs like she was frisking herself.

"The berries!" she replied. Then her face contorted like she was sucking a lemon. "I mean, yes—I'm fine. I thought...

"You! You were there!" She pointed at Johnny. "I guess my mind was playing tricks on me..."

The Half-Boy had turned away from her, his lips quivering as though she had frightened him more than he had frightened her. Louise could tell that Johnny's feelings had been hurt by the girl's initial reaction to him.

"I'm sorry. I didn't mean..." the girl began. Then she paused and lowered her head. "Forget it."

Turning back to Dr. Couney, she extended her hand, and said, "Let me start over. I'm Piper."

"I know," Dr. Couney said, shaking her hand loosely and looking at her in continued astonishment. "I was there the morning they named you. Not long after you were discovered by the drainpipe."

The girl called Piper let the doctor's hand fall. Her green eyes sparkled wildly as she studied him.

"You're Dr. Couney!" she gasped. "You brought me to Hollygrove!"

Couney nodded. "This is my head nurse, Madame Recht," he said, and Louise took a slight bow. "And this is Zip. He was also there when they found you."

Zip smiled at Piper and nodded repeatedly.

"And over here..." the doctor gave her a delicate nudge to face Johnny.

"And over here," Piper interrupted, "is my knight in shining armor who saved me from a gruesome fate."

The girl went down to one knee, took the Half-Boy's hand, and kissed it. Johnny smiled and blushed.

"I'm Johnny Hart, the Half-Boy who's all heart," he said, drawing a heart in the air from the top of his head to the bottom of his torso.

Piper giggled.

"Stargirl missing something," Zip grunted again, his finger also circling his upper body.

"He said that before," Louise said. "What do you mean, Zip?"

Piper flattened her hand to her chest.

"Oh, no! My lock!"

Johnny reached into his coat pocket and pulled out a silver padlock dangling on a chain.

"You mean this thing? I found it on the floor next to you."

He held the heavy pendant out to Piper. She lowered her head and allowed him to put it on her.

"That's two things I owe you for," she said with a smile.

"Zip found that in your blanket the morning you came to us," Dr. Couney said, looking curiously at the What-Is-It? "He also gave you the chain so you could keep it with you forever. *Weiss* was the only name we had for you—until he came up with Piper."

The girl stood and gazed at the dark-skinned pinhead.

"You named me?"

The What-Is-It? lowered his head and nodded. Piper held up her hand and caressed his cheek.

"Thank you, Zip. It's the best name ever."

Zip smiled and nodded faster.

Suddenly, a handful of bruisers from the Fourth Brigade charged up the West 10th Street entrance hauling ladders and lugging hoses over their broad shoulders. Wielding their hefty axes like medieval warriors, the grim-faced volunteers burst through the door leading to the Infant Incubators.

"The reunion will have to wait," Dr. Couney announced. "Zip, come with me. Let's see if we can help. Madame Recht, get the youngsters to safety!"

The doctor and Zip scampered off in the direction of the bells and whistles. Yellows, golds, and reds twinkled and glittered as firefighters battled the blaze with hose and bucket. Louise ushered Johnny and the girl to the relative safety of Surf Avenue where the sirens were now a constant clamor.

But over the din of the sirens and the roar of the flames, Louise thought she heard panicked screams coming from a building two hundred yards east of Hell Gate. The redheaded girl heard it too and bolted toward the source.

"Piper, no!" Louise shouted.

But the girl disregarded her.

Louise and Johnny pursued her to a semi-circular Grecian style building that stood between the east and west promenades. Statues of several life-sized lions stood prominently atop the building's vaulted entrance. At its sides were sculptures of two trumpeting elephants.

"That's the Wild Animal Arena," Louise panted as she reached Piper's side. There was another shriek from within.

"Someone's in there!" Johnny shouted.

"We have to save them!" Piper replied.

The walls of the building had already begun to blister and Louise could feel the heat scalding her skin. But she, Piper, and Johnny continued to push closer. When they reached the entrance, they noticed a chain had been wrapped around the door handles, fastened together with a padlock.

The redhead fumbled through her tattered pockets. Louise saw a look of relief spread across her face as she withdrew a strange-looking pocket knife. Pulling out one of its implements, the girl grabbed the metal lock and yelped. Louise could almost hear her skin sizzle as the searing metal made contact.

"Piper, let me see that!" Louise said, her nurse's instincts kicking in.

"There's no time!" the girl replied, tearing off a piece of her tattered blouse and binding her hand with it. Grabbing the padlock with her shielded hand, Piper fidgeted with the lock mechanism. Louise was astonished when the chain suddenly fell to the ground with a heavy thud.

"Let's go!" Piper called, exploding through the ornate doors.

When they reached the interior, Louise saw that all chaos had broken loose. Cages were lined up against the back of the arena. The wall had been painted to look like a Roman amphitheater where hungry lions had fed on helpless Christians. Inside their pens the big cats had smelled the caustic smoke and were pacing nervously.

The red-haired girl ran to a cage that housed two lions. The animals leaped at the bars as she frantically worked the lock to free them. Louise grabbed her by the shoulders and pulled her away.

"Piper, no! It's too dangerous! You have no idea how to control these animals once they're out!"

"I can't just let them burn to death!" she said, her green eyes pleading through a watery film.

Another cry of panic erupted from the adjacent side of the building. Louise and Piper dashed across the arena as Johnny struggled to keep up. Another row of cages stood against the wall. Peering into the cage, Louise gasped in fright as a gaggle of squawking cockatoos fluttered against the bars.

"*Étonné!*" she screamed, putting her hand to her chest.

The girl giggled at her. "My aunt has a bunch of them. They sound so human, don't they?"

Louise nodded, trying to catch her breath. "I think it's safe to let them out. They won't pose a threat."

The girl unlocked the cage and threw open the door. Louise and Piper covered their heads as the birds flitted out in a colorful frenzy.

Johnny inspected his shoulder.

"What's your definition of *threat?*" he grumbled as a fresh wad of white dripped down his lapel.

Louise suppressed a grin and could tell that Piper was doing the same. But when they approached the next cage, the girl's face went blank.

"Piper, what's wrong?" Louise asked.

"I don't believe it!" she said, gazing between the bars.

Hanging upside down on a wooden perch was an animal that Louise had never seen before. It looked like a silver fox with demon wings. Piper hastily opened the locked and reached into the cage.

"Be careful!" Louise warned. "You don't know what that thing is!"

"I know exactly what it is," the girl replied. The animal's clawed feet embraced her hand tenderly as she wrested it from its prison. "The one I know is much older."

Suddenly a door on the back wall smashed open. A man in his late fifties wearing a safari helmet and khaki clothes leaped into the arena. He was holding a shotgun in one hand and a whip in the other.

"What in bloody hell do you think you're doing?" the man demanded, leveling his weapon at the red-haired girl. The creature fluttered its wings nervously.

Louise stepped defensively between Piper and the man with the shotgun.

"Colonel Ferari, put your gun down this instant! This young lady is only trying to help get your animals to safety."

Colonel Ferari studied the three intruders. It took him a moment to recognize Louise, but as soon as he saw Johnny the tension in his body visibly softened.

Lowering his weapon, he looked at Piper and said, "I had no time to get my keys. You can open the cages without them?"

Piper nodded.

"Then maybe this won't be a mission of mercy after all," Colonel Ferari announced. He took several quick strides toward the Coliseum mural and rested his shotgun against one of the big cat cages.

Louise watched in fascination as the colonel silently directed Piper to unlock the exhibition cages one by one. He attempted to soothe each of the frightened beasts by herding them into the main arena. As Piper freed each animal from its enclosure, Colonel Ferari paraded them around the steel-rimmed oval like it was just another training session.

Most of them cooperated. With a crack of the whip, lions, cougars, leopards, bears, ponies, and gazelles followed the firm yet reassuring commands of their master. The colonel loaded as many of the beasts as possible into their traveling cages so they could be wheeled out of the arena. Louise and Piper helped him haul nine of the big cats to safety.

Then an overhead light flickered and went out.

"Oh, no. Not this again," the redhead said from somewhere in the dark.

Against the rear wall, Louise could make out the dim outline of Colonel Ferari trying to save more of his felines with only the swiftly encroaching flames for illumination.

Suddenly there was a hailstorm of sparks. One of the great cats roared. The others, panicked by the outburst, reacted in kind. Louise could hear an unremitting clicking noise as the girl continued to fiddle with the locks.

"Piper, there's nothing more you can do! It's too dark for you to…"

Her words were cut off by the colonel's anguished scream:

"Sultan, no!"

But it was too late. The fur of a frightened lion had been ignited by drifting embers. Louise could only see the big cat's mane, which looked like a ring of fire, and its tail, which showered sparks like a live electrical wire. She stood frozen to the spot as the fiery ring started racing toward her.

The next thing Louise knew, she was lying flat on the hard floor as the blazing animal soared several inches above her. To prevent the lion from striking her, someone had thrown her to the floor.

"Are you all right?" It was Piper's voice. She was on the floor beside Louise with her arms wrapped around her.

"How could you see that I...?" Louise began to ask.

There was a loud *thud* as the lion sprang through the back door. Sultan roared in anguish as it rushed onto the boardwalk.

The big cat startled a man who looked as though he was about to come inside. He had round, wire-framed glasses and a mustache that looked like two thick caterpillars crawling on each side of his upper lip. And like Colonel Ferari, he too was carrying a shotgun.

The man got to one knee and took aim at the fleeing animal. Piper scampered away from Louise and launched herself through the doorway. The head nurse tried to shout a warning, but the girl was too quick. She barreled into the man at the same time as he pulled the trigger, knocking him over and causing the shot to go astray.

The girl jumped to her feet and shoved a finger in the man's face.

"You can't go around shooting helpless animals! Who the heck do you think you are?"

"Mr. Gumpertz! I'm so sorry!" Louise exclaimed as she rushed through the door. Johnny cantered after her on his hands, followed by an exhausted Colonel Ferari, who was towing the last of the wheeled cages out of the blazing arena.

The man with the gun stood up, brushed off his suit, and addressed the red-haired girl with clear agitation in his voice.

"Name's Sam Gumpertz. I'm responsible for this part of the boardwalk and the safety of everyone on it." He eyed her suspiciously. "Who might you be?"

"I'm Piper Weiss."

The girl choked on the name, as though she were going to say something else.

"Feisty young bird, Sam. But she's got a good heart," Colonel Ferari said. "Helped me corral most of the animals. The profitable ones anyway."

The redhead folded her arms across her chest. She clearly took offense at his implication that she had valued the life of any animal over another.

Mr. Gumpertz considered her for a moment. "Well, Piper Weiss. While I appreciate your concern for these creatures, I can't have a dangerous, wounded carnivore running loose. Bad for business."

He nodded to Colonel Ferari. "Joe, come with me. We've got a job to do."

Piper seized the colonel's ash-stained jacket.

"Sultan only wants to go someplace where he can be by himself so he can lick his wounds," she pleaded.

"This is Coney Island, kid," Gumpertz said, cocking his firearm. "Better chance of finding a three-legged ballerina than a place to be alone." Without looking back, he and the colonel walked off in pursuit of the flaming lion.

"The three-legged ballerina quit last year," Johnny mumbled.

Suddenly there was a spectacular crash. The trio turned to see the walls of the Wild Animal Arena give way as the ceiling collapsed.

"No!" shouted Piper.

Louise had to use all her strength to restrain her from running back inside. The girl might have succeeded in breaking away had a solitary creature not emerged from the blazing ruins.

The silver bat glided across the heated winds and flapped to a midair pause in front of the redhead. Piper held out her arm and the bat instinctively grasped it, flopping to a hanging position from her tattered sleeve.

"You're safe," the girl sighed with a smile. She pet the creature on its fuzzy snout as it preened the soot from its snow-white fur.

A shot rang out in the night, followed by another. And another. Louise and Piper flinched at the sound of each blast and then looked at each other. They both knew that Sultan was dead.

"It had to be done," said Johnny.

Because she was a nurse, Louise would always wonder if there might have been a way the big cat could have been saved.

An hour later, the fire brigade finally brought the Coney Island blaze under control. Colonel Ferari returned to his arena and scattered sawdust over its smoking remains. Some of the vendors had opened their concession stands to hand out free refreshments to the firefighters. Louise, Johnny, and Piper were taking turns feeding popcorn to the silver bat when the fire battalion chief approached them.

"You're one lucky girl, Red" he said to Piper. "I hear the Half-Boy pulled your keester out of Hell Gate before you got roasted."

The girl looked at Johnny and smiled.

"Mind telling me what you were doing in there?" the chief demanded.

With an ardent wobble, Johnny inserted himself between Piper and the fireman.

"I don't appreciate your implication, Chief," he said, inflating his chest.

"Calm down, son," the chief replied. "I have to follow up on every lead, that's all."

"I didn't set the fire!" Piper declared. The white bat flapped uncomfortably at her frustration.

"She's telling the truth! It wasn't her!" Johnny exclaimed. "It was some doll dressed like Theda Bara. She dropped these!" The Half-Boy held up a book of matches.

"Is that so?" the chief said, snatching the matches out of his grasp and inspecting them. "Fire started on the roof. Mind telling me how this Theda Bara lookalike got up that high?"

Johnny and Piper looked at each other in dubious complicity. The silence became so painful that Louise intervened on their behalf. "No disrespect, Chief—but mind telling me how our friend here would have gotten up that high?" she asked, nodding to Piper.

The chief narrowed his eyes at Louise. Then he looked at the matches.

"Not the kind of joint I'd expect to find someone like you, Red," he said, tossing the matches to the freckled girl.

Piper turned the matchbook over in her hands. Louise peered at it over her shoulder and could read the words "Adonis Social Club" handsomely printed between two American flags.

The chief turned away. "No lives were lost here. At least no human lives," he said, walking away from the charred remains. "We'll chalk it up to electrical failure."

He called his company back to their vehicles and then shouted, "Coffee's on me, boys."

The brigade packed up their equipment and returned to their horse-drawn steamers and motorized fire engines. Watching them depart, Louise leaned over to Piper and said, "Coney Island is no stranger to fire. Like a phoenix, a greater and finer place always rises from its ashes."

The sun was rising over the Atlantic, casting an eerie gloom on the smoldering embers. Just outside the ruins, Sam Gumpertz had rigged a makeshift tent. The events of the evening were taking their toll on Louise and she was longing for bed. But she couldn't walk away without learning what Mr. Gumpertz was up to.

Above the tent, in crudely written letters, the showman hung a sign proclaiming, "A Congress of Curiosities: the Dreamland Circus Sideshow." Outside the makeshift shelter, displayed in traditional country fair style, were canvasses heralding the attractions within, including the World's Most Beautiful Fat Lady and the Living Skeleton.

In mute solidarity, Johnny climbed onto the upended box that would serve as his dais until proper staging could be constructed. Zip the What-Is-It also offered his support by ascending to his assigned platform.

Louise understood what Mr. Gumpertz was doing. When the season officially began, crowds would come from all over to see the freaks and barrage them with questions about their heroic deeds during the Hellfire at Hell Gate.

Admission—10 cents.

Admission to the burning ruins—15 cents.

Mr. Gumpertz approached the girl with the white-furred bat.

"That's my latest acquisition you got there. Arctic snow bat—rarest animal in the world," he said to Piper. "Bought it off of Admiral Byrd who got in on his recent trip to the North Pole."

"I'm going to name him Orlok," she said, letting the bat steal another flake of popcorn from her fingers.

"I suppose you earned the right," Mr. Gumpertz conceded with a nod. "You know, they say the snow bat is the only species in existence that was here before Genesis. The last living relative of the dragon."

Louise narrowed her eyes at him. Sam Gumpertz was a ballyhoo artist, considered by some to be the greatest sideshow talker of all time. And ballyhoo artists were notorious story-tellers.

With the sun rising behind him, the showman popped a top hat onto his head and peered down at the redhead.

"Where are your parents, kid?" he asked.

"Not alive," Piper answered. She sounded a bit defensive and Louise wondered if the girl were being entirely truthful.

"Orphan, huh?" Mr. Gumpertz said.

He looked at the girl with awkward intensity, scanning her up and down. Then he lit his stogie and blew a steady stream of smoke into the night.

"So, you want a job?"

WHAT IS IT?

Zip was tired. Helping firemen was hard work.

The sun was out. But he wanted to sleep.

So Zip went home.

He was happy that the Star Girl came back. And he was happy that she liked her name.

A man from England once visited Zip. He wrote Zip's favorite Christmas story—about a mean man who turned nice.

The man from England asked, "What is it?"

That's how Zip got his name.

Before that they called him Last of the Aztecs. Zip didn't know what that meant.

They also said he lived with gorillas. In Africa. Naked. (*Hee-hee.*)

But Zip was from New Jersey. And he liked wearing overalls.

Mr. Gump paid him a dollar every day to keep quiet.

"Just act like a wild man."

So he did. Zip liked money.

He made more money when he played the violin. He didn't know how to play. So people paid him to stop.

Zip made so much money that he became Dean of Freaks. He

didn't know what that meant either. But everyone treated him nicely. So it was good.

Zip walked up to his room. The door was open. He never locked it. There wasn't anything to steal. Zip kept all his money in a bank. He was smart.

Zip stepped inside. A man was standing there. He had a clown face. Zip smiled and clapped his hands. Zip liked clowns.

But the clown's face was all wrong. The painted smile was upside down. He was an angry clown. Zip stopped smiling.

"William Johnson?"

The clown had a funny accent. How did he know Zip's real name?

Zip grunted at him. Mr. Gump would be proud.

The angry clown said some words that Zip didn't understand. Zip laughed at the funny words.

But the angry clown didn't laugh. Instead he punched Zip in the stomach. It wasn't a hard punch. But it wasn't very nice.

Zip wagged a finger at him.

The angry clown tipped his hat. Then he walked out of the room.

Zip watched him leave and scratched the top of his pointy head.

★★★★

Here ends *Piper Houdini: Apprentice of Coney Island.* If you enjoyed this book, please leave a review at your favorite online retailer.

The tale concludes in *Piper Houdini: Nightmare on Esopus Island.* To receive publication notices and regular updates, please join Piper's mailing list at <u>www.piperhoudini.com/newsletter</u>. Turn the page and read the first chapter now for free!

PIPER HOUDINI
NIGHTMARE ON
ESOPUS ISLAND

GLENN HERDLING

TANTUM MORTUUS VINCIT MORTEM

"**M**aster, I've failed you."

The dark-haired girl knelt on the grotto floor wearing a shredded Vionnet dress. She had plucked the shards of glass from her porcelain skin and her wounds had already healed. But the outfit was beyond repair.

"How have you failed me?" asked the hulking figure standing in the center of the raised dais.

In place of the friar's robe that Flapper had grown accustomed to seeing him wear, Master Therion was sporting a casual cotton shirt and Riviera pants. A walking stick, a dagger, and a lifeless snake lay at his feet. The snake had two heads.

"I accidentally zotzed Houdini's niece." Flapper's words echoed off the bare stone walls like they were mocking her. "She's dead."

This time, there were no sycophants chanting around the dais, no public displays of debauchery. It was only herself, Master Therion, and a slender man whose back was to them. The man's scent was familiar to her keen nose.

"What makes you so certain she's dead?" Therion asked.

Beneath their wrinkled lids, the Beast's eyes bulged with froggish strain at his faithful servant. But his lips were curled in mild amusement.

"I lit a fire to smoke her out of her hiding place. It backfired," answered Flapper. At any other time, she might have snickered at the pun.

"Then you didn't stay long enough," Master Therion said. He stepped closer to the other man on the platform. "I made the same mistake thirteen years ago. I was led to believe that the life of a certain child had been terminated by one of your ilk, and I pursued the matter no further."

"Killed by a dewdropper?" Flapper asked, using the term she had coined for her people. She thought vampire sounded fluky. And nightgaunt was just plain creepy.

Master Therion nodded.

"But it has recently come to my attention that the girl was brought to the Island of Coney instead. Interesting that the Houdini girl should now find refuge there."

Beneath the light of a powerful acetylene lamp, the lean man continued to toil over seven coffins that were lined up along the back of the platform behind the stone altar. All but one were connected by tubes that pumped goop in and out them.

"I've arranged for one of my agents to keep an eye on the girl," the thin man said, turning to address them as though it were a laborious chore. Flapper recognized his bookish appearance at once. It was the doctor whose wedding she had attended with Master Therion in Boston eight years ago.

"Flapper, you remember Dr. Crandon," the Beast said flatly.

"Posalutely!" Flapper replied, attempting a curtsy. "Good to see you again, doc."

Crandon ignored her. In his hands he held out a ghastly thing.

"Aleister, look!" Crandon bellowed, completely disregarding the vamp. "I have successfully reanimated the subject by introducing the serum into its bloodstream intermittently over the course of several weeks!"

Flapper looked at the thing. It was a large toad. In fact, it looked like the same toad her Master had crucified on her last visit. It had three eyes and six limbs. But its middle eye and middle legs were now grossly disproportionate. All three eyes glowed red—and the poor creature was very much alive.

A loud belch escaped the toad's mouth, exposing rows of razor-sharp teeth that would have been more suitable for a piranha.

"You see?" the doctor continued. "Creatures that manifest with mutations are more resilient to the procedure! The solution lies in a property of the ectoplasm. It targets and modifies the singularity of a species, not the similarities."

"What's he beatin' his gums about?" the vamp asked her Master in a loud whisper.

"Manners, Flapper," admonished the Beast.

Peering over the rims of his glasses, the surgeon replied, "I'm saying that freaks of nature have what it takes to return from the abyss because they have developed a means to overcome similar afflictions in life," he explained. "Perhaps the parts of them that die in the womb are replaced by some sort of metaphysical coping mechanism."

"*Tantum mortuus vincit mortem*, to paraphrase Cagliostro," said Master Therion.

"I don't speak Martian," Flapper said.

"Only the dead can conquer death," the Beast translated.

Just then, the toad creature leaped from the doctor's hand onto Flapper's upper chest, latching itself to the flesh left exposed by her torn dress. The attack was so swift that even her superhuman reflexes couldn't thwart it.

"Get it off! Get it off!" the vamp screamed, slapping at the amphibian to dislodge it. But it remained on her flesh, dangling by a perverse suction mechanism at the end of its overgrown fifth leg.

The mutant toad bit into Flapper's alabaster flesh. A stream of blood flowed down her chest and she howled in agony.

Flapper's tolerance for pain had grown considerably since the night she had been "revamped" by Master Therion and she wasn't accustomed to unpleasant sensations. The inability to feel had been one of the advantages of her transformation. But the toad's attack not only reawakened Flapper's physical awareness, it dredged up emotions she thought she had buried long ago.

"Get it off me, please!" she pleaded. Tears streamed down her cheeks as she tried to rip the thing off.

"Seems my pet has an appetite for the arcane," Dr. Crandon said to the Beast, showing no regard for Flapper at all. "It's trying to consume the very thing that makes your pet special."

"Enough!" Master Therion shouted, raising his walking stick. The ruby eyes of its cobra-headed tip gleamed with menace and shot two fiery beams at the mutated amphibian. An unearthly croak erupted from the creature's throat and it fell to the bedrock in a smoldering heap.

"No!" Dr. Crandon screamed, leaping off the dais and kneeling before the ashen reamins of the misshapen toad. Cradling the thing in the palm of his hand, Crandon sobbed as its charred sac expanded once, twice, and then no more.

The Beast glared at Crandon from the edge of his altar.

"My dear doctor. You will be permitted to gloat when you can devise a creature that is impervious to the light of this world in all its manifestations—including the light of my staff."

The doctor reeled to face the Beast.

"And I will not be able to produce such a creature until you deliver the wormwood star! I grow tired of all these setbacks, Aleister. The time to strike is now!"

Master Therion shook his head and his jowls bounced like gelatin.

"The time will not be ripe for another few months, Roy. You know that."

Dr. Crandon turned away, dismissing the necromancer with a wave of his hand.

"You and your damned occult timetables. This is science we're talking about!"

"And science demands that we obtain the proper test subject," Master Therion insisted. "We have no evidence that the Houdini girl is anything but a mortal vessel."

The Beast shifted his vast bulk to address his servant.

"Flapper, did you notice anything out of the ordinary about your quarry?"

"She's one smart cookie, I'll give you that," the dewdropper replied. "But I didn't see no earth-shattering miracles."

Therion rubbed his fleshy chin.

"I'm sorry I disappointed you, Master," Flapper said, casting her eyes to the floor.

"Nonsense, my dear. The mission wasn't a disappointment at all. You flushed the prize into the open and pursued her to the one place we can keep an eye on her night and day."

"So my job is done?" she asked with a hopeful lilt to her voice.

"Absolutely," Master Therion replied. Flapper began to smile. "But I will need to keep you here by my side for the next several months."

Her smile faded.

Dr. Crandon sneered. "Don't worry, doll. Your Master's acolytes may not be the most fashionable bunch. But they're real party animals once you get to know them."

The perpetual shadow around Flapper's eyes made her glare all the more insidious. Crandon turned away to avoid it.

"The sun's up outside the cave," he said, trying to change the subject. "You can sleep in one of the unoccupied coffins until nightfall. But you'd better start making other arrangements because I expect there to be one less vacancy by the end of the week."

Flapper glanced at Master Therion who nodded in consent. She floated up to the altar and swanned over to the tubeless casket. She climbed into the pinewood box and thought about the events of the last few hours. All in all, it had been a real lousy evening.

Some milquetoast teen had made her look like a sap.

The toad's bite wasn't healing, nor was the swollen red hickey where the toad had stuck to her chest.

And she was pretty much grounded on this rock from now till Doomsday, which wasn't far off if her Master's predictions about teeny Houdini were right.

She allowed the lid to close. Before slipping into oblivion, one last thought pierced her mind like a stake through her heart…

How the hell am I gonna find anything decent to wear on this god-forsaken island?

ABOUT THE AUTHOR

Glenn Herdling, a graduate of Bucknell University and post-graduate of New York University, began his publishing career in 1987 at Marvel Comics as assistant editor on Marvel's flagship Spider-Man titles. A New Jersey resident all his life, Glenn currently works in the financial sector as a communications specialist. He has contributed to numerous published works and has written over 80 comic books. **Piper Houdini: Apprentice of Coney Island** is his first novel.

Discover other published works by Glenn Herdling at http://glennherdling.com/

Connect with Glenn on:
Twitter at https://twitter.com/GlennHerdling
Goodreads at https://www.goodreads.com/author/show/191422.
Glenn_Herdling
e-mail: me@glennherdling.com

Connect with Piper on:
Facebook at https://www.facebook.com/PiperHoudiniFanPage
www.piperhoudini.com

Printed in the United States
By Bookmasters